I0735455

The Things That Matter Most

The Beginning

sands press
Brockville, Ontario

The Things That Matter Most

The Beginning

Perry Prete

sands press

sands press

A division of 10361976 Canada Inc.
300 Central Avenue West
Brockville, Ontario
K6V 6K8

Toll Free 1-800-563-0911 or 613-345-2687
http://www.sandspress.com

ISBN 978-1-988281-07-0

Cover concept and design by Wendy Treverton
Formatting by Renee Hare
Publisher Sands Press

Publisher's Note

This book is a work of fiction by the author. Characters, names, places and circumstances are the product of the author's imagination and are used in a fictitious manner. Any relation to any persons, alive or deceased, place, location, event or otherwise is purely coincidental.

Medical protocols differ from year to year, region to region, province to province, and county to county. Although I strive to be realistic, this novel is a work of fiction and not meant as a medical textbook for paramedics.

1st Printing April 2017
To book an author for your live event, please call: 1-800-563-0911

Submissions

Sands Press is a literary publisher interested in new and established authors wishing to develop and market their product. For more information please visit our website at www.sandspress.com.

To every medic who has ever put the needs of their patient before their own, to every medic who has ever missed a family event because of a late call, to every medic who has cared for a patient as if they were a family member, to every medic who gets just a little tired of being called an "Ambulance Driver" and just smiles back at the patient, to every medic who…
There are too many "who"s to mention.
To every medic, regardless of where you work: we always seem to hear the bad stuff from management or patients, so let me say it for them…

Thank you!

I sincerely hope you enjoy all my novels.

Perry

Disclaimer

I've been very lucky to have had an EMS career that started in 1982, serving the sick and injured and still work on the road today.

During that time, I've come to know some great police officers and firefighters. Quite often, at the crime scene, a police officer will ask our opinion of what happened or what we think might have happened, not unlike asking a firefighter what he/she may think caused the fire.

As paramedics, we offer a unique perspective on the human body that a uniformed officer or detective may not immediately see.

In my Ethan Tennant books, I've taken those times when I've been asked for my unique perspective at the scene of an accident or crime scene and turned it into a work of fiction where the police and paramedics work as a team. Does this happen in real life? Yes, it does. Does it happen to the extent in does in my books? Well, my books are a work of fiction after all.

August 2000

1

Tom Lister grabbed the foot end of the ambulance cot and pushed it into my back. The impact caused me to fall forward into the nurse with whom I was speaking. We were almost the same height, inches away from each other, looking into each other's eyes. There was a pause, not an uncomfortable one, but a single moment in time that seemed to last forever. I stepped back, reached behind, and pushed the cot back into my partner's stomach.

The nurse smiled politely at the childish games my partner and I were playing.

"So you have my number now. See," she smiled, "persistence pays off." She handed me the piece of paper with her home telephone number scribbled in pen. Like a high school kid feeling the surge of emotion of his first crush, my heart pounded in my chest, little beads of perspiration formed on my brow, and my palms became damp. As I reached for the scrap of paper, our fingertips touched. I swear I felt electricity pass between our fingers. She held her end of the paper a little longer than needed, looked at me, - no, into me, - smiled, and released her grip.

"Don't lose it!" she ordered. "I'll be waiting for your call."

"I have it memorized already." I placed the paper in my shirt pocket and secured the dual Velcro closures. I placed my hand over the pocket, felt the paper inside, and was confident that it was safe.

She turned and walked down the hall. The other nurses at the triage desk were smiling and laughing at our juvenile behaviour. I stood, unmoving, as she walked away.

"Turn and look back. Turn!" I screamed loudly in my mind. At least I hoped I was speaking with my inner voice.

Mid-stride, she turned and looked back at me, smiled, and kept walking. Her light brown, wavy hair bounced with each step and flowed down to her shoulders. It was all in slow motion as if it were a video playing back in my mind.

"You plan on coming back down to earth, Nash?"

Tom knew how much I hated that name and it did break my concentration. He insisted on calling me "Nash" because I chose to support the Nashville Predators instead of the home team Ottawa Senators. That NHL season, Ottawa had made the playoffs, and the Nashville players had hit the golf course early. Something Tom bugged me about constantly.

"Come on, buddy. We have to get back in service." Tom was tugging at my shirtsleeve. She was already out of sight, but I continued to stare down the hall where she had turned to look back at me.

"Yeah, I'm coming." I grabbed the head of the stretcher and followed Tom's lead out the Civic ER's door.

"So you finally got her number! How long did that take? Three, four months?"

I held up two fingers. "Two! Two months! And besides, the nice ones are worth the wait."

"Sure they are! What's her name again?"

"Madeleine. Maddy. Funny thing was she said she knew you. So how come she knows your name? Would you care to explain?"

"I asked her out last year. She turned me down flat. I thought she was a lesbian. Turns out, she just has really bad taste in men."

"What? You asked her out and you couldn't remember her name?"

"I ask a lot of women out. I play the odds, ask enough of them out, and eventually a good number of 'em say 'yes.' I don't remember the ones who turn me down. Besides, who would ever imagine she would say 'yes' to you and not me?"

I pushed the foot end of the Ferno cot hard into Tom's back as we approached the rig parked outside. He turned and laughed.

We loaded the cot. Tom walked around the rig and took the driver's seat; I climbed into the passenger side. Tom cleared our truck from the Civic and we were assigned a roving standby in the east end of the city.

Driving east on Carling Avenue, I pulled the small piece of paper from my shirt pocket and looked at it: "Maddy 686-3794." Black ink on white paper. Handwritten, so beautiful and so important. I closed my eyes, and repeated the number over and over again.

"What's the number?"

With the paper folded, I repeated the number back to him from memory.

"Why?"

"I'll put it in my Palm Pilot for safekeeping."

"No way."

"Don't worry, buddy. No way I want your seconds. Besides, I had my chance. Half of the guys and most of the gay women at the Civic asked her out and she turned 'em all down flat. It's fate, bud. She's yours."

Tom handed me his new Palm Pilot device, shiny, silver, and blue with a full colour touchscreen. I pulled the stylus from the back and was confused about what to do with it.

"How does this thing work, anyway?"

Tom reached for his new Palm Pilot. "I'll do it at the next light. Really, Ethan, you should get with the eighties. You still have a rotary dial phone at home, don't you? Just imagine if they combined this thing with a mobile phone, what it could do. It would change our lives."

At the next traffic light, as promised, Tom stored Maddy's number in his Palm for safekeeping. As he pocketed the device and handed me back my precious piece of paper, dispatch called our vehicle number.

Tom reached for the mic. "Go for 4198."

"What's your 10-20?" Dispatch was asking for our current location.

"Carling Avenue and Champagne Avenue."

"10-4. Proceed priority four to 540 Cambridge Street, apartment 306. It's the Lake Lander apartment building. Possible hanging. 10-200s are also dispatched. Advise if you need further assistance."

"4198 10-8." We booked in service. Tom reached down, activated the emergency lights, and powered up the siren. "That's only a few blocks up the road, right on the corner of Carling."

"There's a median between the lanes. You gonna drive to Bronson and pull a U-y?"

I turned to see Tom grinning again.

Even though we only had a few blocks to travel east on Carling Avenue, Tom pushed hard on the accelerator and blared the siren. Cars pulled right or stopped dead in their tracks. Tom weaved in and around the cars, and activated the left turn signal as we approached Cambridge Street. A solid concrete median separated traffic flowing east and west almost along the entire length of Carling Avenue.

Westbound traffic on the opposite side of the barrier didn't stop or pull over, and when Tom saw the break in the traffic, he took his chance.

"Hang tight."

Tom jerked the steering wheel to the left. The front tires hit the barrier and the ambulance jerked upwards, then landed hard on the pavement. The back tires followed suit, causing me to smash forward into the dash. My outstretched arms prevented a face plant into the plastic dash.

Tom regained control of the rig and came to a stop in front of the Lake Lander apartment building, facing north in the southbound lane.

"That," he said as he put the vehicle in park, "that was fun."

The Lake Lander apartment building was a modern, five-storey,

U-shaped brick apartment building with a recessed, patio-stone, ground-level entrance way. To the right, a wheelchair accessibility ramp snaked its way from street level to the ground floor of the apartment building. Ramps, the paramedic's best friend, I thought. Well, that and coffee!

Tom keyed the mike, "Ottawa 4198 is 10-7 scene. 10-2's not here yet. Do you have an ETA?"

"Police Dispatch said a cruiser would be there in a few minutes. Caller stated they came home and found a young male hanging in the closet. Patient is possibly VSA."

"Great."

Tom hated VSA, or "vital signs absent," calls. Not that he couldn't do them. They just affected him more than they did me.

I regained my composure and shot Tom a dirty look. "I'm wearing my seatbelt from now on. And to top that ride off, we have a dead guy upstairs."

I stepped down from the passenger side and walked around to the back doors of the rig. Fumbling with the portable radio, I couldn't get the radio holster to lock into the half-moon clip that permitted the radio to swivel on my belt.

Tom released the cot-restraining bar on the sidewall of the ambulance and pulled the cot from the back of the rig. The cot's swing arm caught the yellow safety hook on the ambulance floor, preventing it from dropping to the ground. I threw the radio onto the cot instead of continuing to fumble with it and trying to secure it to my belt.

I grabbed the carriage and lowered it to the ground. Looking up at the building, I admired the modern brick styling, large windows, enclosed patios for some of the apartments, and open patios for the apartments facing the centre courtyard and the end units.

Tom pulled and I pushed the cot with the defibrillator, med/drug bags, backboard, and spinal kit. We should have called for fire backup, too. At least they could have helped carry some of the gear up to the apartment. "Correction, the paramedic's best friends are ramps, coffee, and fire fighters," I thought. Not necessarily in that order, and the list is subject to revision.

We stopped in front of the elevator, and I let whatever gear I was shouldering fall uncaringly to the tile floor. I pushed the up button several times in rapid succession and waited for the bell to indicate when the elevator arrived at our floor. I patted my shirt pocket to make sure I hadn't lost Maddy's telephone number.

"Do you still feel it?"

"Yeah."

"Are you going to move it?"

"No way."

"Then let it be. It's not going anywhere. Relax, bud. That girl likes you."

My chin rested on my chest, trying to hide my embarrassment. I was acting like a fifteen-year-old boy with a crush on the hottest girl in the school, the city, or, in Maddy's case, the whole country.

I slipped my nitrile gloves on, pulled them up high, and fitted them between the fingers. Twisting each finger, they cracked as the nitrogen gas was released from each joint. I wasn't nervous about the call upstairs; I just couldn't stop thinking about Maddy in the ER.

"Calm down, Ethan. Call her tonight when you get off shift." Tom saw me fidget.

"That's not too needy?"

"Oh, you're needy, but I think that's what she goes for."

Ding. The elevator doors opened. This was a brand new building, and, unfortunately for us, they had installed tiny little elevators barely large enough to fit a stretcher to save money.

Tom raised the head of the cot and lowered the push bar while I reached into the elevator and held the hold button. I placed the backboard upright in the corner and kicked the medical bag into the tiny room. We jostled the cot into the elevator and heard the portable radio fall to the floor.

"I'll get it when we get to the third floor," I promised Tom. Tom pressed the number 3, and we waited while the doors closed. Between the two of us, the cot, and the equipment, there wasn't any room left for another rider. If the patient was alive and needed to be boarded, we would have to almost stand him upright.

The elevator doors opened on the third floor and we spewed out, gathered our gear, and checked the apartment number signs to point us in the right direction. I looked to the right and saw a panicked woman open an apartment door and frantically wave us towards her. The dimly lit hallway offered little assistance in revealing any physical details of the woman who ducked back into the apartment.

As we approached the open door, we heard loud voices arguing back and forth, and footsteps running about the apartment.

Tom and I pulled the cot to the front door, peered in, and found the hallway too narrow to manoeuvre the stretcher. We lowered the cot, removed the bags and defibrillator, and entered the apartment, following the voices down the hall to the right. The older lady who had waved us down in the hall was pacing in the small bedroom to the left. Her hands covered her mouth, and her tears flowed freely. In front of her, a younger man was kneeling in the closet. It was only when I entered the room that I saw what he was doing.

The man was on his knees, holding up a younger man by his waist. A belt or strap was still wrapped tightly around his neck. The younger man's head was cocked back and to the side. Whatever he had used to constrict his trachea, it had done its job. The belt had cut deeply into his neck, and the skin was swollen around the ligature. His lips were engorged, and looked white, waxy, and almost fake. The tip of his tongue stuck out slightly between his lips.

Tom dropped the defibrillator and rushed over, bent down, wrapped his arms around the hanging body, and lifted him up. I let the gear fall to the ground, grabbed the scissors from my holster, and was about to cut the belt up high above his head to preserve the knot for the police when Tom released the body from his grip. I stood back, stunned, until I realized why.

The body was in full rigour mortis. It swung slowly for a moment, and then stopped. His extremities stayed in the same positions, failing to move with the momentum. His facial expression— everything—remained motionless. The belt was tied around the closet rod, wrapped tightly around his neck, and he'd simply let himself hang until he passed out. The closet was low enough that he could have stood up if he had changed his mind. Obviously, he was determined. Or drugged.

"What are you doing?" The lady who had rushed us into the apartment was now screaming and crying at the same time. Her arms were outstretched, as if pleading with us to help, wanting to push us forward to do whatever we could.

"Please, please help my son!" She placed her hand over her mouth and wiped her nose with the back of her other hand. "Please!" Her plea for help was now more of a whimper. She had realized that the reason we'd stopped was because her son was dead, and had been for quite some time. She slid down to the bed, sat on the corner, and cried, her stare never leaving her son who still hung in the closet.

The man who had been kneeling in the closet holding up the younger man stood up slowly. He walked over to the woman and touched her arm, coaxing her to leave the room. He shot Tom and I a look of appreciation. It was a silent confirmation that he understood. Sometimes even a simple look from a family member in these situations sets our minds at ease.

When they had both left the room, Tom stepped in closer and looked at the body still hanging in the closet. He pulled out his notepad and pen, and began taking a few notes.

Moisture had begun to form under my nitrile gloves. Little pockets of sweat rolled between the gloves and my skin, making me feel uncomfortable. I took notes as well, detailing the way the belt was tied around the rod and around his neck, the clothes that still hung in the closet, what the young man was wearing, and general observations around the room.

I looked for a wallet, prescription medications, anything that would reveal clues as to who our patient was and what had made him decide that this was his only option. I've always found it hard to understand why someone would choose suicide as a way to deal with whatever it was that was causing them stress.

After all of the socially acceptable discussions of why I became a paramedic are exhausted, the real reason is simply because I hate death. "Hate," in this case, is not a strong enough word. "Despise" is more precise. I despise the thought of growing old, the body beginning to break down, the inevitable aches and pains of old age, the body failing its host, and the undignified end that consumes us all. I plan on going down fighting all the way and holding on with my fingertips, never wanting to let go of life. Due, in part, to not knowing what lies ahead. Does it simply end? Is there something more? I only know what is presented before me. What I see, I like.

Tom bumped me to bring me back to reality. I went back to my scene notes.

The man in the closet appeared to be young, but his condition made it difficult to gauge his age or what he'd looked like. There was no beard stubble, no sideburns, no facial hair at all. He had delicate features; even his arms and hands, now swollen, sported little hair.

"I just spoke to his mother. Apparently, he had been bullied something fierce at school since he came out of the closet." I turned around to see my old friend standing in the doorway. A red-haired city of Ottawa police officer stood behind us, one hand resting on the edge of his belt, the other on the handle of his holstered gun.

"Hey Galen. Didn't hear you come in."

"Here, you dropped this in the elevator." Galen handed me our portable radio. I clipped it on my belt and adjusted the volume to make sure it was turned on.

Galen and I had gone to high school together and continued to hang out together. Galen had decided on law enforcement instead of college and gotten married, whereas I'd gone to college before going to work for Ottawa EMS.

"Is this not the definition of irony: a young guy comes out of the closet, only to be bullied and then hang himself in one?! Jesus Christ, what's this world coming to?" Galen stepped in closer to the body that still hung from the leather belt, carefully scanning it for clues.

"Fuck! What is he? Twelve? I can't believe someone would hate life so much that he'd want to leave the theatre even before the credits start to roll." Galen stood upright, leaned back, and cracked his back. "These fucking belts are going to cripple me." He spun circles from the waist to stretch. "They keep adding crap for us to wear. I'm going to apply to be a detective, just so I don't have to wear this stupid uniform anymore."

He turned towards Tom and me and ran a hand through his red hair. "You guys writing up the report for the murder scene here?"

"What?" I looked at Galen, startled at his declaration.

"Didn't young Sherlock here," he thumbed me, "notice the belt is a large men's size? It's long enough to wrap around me twice. I take it for at least a size forty-six leather belt." He turned back towards the closet, got down on all fours, and looked at the waist of the young man still hanging in the closet. "I doubt if he's even a size thirty." He stood back up. "The belt size is usually stamped into the leather near the buckle, and since that part is around the kid's neck, we're gonna have to wait until they cut him down. Not one pair of the pants hanging up in here is anything big enough to carry a size forty-six belt. Besides, it's brown. I don't see any brown, tan, or grey pants, do you? Plus, there's a wear mark a couple of holes in. The belt is used. The welt on the left side of his forehead might tell us something later, too."

"Son of a fucking bitch!" Tom stood and walked over to the closet. "You've been here for thirty seconds and got all that already? Impressive! OK, what if he just bought the belt?"

Galen turned to Tom. "You decide to kill yourself. You've been thinking about it for days, weeks maybe." Galen slowly looked back into the closet. His voice became slow and quiet. "Finally, you've reached the end of whatever you can endure. You decide, 'Yup, I'm going to kill myself.' Do you go down to the local department store to buy a belt instead of rope?"

Tom cocked his head in agreement.

"Then you come back here and hang yourself with a belt, only after putting a wear mark a few sizes down from the end. Someone was wearing that belt before he decided to hang himself, or he was hung to make it look like a suicide. And there ain't nobody here who's a size forty-two or bigger. If I ever get that fucking fat, shoot me!"

"So, either he borrowed the belt or someone helped."

I stood beside my old friend and looked into the closet, and realized how much more I might have missed on other calls. I slapped Galen on the back and felt the rigid bullet-resistant vest he wore over his uniform shirt. Feelings of remorse for our young patient built up in my throat. I swallowed and it felt like I'd just downed a hockey puck.

Galen stared down at the young man who hung silently in the closet. "We just have to wait for the suits to come and investigate and see if I'm right. Being a uniform, I don't have to do much but secure the scene. That and make sure the Ambulance Drivers don't fuck with the evidence." He smiled at Tom and me, knowing full well that we both deplored that moniker.

2

I unlocked my apartment door, went in, and tossed the keys into the key bowl. I was already retrieving the sheet of paper with Maddy's telephone number from my shirt pocket before the door closed behind me.

Pulling the cordless phone from its cradle, I walked over to the couch, fell into it, and stared at the number. I held it nervously, like the winning lottery ticket, still not believing I held the lucky numbers. Holding the paper in my right hand, my left thumb dialled her number and hovered over the "TALK" button. I tossed the phone to the seat cushion beside me, turned on the TV, and pulled off my uniform, letting my shirt and pants fall to the floor as I headed for the bathroom.

Standing under the showerhead, the water cascaded over my face, forcing me to spit every few seconds. It felt good. Normally, a suicide wouldn't affect me at all. I had been ready to dismiss the call as just another suicide by a kid who felt the world had abandoned him and chosen to take his life instead of fighting. Galen's detective work had changed my perspective on the scene.

Thoughts of Maddy kept poking in and out of the suicide scenario. Eventually, my focus shifted completely to her, and I continued to deliberate calling her. Should I call? Should I wait? Tom had said I should call her when I got off shift. I was pretty sure Maddy wanted me to call her. The water continued to pound down on me.

As I wavered back and forth about calling her, the cadence of the water hitting the tub around my feet started to sound like a ringtone. Pulling myself from under the showerhead, I slicked my wet hair back behind my ears and heard it: the phone was ringing.

I slid the shower curtain aside, and ran out of the bathroom and down the hall. Hitting the hall floor mat, my feet suddenly flew out from under me. I landed on my back and felt the breath being forced from my lungs. The phone continued to ring.

I crawled on all fours to the couch, grabbed the phone, and looked at the call display, but I was so out of breath that the number on the screen was just a blur.

I pressed "TALK". Silence. I couldn't speak. A voice came over the other end. A woman's voice.

"Hello?"

I grunted. "Wait." I forced a word out.

"OK?"

"Wait… please." My voice still echoed my inability to breath. I stood to expand my lungs. My mind was trying to process the voice. A woman's voice—breath—was it Maddy? Breath. She wanted me to call her. Breath. Maybe my mother? My lungs finally accepted air.

"Whew! That's a little better."

"Ethan, are you OK?"

"Yeah. You wouldn't believe what I just did."

"Try me."

My heart skipped a few beats, my stomach dropped, and my pulse quickened. It was Maddy.

"Maddy?"

"Yup!"

"How did you get my number?"

"I called Tom and he gave it to me. Well, that and your bio: likes, dislikes, tastes, favourite colour, you know. I grilled him until he folded like a cheap suit."

"Remind me to thank the guy! Wait, how did you get Tom's number?"

"He's given it out to every nurse, female porter, well, every woman with a pulse at the Civic. One call to a friend of mine and she had it. I called Tom and here we are."

"That's some detective work, but I thought I was supposed to call you?"

"I didn't want to wait for your call. I figured you were gonna call me as soon as you got home. Did I catch you doing something?"

"I was taking a shower." I suddenly realized that I was talking to her naked and dripping wet all over my living room floor. The shower was still running in the bathroom.

"Oooh! Really! Damn. Too bad we don't have video capabilities on these phones." Maddy chuckled.

"Funny! I think I broke my coccyx when I slipped and fell running to get the phone."

"That explains why you were out of breath. I thought you might have been doing something else in the shower!"

"Funny girl."

We continued to talk while I walked back to the bathroom, shut off the water, and grabbed a towel. Sitting on the edge of the bed, I towelled myself off while I listened and put on a pair of gym shorts and an old KISS t-shirt. We chatted for quite some time as I walked about the apartment. I imagined what she was doing; what she looked like on the other end of the line.

As Maddy continued talking, I opened a can of Diet Coke and sat on the couch. The conversation went on as the room slowly faded into darkness. Eventually, two empty Diet Coke cans stood beside the phone cradle on the end table, and the time on the VHS machine shone glowingly in red digital display at 11:13.

"I have to work at seven. Otherwise I would ask you if you wanted to go out and get a drink," Maddy offered.

"If I didn't have to work tomorrow, too, I'd invite you here for a drink so we could keep talking," I countered.

"Since we're both working tomorrow at seven, I may as well come over."

"Wait? What?"

Laughter filled the earpiece. "You should've heard yourself stammering to say something. Don't worry, Tiger; I'm not that easy." Pause. "But I'm worth the wait."

3

I dragged my ass into the Ottawa EMS headquarters the next morning. Tom was already booking us into our assigned rig for the day. Passing a washroom on my way to the garage, I went inside, leaned over the sink, cranked the cold water, and let it run until it got as cold as possible. With my eyes closed, I cupped my hands, filled them with water, and splashed it on my face. I still felt horrible. The water dripped from my chin onto my shirt, turning the midnight blue uniform black. Blindly, I brushed the excess water from my shirt, reached down, and fumbled for my bag. I turned and bumped into someone.

"Watch it, son."

I opened my eyes. Before me was the new EMS Chief, Andrew Krycek, in his crisp, white, and obviously dry shirt.

"You look like shit." He rubbed his cheeks.

I took the cue and rubbed the remaining water from my face. "Sorry about that. Yeah, I look and feel like shit today." Great! I thought. First time meeting the new boss and I looked like I had taken a shower with my clothes on.

"Rough night?"

"Yeah. You might say that."

"Sick? Hungover? You OK to work?"

"Tired. Stayed up late talking to a girl I met."

"Go get a few coffees into you. Don't want any of my medics making mistakes because of lack of sleep."

"Good idea." With my eyes barely open, I brushed past the chief and pulled the door open to exit the bathroom.

"Is she worth it?"

I turned to face Chief Krycek. "What?"

"Is she worth you feeling and looking like a pile of shit?"

"Oh yeah!" I smiled and woke up a little. The door closed behind me.

Later, I sat in the passenger seat of the rig as we left the Ottawa General

Hospital ER. With my eyes closed, I used my right hand to shield the sun. Tom cranked the wheel hard right, then hard left. The coffee cup I held in my left hand spilled its contents over my thighs. My head bounced off the window.

"Awake yet?"

I grunted and kept my eyes closed while I sipped what was left in the mug.

"How much, or should I say, how little sleep did you get?"

"'Bout two hours."

Tom cranked up CHEZ 106 on the ambulance radio. Matchbox 20 played their newest hit as Tom turned west on Smyth Road, then south on Alta Vista Drive. I kept my eyes closed and tried to get a little sleep. My body was betraying me. In my college days, this was a normal routine: stay up all night partying and drinking—a total lack of sleep—then working a part time job the next day, and sometimes even attending a class. Only a few years later, and I can't even handle a single night without much sleep.

I drifted in and out of a light nap, but any rest at this point would have been worth it. When Tom pulled into Lick's Homeburgers on Alta Vista Drive at Bank Street, I crawled into the back of the rig and sprawled out on the stretcher. I laid back, covered my eyes with my forearm, and let myself drift off. Thirty minutes of undisturbed sleep. I needed it badly.

After what seemed like only a few seconds, a sharp rap on the side of the rig pulled me back from my coma. It was followed by the sound of the driver's door slamming shut.

"Wakey, wakey, sunshine."

I straightened up the sheets, fluffed the pillow, exited through the side door of the rig, and hopped into the passenger seat of the cab.

"I thought you were starting your new health regime. You know, eating right, no carbs, no fats?" I asked Tom.

"Rumours are Lick's is closing and I want to get in every last burger I can before they're gone. Besides, I got one for you." He tossed me a brown bag. The weight of the bag indicated a large burger, which, no doubt, Tom would have had "dragged through the garden." That was Tom's way of saying to put everything and anything on it. With no breakfast and only coffee since I had woken up seven hours' prior, the burger would hit the spot.

Tom booked into service and turned south on Bank Street. Mid-afternoon traffic was heavy; nothing unusual about that. The smell of the burger still in the bag only made me hungrier. I barely had the burger out of the waxed paper wrap and was chomping down on it as dispatch called our rig number. I chewed faster, taking another bite.

I pulled the zip pack from between the seat and the centre console, ready to copy the call information.

"4287, call Ottawa."

Tom keyed the mic. "Go for 4287."

"Code 4, 304 Kitchener Avenue. Caller stated father fell. Found him unconscious when he came home. Caller thinks his father is VSA. He can't wake him. Son is too scared to verify patient is VSA or try CPR."

4

Little hearts, flowers, rainbows, and whatever other feminine shapes could be cut from the floral coloured material were carefully traced out, cut, and glued to the wall of the bedroom. Special care had been taken to cut as precisely as possible, keeping the lines crisp and exact. Slowly, meticulously, each project took shape and the material morphed into something new and wonderful.

The orange cap to the glue bottle was twisted loose and an exact amount of white glue spread evenly over the back of the cloth. Finding the right spot for a new cut-out was actually the most difficult task, but once discovered, it only made the wall look that much better.

There were only four different patterns of material used for the wall display, but dozens of hearts and flowers and rainbows. Hearts were the most popular, then flowers. Everything after that was a tie.

The room was brightly lit, the walls a pale shade of pink, the trim around the floors and windows painted a brilliant white and kept immaculately clean. The sheers on the window were tied back and swept upwards, letting them fall in a cascade of pink, and ending with a darker shade of lace trim.

Hundreds of hearts of different sizes and colour patterns far outnumbered anything else on the wall. Some of the hearts were barely visible, while others were larger than the dinner plates used when company came over.

Head cocked back, eyes closed, arms outstretched, the spinning started. Tunes hummed from children's television shows filled the room. The spinning continued, dizziness set in, and only stopped when laughter took over. Hands were braced firmly on the back of the wood chair to prevent falling over. But even falling to the floor would have been fun.

Once the dizziness abated, looking down, it was noticed that the little material left on the table was now only tiny scraps. Not nearly enough to cut any more shapes to glue on the wall. The scraps were brushed into a wastebasket, and the white plastic liner was tied and carried to the garbage can. Scissors were put in the drawer along with the glue. All the books used to trace the favourite shapes were placed on the shelf beside the schoolbooks. Mom would be upset to see the room in a mess. Mom would be pleased to see the new hearts and flowers added to the wall, and how clean the room was.

Everything has a place, so everything in its place, Mom always said. The room was perfect again. Clean, smelling of flowers and drying white glue. Soon the glue smell would leave the room and all that would remain would be the flowers and their aroma.

The afternoon sun was still high in the sky, but it was naptime. Naps were important to the keep the body fresh and alert. Time to crawl into bed, pull the covers up high, and fluff the pillow. Eyes closed, and soon sleep took hold.

5

The father was lying supine on the kitchen floor. The son who'd called 911 was standing far off in the corner, not wanting to touch his father or even look at what we were doing. He was still holding the phone, hiding around the corner, sneaking a quick peek every few moments. It seemed like he was afraid that he might catch whatever had overcome his father.

Unlike the Emergency Department, where the ambient temperature is controlled, the lighting is always perfect, family is kept away, and the bays are clean, we work in a totally opposite environment. The kitchen here was dirty, smelly, and dark, and the family was peeking from the corner.

I knelt on the man's right side and looked down at the father whose chest I was crushing with my compressions. CPR is not a dignified procedure. It violates so many social taboos. You assess the patient to make sure they are actually dead. With enough experience, most medics can tell if a person is dead from twenty feet away. This guy had been VSA for at least ten minutes. His skin was pale, his temperature had already started to drop slightly, and, this close after death, even slight changes were noticeable. He did not respond to any verbal or painful stimuli.

Once we determined our patient was actually VSA, we had to expose the chest. Male, female, young or old, we don't care. Just another one of the indignities we perform. So many people would be embarrassed to expose themselves like this, but we forego any shame and rip the shirt open by grabbing the material from the waist and yanking. Buttons usually fly in all directions as threads give way to the pressure placed upon them.

One medic usually starts compression at a rate of fifteen compressions to two ventilations. However, I don't know any professional medic who would ventilate a patient without a BVM. The Bag Valve Mask device provides a barrier between the patient and medic, and a simple squeeze of the bag pushes air into the lungs. We always wait to ventilate with a BVM. No self-respecting medic would ever do mouth-to-mouth.

The other medic applies the defib pads to the bare chest. One of the large sticky electrodes is applied vertically below the right collarbone or clavicle. The other is applied horizontally under the left armpit below the breast. The pre-attached defib electrode cable is then plugged into the defibrillator. If the defib computer sees a shockable rhythm, it will charge to a pre-set power level and tell us when it's ready to shock; unlike on television, few people actually receive a jolt.

The defib allows for manual or semi-automatic operation. The Memory Control Module in the defib had been set for semi-automatic mode at shift change. I could have changed the MCM to manual, but decided to leave it on semi-automatic. My blue-gloved hands pushed hard on the man's chest as Tom pressed the "Analyze" button. I lifted my hands and rested them on my lap. The Laerdal 3000QR paused and then started to buzz loudly. The mechanical voice reminded us to "Stand Clear". You could see the cardiac rhythm, or ECG, on the monochrome screen. His heart was in a fast uncontrollable rhythm. It needed to be shocked out of this rhythm or he would die. The tone grew louder as the power level increased, then stopped. Tom looked around to make sure no one was around to touch the patient as we shocked him. He pressed the "Shock" button. 200 joules of energy surged from one pad to the other, through his heart in the hopes that the electrical current would shut down the bad rhythm and allow the normal rhythm to take over. The patient gave a little jerk, his arms raised slightly, nothing like what they show on TV when the patient almost hops out of bed.

We paused and looked at the screen. The rapid, unstable rhythm had stopped, a single flat line appeared, and then a normal sinus rhythm started; slow at first, then it picked up.

Tom ripped open the BVM package and started to ventilate the patient with high-flow oxygen. I felt for a carotid pulse in his neck, beside the trachea. The pulse was even; weak, but I could feel it. The colour almost instantly started to return to the man's face, and there was a frail inspiratory effort. One breath, followed by another, and yet another. The effort wasn't enough to sustain the body. Tom continued to ventilate.

In between ventilations, Tom managed to get a blood pressure. "Still low, 60 over 42. Pulse on the screen is 48, regular."

Tom pulled an endotracheal tube from his bag, ripped open the package, and squeezed lubrication on the tip. He flipped open the laryngoscope like a switchblade knife, lay down on the kitchen floor, and tilted the patient's head back. He inserted the Macintosh curved blade over his tongue and pushed the handle up and forward. With the first attempt, the tube slid into place.

I unzipped the IV bag and spiked into the IV line, opened it wide, and let fluid flow through the line until it ran freely on the kitchen floor.

Tom attached the BVM to the end of the ET tube. I stopped what I was doing and auscultated the patient's lungs for the sound of air being pushed through as Tom squeezed the BVM. I nodded in agreement and Tom secured the tube in place with tape to the patient's face.

The IV was set in the man's right dorsal vein on the back of his hand. I looped the line, taped it in place, and opened it up wider in an attempt to raise his blood pressure. I was about to ask the son to help hold the IV bag when I heard the side door to the kitchen open and slam shut.

"Gents! What can we do to help?"

Another Ottawa paramedic crew had shown up to help. On cardiac arrest calls or other difficult scenes, two crews are often sent to assist each other.

Without looking up, Tom quipped, "One shock and badda-bing. Got him back. Let's see if we can get him to the hospital alive." He looked up at the young crew. "This, my friends, is what you call experience." Tom shot me a look, smiled, and then his attention went back to the patient on the floor.

"Or dumb luck," the younger medic shot back.

The patient's condition continually improved as we prepped him for transport. His respiratory effort grew stronger with each breath. Within minutes, the old man was strapped to a backboard and secured to the stretcher.

Outside, as Tom and I were loading the cot into the rig, a woman came up from behind, screaming. I locked the cot in place and released the sidewall handle as she grabbed my arm and spun me around. A young woman, with short, dark hair, eyes wide with tears flowing freely down her cheeks, and panic and desperation in her voice, she tightened her grasp around my arm.

"Please… my baby!"

She turned and started running, dragging me along. Her grip was so tight, I had no choice but to follow or risk having my arm pulled from its socket.

"Have you got your portable?" I yelled at Tom.

Tom nodded. "I'll go with the patient to the General and send one of the PCPs down to help you out. I'm calling the 10-200s and dispatch to tell them you're on another call."

I could see one of the medics hopping into the other ambulance to follow me down the street. As I was being pulled around the corner, the woman didn't let up on her grip. Apparently, I was holding her back. She pulled and wanted me to run at her pace. Not knowing what I was in for, I scanned the street looking for, well, anything.

Partially hidden by a tree, neighbours stood in a small crowd looking at something on the ground. One woman was holding her hand to her mouth, with her other arm wrapped around her chest. There was a lot of talking, yet no one appeared to be doing anything.

The frantic woman punched through the crowd, dragging me with her. The rest of the crowd gave way.

When the woman released her grip, she fell to her knees, landing beside a young girl lying supine on the grass. I stopped, taking in the scene before me: the woman—the mother—raised her child's head, rested it on her lap, and began stroking her hair back and away from her face while she continued to cry and mumble something to herself.

A young girl, five at the most, pretty, with dark hair like her mother and huge piercing brown eyes stared upwards, seeing nothing. She lay motionless, quiet, as if sleeping in the grass and enjoying the summer sun. There was no visible trauma, no blood. Her arms and legs appeared to be uninjured. No obvious fractures were noted.

"Did anyone see what happened?" I asked. "How long has she been here?"

Silence. No one answered, the only response silent head shaking.

I bent down and felt for a radial pulse in her right wrist. Nothing. I gently pulled the young girl from her mother's lap and laid her back down on the hard ground. I knelt beside her and felt for a carotid pulse in the neck. There was no pulse, but there were several red spots on her neck. Mental note!

As I palpated her carotid artery, I felt crackling under my fingers. No pulse, but there were definitely fine crackles?

Another note!

I checked her breathing; nothing. The young girl was VSA just like the older man on the kitchen floor only minutes earlier.

"Anyone know CPR?" I looked at the crowd as they surrounded me.

Heads again shook from side to side. Either no one knew how to perform CPR or they didn't want to get involved.

Not wanting to cause any more hardship for her mother, I chose not to open the young girl's dress to perform CPR. I found my landmark and I started compressions. With one hand, I reached up and grabbed the woman standing closest to me and pulled her to the ground. She dropped to her knees.

"You've seen CPR on TV, right?" She nodded. "When I pause my compressions, pinch her nose, blow slowly into her mouth, pause, and repeat. Got it?"

"I can't." She was shaking so badly, I thought I had chosen the wrong volunteer.

"You can and you will." I spoke calmly, but with authority. She nodded in agreement and positioned herself to ventilate. Normally, medics would never do mouth-to-mouth or ask non-family members to do artificial respirations. Common sense no longer applies when kids are involved. I also couldn't ask the mother to do CPR on her own five-year-old child.

The crowd parted as one of the Primary Care Paramedics arrived on scene. I had been so focused on the young patient that I hadn't even heard the ambulance pull up.

The other medic dropped the oxygen bags beside me, attached the BVM, cranked the tank stem, and started the flow of oxygen. He placed the BVM in the reluctant volunteer's hand and the mask over the child's face, and showed her how to squeeze.

The model of defib used by PCPs was not meant for patients this small. Besides, I suspected the young patient hadn't died from cardiac arrest, and the defib would have little effect on someone who had been choked to death. The medic applied the monitoring electrodes instead of defib pads, and the defib-monitor showed asystole—a flat line—when I stopped doing compressions. A semi-automatic defib will not shock this rhythm.

Not wanting to speak out loud with the mother standing over us, watching our every move, I caught the attention of the other medic and cupped both my hands around my neck, a non-verbal cue for a cervical collar. He simply blinked his acknowledgement.

The cot was placed on the opposite side of me and dropped to its lowest position, and the medic placed a backboard behind the woman who was providing ventilations. The medic instructed someone else to hold the stretcher to prevent it from rolling away and took over ventilations. Between ventilations, he slid a cervical collar around the child's neck and set the Velcro to secure it.

"Ready?" he asked me.

I stopped compressions for only a moment and carefully logrolled the patient to her side, keeping her spine in alignment. The other medic stopped doing ventilations and placed the backboard behind her as I rolled her up and back onto the boards. Not done according to protocol;

sometimes protocols were meant to be broken.

We locked the stretcher in place, and I climbed into the back patient compartment, cranked on the oxygen, and felt myself getting pushed from behind.

"I'll take over pumping, you do the blowing. You look tired."

I looked over my shoulder to see Galen ripping the Velcro sides open on his protective vest and unclipping his duty belt, gun and all, letting it fall to the bench seat. Galen had done CPR on as many patients as most medics, and we usually like to have the person assisting us doing compressions anyway. Managing the airway is much more difficult and better left to the medics.

"There are enough officers to manage the scene until I get back. Where's Tom?"

"Took another patient."

Galen looked down at the young girl. "Jesus fucking Christ! Are you fucking kidding me? She can't be more than what? Six? Your new partner told me you think foul play." He began compressions.

"Not think! I know! When we get to the hospital, check under the c-collar. There are fingertip bruises around her neck consistent with being choked. No other trauma."

I hooked up the BVM to the oxygen and began ventilating.

6

Stepping through the Civic emergency room sliding glass doors, I walked to the centre of the parking lot, closed my eyes, placed my hands in the small of my back, leaned back, groaned, and let the warmth of the August sun beat down upon me, washing away the stress of the last call.

With my eyes still closed, I heard Galen as he walked up to me.

"You're right. Once she was pronounced, the doc took off the collar and there were distinctive fingertip bruises around her neck." He looked up into the sky where I would've been looking if my eyes had been open. "Whatcha' looking at?"

"De-stressing."

"How do you do this? Tom is still inside the ER with the old man and he said you did back to back codes!"

"Yup!" I straightened up and turned to face my friend. "Nice, eh! Calling them codes is easier than saying we dealt with two dead people."

Galen walked towards my rig and pulled open the back doors.

"Inside."

Curiosity got the better of me. I looked at my friend, puzzled, but chose to follow his orders. I brushed past him and sat in the captain's chair.

Galen shut the doors and pushed/pulled on them to make sure they were secure. He sat down on the bench, his elbows resting on his knees, and contemplated what he was about to divulge.

"What I'm about to tell you can get me fired!" Galen looked through the glass to see if anyone was close by. "This little girl is the fourth to be killed in the same manner in the last eight months."

"What?" I leaned forward. "How the hell does something like this get past the press?"

"We—well, the detectives—have been working hard with the families to keep things quiet. After the second one, police brass knew we had a problem. They asked the family to keep the details private until we could build a case. We have the same arrangement with the third family. Now we have to talk to this family. I can't see this staying under wraps much longer, though."

"What've you got so far?" Galen had me hooked.

"Free tonight?"

"I am now."

Later that evening, I buzzed Galen up to my apartment. As usual, he'd brought pizza and beer. Making himself at home, Galen dropped the pizza box on the counter, pulled out a slice, and started eating as he twisted off the cap of a beer bottle. Before sitting down, he dropped a file on the dining room table. The file folder spilled its contents.

Papers and photos slid across the varnished wood table. One of the pictures stopped before me. With my index finger, I turned the colour picture so it was square in front of me. My heart sank as I stared at the portrait of a beautiful young child with ginger red hair, similar in colour to Galen's. Her eyes were closed, her skin pale, with the cold, unfeeling stainless steel table as the background.

In disgust, I pushed the photo back to Galen. Like the winner in a poker game, Galen swept up all the papers and photos and tucked them back into the folder.

"This," he tapped the folder, "this bothers you? You see this shit every day."

"I work on them every day. I don't see them as a person, who they are. I think Tom does the same. To me, they're faceless patients, bodies to practise my skills on. If I actually had to look at the faces of my patients every day, I would be on psych meds."

Galen twisted the cap off a bottle and placed it in front of me. "Drink!" He tilted his bottle back. "You couldn't pay me enough to do your job."

"Give you a little hint, we get paid shit."

I swallowed half of the bottle in the first gulp. Something, anything, to get the image of that little girl out of my mind.

Again, Galen pulled the papers and photos from the folder. He arranged them chronologically, with occurrence report papers clipped to photos. Each occurrence report number corresponded to the number on the photo.

"How did you get these?" I asked my friend.

"Would you believe me if I told you I stole them?" I looked up from the table. "Serious. When the lead detective on the case asked for my help making backup copies on our new server, I made an extra copy of the entire case for myself to study at home."

"You stole from the police department?"

"I'll give them back when I'm done," he countered.

Galen grabbed the first bundle dated "January 13, 2000" and pulled the photos of a young girl, aged five, who went missing from her fenced-in backyard. Galen went on to tell me the circumstances of the abduction.

The mother was outside watching her child play in the snow with the family dog. The mother left to answer the phone and when she came back less than a minute later—or so the mother said—the girl was gone. The dog was still running around, barking at the fence. The dog had trampled over any possible footprints in the snow in the family's yard, and there were too many footprints on the opposite side of the fence to track.

When they found the girl's body, it, too, had the fingertip bruises indicating that she had been strangled. The person who had strangled the young girl must have been wearing gloves and left no prints. The handprint size on the neck didn't match up to the father's.

The media had played it up that the estranged father might have abducted the child. Since the father had no alibi for the time the child went missing, everyone had made up their minds that he was guilty. The father had denied any involvement, and with the stress of the media coverage, he committed suicide shortly after. That seemed to quell the media's desire to sensationalize the case. Whether it was accurate or not, it fit the cover story for the police.

Each subsequent case had similar circumstances: no one had seen the victim disappear, no one had seen anyone suspicious around any of the scenes, and each victim had the tell-tale ligature marks around her neck.

After drinking several beers and finishing off the pizza, Galen and I sat side by side, quietly comparing notes and looking for clues; anything that may have been overlooked. A knock at my apartment door broke the silence. I looked at Galen; he looked back at me and shrugged his shoulders. Neither of us were expecting someone this late.

Pulling the door open, I found Maddy standing before me, holding a bag of Chinese food and another large paper bag of drinks. She was dressed in a simple, tight white T-shirt and faded jeans. It occurred to me that I had never seen her in anything except for scrubs.

"Hungry?" Maddy smiled and passed the brown bag to me.

I stood silently before her, wondering what she was doing at my door.

"Thanks." I looked down at the bag, feeling the warmth of the food it held. Like a teenager, I was lost for words, I wanted to invite her in but instead, kept looking at her.

Maddy stood smiling, waiting for me to do something. I took a few steps back as Maddy walked past me into the living room. Off to the left in the dining room, Galen heard the voices and stood as Maddy walked in.

"I spoke to Tom in the ER today. He said you were spending a quiet evening at home and that you love surprises. So I thought I would violate your privacy and come over with Chinese food and beer." Maddy stood before me, smiling. "My bad."

"Not a problem. Galen decided to stop by with some police homework."

Galen walked over, grinning, and extended his hand, "Hello." His voice was musical. "Galen. Married, but soon to be divorced, if you're single."

Maddy smiled. "Sorry, I'm taken." She glanced my way. Galen smirked and looked at me.

Seeing the papers and photos scattered on the table, Maddy looked at me. "Am I disturbing you guys? I can leave."

"No, not at all. It's nothing, er, official. Galen just asked for an outsider's opinion on something he's doing after hours," I offered.

Looking around the room, Maddy suggested, "There should be enough food for three. Do you want an extra set of eyes…?" she asked, fumbling to remember Galen's name.

"Galen," he said softly, reminding Maddy. "Sure, come on over and take a look. I'll get the food on the table." Galen grabbed a few plates from the kitchen as I sat beside Maddy at the table and gave her a quick breakdown of the case presented before her.

Galen opened each of the food containers and piled the plates beside them. The empty pizza box lay open in the kitchen, now filled with empty Chinese food containers, and the empty beer bottles stood like soldiers at attention on the counter.

On the table, photos and police occurrence reports were stacked in chronological order. Galen, Maddy, and I argued over minute details of the abduction and death of each child.

The beer bottles emptied quickly, the empty plates got stacked at the far side of the table, and napkins had fallen to the floor.

"Other than the ligature marks, ages, and genders of the victims, there are no other similarities." Galen slammed his open hand down on the table. He stood and paced around it. "Come on," he yelled in frustration.

"OK, OK, wait. Each girl is under the age of seven, each was taken close to home…" Maddy started another avenue of thinking.

"Really? What seven-year-old is away from home without their parent?" Galen burst out.

Maddy stopped short.

I looked at the map of the city of Ottawa. Four different coloured dots, each representing one of the children, indicated the sites of the attacks.

One in the north end of Ottawa, in Britannia Heights; one close to Cyrville Park in the east; one on Debra Avenue off Meadowlands Drive; and finally our call on Kitchener Avenue. I scanned the four neighbourhoods and drew circles in pencil representing approximately ten blocks around each site, to see if I could find an area that intersected as a safe zone for the attacker.

Two areas overlapped: Kitchener and Debra Avenue. I almost jumped out of my seat. I sat back down when the other two circles did not intersect or even come close to the other two.

"What?" Galen asked.

"Nothing. I thought I had something. I have to take a leak." I realized this was technically our first date and I had just told Maddy I had to pee. I looked at her and she simply smiled.

I sat on the toilet, not wanting to make any noise, and closed my eyes. I rubbed my face; my lips felt swollen from all the salt in the pizza and Chinese food. I was tired and frustrated at our lack of progress in trying to help my friend.

"Hey, wipe up and get your ass out here!" Galen yelled.

I finished what I was doing, washed up, and rushed down the hall.

Maddy was smiling, glowing as if she had just pulled Excalibur from the stone. Galen had his arm around her.

"You'll never believe who found a link?"

"What've you got?" I walked over as I dried my hands on my jeans.

Maddy pulled me in close to her. Our arms were touching. Her long brown hair fell down off her shoulders and the air around her smelled of, I wasn't quite sure, but something feminine. It was nice; very nice.

"…and that's when I noticed it." Maddy turned to look at me. "Are you paying attention?"

"Yeah!" I exclaimed.

Maddy reached down, held my hand, and squeezed. "Look!" She pointed.

Four photos were side by side, each showing the lifeless face of a young child—a young girl—taken from her family too soon. I couldn't look past their faces.

"Do you see it?" Maddy asked.

"See what?"

Galen interjected. "I didn't see it either until Maddy pointed it out."

"The only thing the four girls have in common. We looked at neighbourhoods, social status, hair colour, eye colour, race, everything except one thing." She stopped short.

"What?" I yelled.

Maddy tapped each picture in a row, hard, to emphasize her point.

"Each girl is wearing a floral print dress. Each dress was ripped at the scene."

"Yeah, so the police report said each dress was ripped. They figured it happened during the assault."

"I read that. They're wrong. Look real close. The dresses are not just ripped; the print edges don't match up. There's a piece missing from each dress. That's what the killer took. He attacked each girl because of the dress she was wearing that day. And that," she squeezed my hand tighter, "that's the trophy!"

7

Galen pulled out a magnifying glass and studied the photos more closely. He moved the lens in or out to adjust his focus on the edges of the torn dresses. Maddy was correct. The torn sections of the floral prints didn't match up on any of the four dresses.

Maddy leaned over the table, looking over the photos and holding my hand tightly, out of Galen's view. She was proud of herself, smiling and gripping my hand tighter with anticipation as she waited for Galen's approval.

Galen said nothing. He was concentrating on the images being scanned carefully under the magnifying glass. When he finished with the first, he picked up the second, then the third, and finally the fourth. He put the magnifying glass down and slid back from the table. He slowly got up and went to the kitchen, cracked open another beer, and sat back down.

"Seven detectives missed it. Not once, but four times." Galen looked at Maddy and I as we stood on the opposite side of the dining room table, Maddy still holding my hand out of sight.

"I'm not even supposed to have this stuff. You guys can never say anything about this and I can't give you credit for your find." He stared at Maddy. "At least you both know that you played a part in the investigation." He tilted the beer bottle back and swallowed. "You guys OK with that?"

We nodded in agreement.

"I've got to find a way to pretend to suddenly find the discrepancy in the material and tell the investigative team about it."

Maddy was beaming. Her grip on my right hand almost cut off the circulation to my fingers.

"Is there anything else we can do?" Maddy offered.

"It's late. We better call it a night. I have to work tomorrow." Galen started to gather up the pieces of evidence and place them all in their respective folders and envelopes.

Maddy finally let go of my hand, walked around to the far side of the table, and started to collect the dishes and food containers.

"I'm calling a cab. Wanna split the fare?" Galen asked Maddy as he picked up the phone.

"Thanks, I'm good. I only had one beer all night. I'm gonna stick around and help clean up before going home. I don't have to work tomorrow."

Galen shot me a look. It was the subtle, quiet, mind-reading look that only guys can read. I'm pretty sure Galen understood my silent reply.

Galen thought for a moment. "My God, it's only Thursday tomorrow. Man, I have to get off this shift work. It's great if you're a firefighter and you get to sleep all night, but we have to drive around and protect people. Fuck that." He air-quoted "protect."

*****

Across town, the bedroom door was locked, the lights were turned off, and the window curtains were opened wide, permitting the light from the full moon to fill the room. It was mid-month; the moon was high in the sky and lit up the bedroom with an eerie calm.

The leaves from the trees in the backyard fractured the moonlight and made the floral cut-outs dance on the wall.

Smiles became wide, and eyes became heavy as they strained to see all the beautiful, tiny shapes cut from the material taken from the young girls' dresses.

Memories drifted back to younger days; carefree days when the stress of being an adult seemed like a far-off, make believe land, like in the books read by parents at bedtime. Those memories were good; everything about childhood had been enjoyable, and bad times hadn't been discovered yet.

Adulthood can tear into childhood like a ravenous wolf ripping the flesh off of a fallen deer. Adulthood crashes in and changes the life of a child abruptly, sometimes violently, forever changing who and what you are. Those metamorphoses can alter the very being in more ways than just the physical.

Lying on the carpeted floor, looking up, seeing those cut-outs, whatever had changed was no longer relevant. Only the good childhood memories returned when viewing the delicate floral designs. Simple, elegant shapes, childlike shapes, rekindling the who and what of childhood. The problems of today slipped away in the moonlight to be temporarily forgotten, always to return when the sun rises and washes clean the mind of the night before.

Outside, the stars and the moon acted as guides from one realm to the other, tracing their paths in the darkness, blurring the mind free of adulthood responsibilities.

But for now, it was night. Sleep came peacefully, safe in the knowledge that, whatever tomorrow brings, this room was a sanctuary from life and all it produces, good or bad. It would always be here to protect and serve in ways only the mind could imagine.

Curled on the carpet, covered by a knitted blanket, eyes grew heavy as they watched the shapes dance on the wall bathed in moonlight.

"They are mine. Mine."

Eyes closed, darkness set in. Sleep came easily.

8

I rolled over and tucked my arms up and under my head. The sweat on my back had made my skin stick to the leather couch. Even with my eyes still closed, I could make out the brightness in the living room. The morning sun had burst through the patio door and the room was awash in yellow light.

I had forgotten to draw the curtains or put a sheet on the leather couch before bedding down for the night so that Maddy could sleep in the bed. The couch was not that uncomfortable. Despite sticking to the leather, I'd actually slept pretty well.

I pushed my face into the back cushion to block out the light, but my nose filled with the scent of breakfast cooking. Fresh coffee, toast, I thought, maybe muffins. Meat? I knew I didn't have bacon in the fridge, but I did have some ham left over from dinner a few nights prior. I really didn't want to wake up just yet. An hour more, half an hour would suffice, fifteen minutes even.

I heard a soft thud behind me on the table. The smell of coffee permeated the air and stirred my senses awake. I was really beginning to like this woman.

I rolled over, rubbed my eyes with the backs of my hands, and then stretched the night away. I opened my eyes to see Maddy, awake, showered, dressed, and ready for the day. She looked amazing. Even better than she had the night before. She stood over me, smiling.

"Morning."

I wanted to reply, but my mouth was pasty and I'm sure my breath would have knocked her over, even from this distance. I sat up, reached for the cup, warmed my hands, and took a sip before speaking.

"Thanks. How long have you been up?"

"Not long. I took a quick shower before making breakfast. You have about ten minutes before everything is ready if you want to wash up first."

I stood, coffee cup still in hand, and made a beeline for the bathroom.

Breakfast was laid out on the table by the time I'd finished my shower. Maddy and I chatted about the details of the case and work, and then just got to know each other better. The conversation never stopped. The cups of coffee continued to be refilled, and the plates got pushed aside to make room for elbows on the table. Time passed with total disregard for the outside world.

Eventually, the talk moved to the kitchen. Dishes were cleaned, food was put away, and the kitchen was tidied.

Finally, Maddy grabbed her keys and stood at the door. The banter continued, then just stopped. There was an awkward moment when silence filled the apartment. We looked at each other. Maddy then leaned in and gave me a slow kiss on the cheek. She pulled back and smiled the kind of full-face smile that shows its true meaning.

Maddy forced herself from the doorway, walked slowly down the hall, and, just like she'd done in the ER, spun around. She looked back at me, smiled the same smile, continued her spin, said nothing, and walked to the elevator. The button was pushed. The bell chimed. She turned my way again and leaned back against the wall, one foot on the wall, one hand on her hip; the other hung loosely at her side. Her head tilted ever so slightly with the smile that hadn't faded from the time she left the doorway.

I forgot to breathe, my heart flipped like a coin tossed into a fountain. It turned one way, slid the other, turned over, and then hit the bottom hard. I think I actually felt a little nauseous. My palms became clammy, and sweat formed on my back. My heart raced and pounded in my chest.

The elevator door opened and she entered slowly, her gaze never leaving me until the silver doors closed before her.

I would always remember that pose.

I turned back into the apartment, closed the door, and rubbed my palms on my jeans. It was then I finally took a breath.

"Whoa! That was freaking amazing!" I said out loud without realizing it.

I sat on the couch, retrieved the phone, called the police station, and left a message for Galen.

Within a few minutes, my phone rang.

"What the fuck do you want?" The voice was buried in static.

"Nice to talk to you, too!" The connection was bad. "Where are you? I can barely make you out."

"Sparks and Kent. Pulled a guy over for picking up a hooker. This time of the day, and this asshole needs to get laid. These buildings blocking my signal or you just hard of hearing?"

"Yeah, you're all static. Did you get a chance to talk to the detectives about what Maddy figured out?"

"I've got to write this fuck up, dipshit, for soliciting. Can you meet me for coffee at our Tim's in twenty minutes?"

"Done." I hung up.

Galen and I always had an ongoing coffee thing whenever we needed to talk. We would go to our favourite Tim Hortons, order a few coffees, and bitch about whatever topic was at hand.

I grabbed my keys and ran down the hall to the elevator, secretly hoping that Maddy would still be in the parking lot. When I got outside, I realized that I had no clue what kind of car she drove or where she had parked. I scanned the lot; not seeing her, I sat down hard into my car and froze.

Last night was actually our first date and I felt like I had known Maddy for decades. I shook my head, started the car, and headed to the coffee shop.

I was on my second coffee by the time Galen showed up. Galen's coffee had grown cold. He brought it to the counter to have it heated up in the microwave. Instead, seeing a customer in a police uniform, the worker poured out the cold coffee and made Galen a fresh cup.

With his hot coffee in hand, Galen sat down, pulled the Velcro strips on his bullet resistant vest to loosen them, and allowed air to circulate.

"I wish I could take this fucking gun off, too." He squirmed in his seat. "Seriously, if some asshole is going to run, I'm not chasing him or pulling my gun. Do you know how much paperwork we have to do every time we pull our gun from the holster in public?"

"I know, only because every time we get together, you bitch about the vest and the belt." I pulled my chair closer to the table. "So what did the detectives say?"

Galen placed both elbows on the table and leaned in close. "I gave them some bullshit story that, when I made the copies, I noticed the pictures and I couldn't get them out of my mind. I went in this morning and asked to look at them, and pointed it out to the chief investigator."

Galen removed the lid from his cup, blew across the top, and took a sip. He knew I wanted to hear what had happened, but thought he would torture me for a while longer.

"So I pointed out the rips in the material that Maddy noticed and he looked at the pictures like he'd just spotted the shooter who killed Kennedy on the grassy knoll." Galen took another sip. "He flipped back and forth from one picture to the next, and sure as shit, he was floored. Not one of the guys assigned to the case noticed the edges of the material didn't match except for your girlfriend."

"Maddy is not," I made a point of emphasizing "not," "my girlfriend." I smiled. "Yet!" I couldn't stop smiling. "Did I mention she made breakfast?"

"She stayed over? Really?" Galen looked surprised.

"I slept on the couch."

"Idiot. If I wasn't a cop I'd shoot you and ask her out." He took a sip of coffee. "Anyway, turns out that not one of the girls was sexually assaulted, they each had ligature marks from strangulation, and now we know the trophy was a piece of material from the dress."

Galen's radio squawked. He keyed the mic, spoke, put it down, and looked at me.

"It was nothing. Gotta go soon."

"So where do we go from here?" I asked.

"We don't do anything. The investigative team has a few leads to follow up. They told me they are going to see where the dresses were purchased. See if they can find anything in common with the stores, clerks, shit like that."

"I still have a copy of the map we made of the four neighbourhoods where each attack took place. I thought about it. The guy who attacked all four girls would want to be familiar with the area, right?"

"We discussed this last night. None of the four areas of the city have much in common. Each section was a different social economic class; one is more English than French. One is more ethnic than the others."

"Except?" I raised my eyebrows.

Galen shrugged his shoulders and took another sip of coffee. "Except what?"

"Each section has a major road close by: the Queensway Parkway and Riverside Drive."

The Queensway is a major four-lane highway that runs east-west across the upper part of the city. Riverside Drive branches off the Queensway and snakes its way south along the Rideau River.

"You're a fucking moron, you know that. This is Ottawa; every section of town has a major artery that runs through it."

I held up two fingers. "Those two roads seem to be awful close to all four attacks. A bus driver or cabbie or delivery guy would probably drive through each section daily. If he has a thing for little girls, he would see them playing all summer long."

Galen sat upright, put his coffee down, lowered his head, and covered his eyes. There was a long pause as he thought.

"Who the fuck do you think we are?" he said with his head low. Galen looked at me. "Do you really think we hadn't thought of that, like on day one?"

Galen tilted the cup back and finished his coffee. The cup made a hollow sound as it hit the table.

"I know you're trying to help, but looking at the city grid is basic policing 101. They looked at the city buses and drivers who worked that route six months before the first killing until now and ruled them out. As far as cabbies go, they're still working that angle."

He stood and re-attached the Velcro on his vest. "Right now, they're looking at the stores that sell the dresses, each manufacturer and style. It's a long shot, but we have to look at everything without discounting anyone. Or anything." Galen patted me on the back. "I really appreciate the work you've done on this. It won't go unnoticed."

Sitting alone at the table, watching Galen drive away, I realized that there was a reason I was a paramedic instead of a cop. I, too, would feel a little uneasy if Galen tried to tell me how to do my job.

I ordered another coffee and sat at my table, sipping my drink and watching the traffic go by on Alta Vista Drive. The traffic was like a living organism. Cars, trucks, pickups, cabs, buses, motorcycles all went by as I sat there. The traffic would pause when the light turned red farther up the street, causing the flow to stop and wait for the light to change.

I couldn't get the cab or bus angle out of my mind, convinced that they would have the right opportunity to drive through any neighbourhood without raising any concerns.

In the distance, an ambulance siren wail was becoming louder and closer. Traffic was already beginning to pull over in front of me. The dual tone yelp increased in intensity and began to echo off the houses on Alta Vista until the emergency crew screamed past the Tim Horton's restaurant. I only hoped it wasn't for another little girl. Another siren was following the vehicle that had just passed, but this one was not an ambulance. Each service siren may sound the same to the public, but each vehicle has its own tone and pitch. If you listen closely, you can tell the difference between a police cruiser, an ambulance, and a fire truck. In this case, a cruiser blew past, following the ambulance, possibly responding to the same call.

"Holy shit!"

9

I called Tom from the pay phone to see if he could help me track down a new lead. No answer. I left a message on his answering machine. He was probably at the gym. I called his pager, hoping he would call me back quickly.

Excited, I finished my coffee and ordered another. I would be banging off the wall shortly! Minutes passed, then half an hour, without a reply from Tom.

I called Maddy at home. She picked up on the second ring.

"Aren't you supposed to wait a day or two until you call me?" She chuckled. "I had a really good time last night, by the way. Well, and this morning."

"Me too."

"We should do this again. Soon."

"Great!" I was hyped. "Glad you said that. Are you busy? Can you meet me at the Tim's on Alta Vista? I have a lead." The line went dead.

I can't recall how many coffees I'd had by the time Maddy arrived. My heart pounded in my chest, either from seeing Maddy again, or the caffeine, or both.

Maddy didn't order a coffee. She slipped into a chair across from me and placed both her hands around mine as they cradled the coffee cup. My heart skipped a beat.

"What've you got?" Maddy asked. She was wearing denim shorts and a tan short-sleeve button-up cotton shirt, and her long hair was pulled back. Lost in thought, I stumbled for words.

"Remember we discussed the locations of the murders last night?" Maddy nodded. "And who would have the ability to drive around all those neighbourhoods virtually unnoticed?"

"So?"

"Cabs, buses, and delivery services could drive those areas completely unnoticed. So any one of those guys could cruise around, on or off duty, looking for the next victim. Galen said that was angle number one."

Maddy thought about it. "Makes sense. They would know who could come and go without ever really being noticed."

"Let's play a little game." I didn't want to pull my hands away while she was still holding them, but I was on a roll. I pulled out a pen and napkin. "Let's see how many different services we can name." I looked at Maddy. She was smiling.

"OK."

With pen in hand, I waited for her to start naming off service vehicles.

Back and forth, we rhymed off: cabs, buses, hydro, public works, various delivery services, cable companies, any commercial or private company doing home repair or renovations, until we exhausted all possibilities. I put the pen down.

"So, did we forget anyone?"

Maddy turned the napkin around so she could read it. "Nope, think we covered it all."

"What about…" Hidden from view, I wrote down three more possible suspects and passed it back to Maddy. "These?"

She read the names I had added and looked up at me. "Impossible!"

"When everything else has been discounted, whatever remains, however improbable, must be considered," I quipped.

"But this makes you a suspect."

"It makes all emergency services a suspect: police, fire, and ambulance." I took a sip of coffee. It was cold. "It's not unfathomable that two medics could be doing this as a team. Fire is less likely, unless it's a fire inspector, but my guess is it's a cop."

"Seriously. Have you spoken to Galen about this?"

"Nope. Think about it. He could drive around and anyone who sees a cop cruising wouldn't pay any attention to it, right? How many times do you see a cop just driving around? If you see an ambulance driving slowly down the street, I think that would register and would be something you'd remember. Same goes for fire. You see a fire truck driving down your street slowly, you think a house is on fire. You're gonna go and check. If you see a stranger walking around the neighbourhood, and if you have kids, you'll notice that, right?"

"Agreed."

"Do you really remember how often you see a police cruiser driving around?"

"Never. I don't think you notice the police unless you have something to hide."

I shook my cup. Empty. I stood. "Would you like something?"

"Something cold, please."

I smiled and returned with two cans of Diet Coke and straws. Maddy pulled the tab back and chugged back half the can.

"Thanks."

No straw, right from the can. I was really beginning to like this girl!

We continued to make a mental list of who the suspects might be. It may have been the fact that we were focused on the suspect being a cop, but every time we tried to look elsewhere, we seemed to go right back to that theory.

Maddy finished the can of Coke, looked at the list on the napkin one more time, and slid it across the table. "Do you think the detectives even considered one of their own? I mean, there's a reason we're not cops. We have no expertise analyzing crimes."

"A crime is no different than a patient with an undiagnosed illness presenting in the ER. You have a presenting problem: a crime versus an illness. The clues will lead you to a suspect. Signs and symptoms and lab work will lead you to a possible diagnosis. We're looking at the signs and symptoms of the crime. Besides, it's a fun way to spend the afternoon."

"It is." Maddy reached across the table and with one finger rubbed the back of my hand.

The touch made me smile. "Feel like going for a ride?" I offered.

"Sure. Where are we going?"

"Feel like visiting a few crime scenes?" I stood and picked up the garbage from the table.

"You want to talk to the people on the street where the kids were killed and see if they noticed anything odd the day of the killings, don't you?"

"Only way to tell if our theory is worth pushing to Galen. Besides, do you really think the cops are gonna like it if we're right? I actually hope we're wrong."

Maddy stood, finished the last of the can of pop, and tossed it into the garbage. "Are we ever going to have a regular date?"

"Seriously, would you want to go on a real date after this?"

As we walked to my car, Maddy quietly reached down and squeezed my hand.

"Nope."

10

The detectives were gathered in a conference room. Papers were scattered about the tables, and pictures and reports were taped to the four by eight-foot whiteboard that was hanging from the wall. Bankers' boxes lined the far wall under the windows.

The five men sat around the table, ties pulled loose from around their shirt collars, sleeves rolled up, and suit jackets draped over the backs of their respective chairs. The air conditioning was blowing full blast into the room, but they all looked exhausted and tired. They were all focused on the case before them: the killings of four young children and the new evidence brought to their attention that morning by a uniformed officer.

A slender man, with an olive-skinned complexion, dark charcoal-black hair, and a light grey suit walked into the room, reading from an open file folder.

"Hey, guys, listen to this. Hoese was right. I've got the report from the techs downstairs. They confirmed the dresses weren't just ripped, but that a piece was missing from each dress. None of the families reported anything else missing from any of the bodies. That's the guy's trophy."

He pulled the report out and taped it onto the whiteboard, then tossed the folder onto the centre of the table and took a seat.

"How is it possible that we missed that? We studied every aspect of the photos, looked at the clothing up close, and we still missed it. Christ, how much more have we missed?" one of the five men, a French detective, said. For mid-afternoon, he appeared tired, and upset with himself for not having spotted the obvious clue earlier.

The olive-skinned man stared at the board, and did not turn to face his colleagues. "I think bringing in some fresh eyes on this might help." He turned to see most of the team nodding in agreement. He got up and left the room.

The French detective stood and walked over to the board. "Do we have a hand size estimate from the fingerprint spacing around the necks yet?"

Another detective rifled through some reports and pulled out a forensic analysis on the handprints. He held up the report and read aloud:

"The palm diameter is suspected to be two and one-half inches or five point five centimetres. Due to the various sizes of the victims' necks, the fingertip spacing is inconclusive. On all four victims, both the right and left hands were used. No useable prints were obtained. The suspect was most likely wearing leather gloves, or some thin material gloves like latex or nitrile. There was a small piece of a blue nitrile glove found on one of the victims, but the medics who treated this particular victim state that they may have torn or ripped a glove on scene. During the interview with the medics, they admitted that they seldom pay attention to discarded gloves if they rip one on scene. The brand and style of the glove is very common, sold by most medical supply companies and used by Ottawa EMS, Police, and Fire, and the same brand was awarded to a city tender over a year ago."

He was going to tape a copy of the handprint report to the board, but realized there wasn't any room left. He placed the sheet of paper back into the file and sat down.

The olive-skinned detective returned with two uniformed officers. They both looked surprised and confused at being pulled into the detectives' conference room.

"Guys, we all know Galen Hoese." Galen gave an uncomfortable wave to the room.

"And this is Erin Rodda. Erin has been coordinating the media releases for us." She offered the same uncomfortable wave.

"I got permission to have Galen and Erin join our team for the balance of the week to give us some fresh eyes and ideas. We missed the ripped dresses. Let's see if they can find anything else we could've missed." The olive-skinned detective offered Galen and Erin chairs. They took a seat and remained silent.

The olive-skinned detective walked to the front of the room with the whiteboard framed behind him. "We really need you two to help us with this case. Galen, we want to thank you for bringing the dresses to our attention. Erin, as you can see, our team is all male and obviously it's a weak link. We need you to give us a woman's perspective on this case."

Erin turned to Galen. "What did you find?"

"Each dress had a straight vertical section removed; ripped away. It was missed because they thought the dresses were simply torn in the attack. I found out there was actually a piece missing from each dress. I thought this was important and brought it to their attention this morning. I figured it might be this guy's prize for each killing," Galen explained.

"I will be the first to admit, we're not only stumped, but we aren't thinking clearly. Whether it's the age of the victims or what, but we just can't get a clear picture of the suspect." The French detective stood at the front of the room with both hands resting on his hips. "There hasn't been one single sighting of the suspect at any one of the four murder locations. No one can even give us a shred of evidence one way or the other of who this guy is. Before we go home, I want a full profile on this guy; age, race, preferences, hair colour, where he eats, what he eats, how often he takes a dump, everything. I hope you don't have plans tonight, because we have a long day ahead."

Galen and Erin stared at the detective, then glanced to each other. They both knew this case could be the one to help them get promoted, and both felt privileged to have been selected.

Galen felt his pager buzzing, checked to see who was calling him, and saw the number, but chose to ignore it.

Erin looked at Galen. "What's up?"

"Nothing. Some guy keeps buggin' me. I never should have given him my pager number."

Galen sat up, pulled the pager from his belt, and turned it off, then laid it on the table. He straightened himself in the chair and turned his attention to the detective standing in front of the whiteboard. As the detective spoke, Galen took notes in his pad, scribbling side comments for future reference.

Galen kept glancing down at the pager. Ethan and Maddy were the ones who had helped him the night before, and now he was ignoring them. He hated that he wasn't answering Ethan's messages, and that the calls were going unanswered. *For now.*

Galen stood and walked over to the coffee stand, his gaze never leaving the man going over the details of the case. He poured two coffees, returned to his chair, and placed one on the table for himself and the other in front of Erin.

Wanting to make a good impression and be part of the team, Galen and Erin paid attention to every detail of the case being discussed. The detectives, one at a time, stood before the group and recounted their areas of expertise. Details were discussed and argued, key points were accepted or discounted, and notes were taken. This procedure went on until all five detectives had had the opportunity to present their assigned portion of the case.

*****

Maddy and I stood on the street where earlier I had tried to resuscitate the young girl who had died later in hospital. We looked around, trying to get a feel for the neighbourhood.

The mid-August sun was hot, but fall would be here shortly. It seemed that the weather patterns could read calendars and as soon as September hit, the weather would take a turn for the worse. Everyone was taking advantage of the sunny day. Those who worked shift work or stayed at home were outside doing something or absolutely nothing; just being outside was enough.

A young woman pushing a stroller on the sidewalk made her way closer to us. I realized we probably looked less intimidating as a couple than two men would. As she approached, not once did she try to avoid us or not make eye contact.

Maddy took the cue and, without hesitating, asked the woman if she knew anything about the young girl who was killed.

"Who did you say you were with?" the woman inquired politely. She was neatly dressed, and pushing an expensive-looking new stroller with an oversized shade protecting a young sleeping child from the sun.

I explained that I was with EMS, leaving Maddy out of the introduction, and we were unofficially looking into the case of the young girl who was found murdered. There were some unanswered questions that needed to be addressed.

"Shouldn't you be in uniform or have ID or something?"

Maddy bent down close to the stroller and pulled the hat back on the baby. Blond hair stuck out from underneath his hat. He was young, less than a year old, sleeping, and his lower lip was sticking out. It quivered with each breath.

"What a darling! How old? What's his name? I could just hug him."

"Trevor's six months, last week. If that lip thing keeps up, the girls will be all over him." The mother smiled proudly. Maddy stood beside me.

I had pulled out my Ottawa ID card while Maddy was looking at Trevor. The mother glanced quickly at it, having lost interest in knowing who we were. A black and gold laminated plastic card, along with interest in her child, was all she needed in order to answer our questions.

Placing the ID back in my wallet, I asked her if she had been outside or had seen anything unusual the day of the attack.

"I take my son for walks a couple of times a day. I've gotta lose this baby fat you know." She grabbed the fold under her shirts and held it tightly as she giggled. "I take the same path around the neighbourhood when the weather allows. Everyone likes to see Trevor and I get some adult conversation instead of listening to a purple dinosaur singing all day. Is it illegal to kill a costume of an extinct species because I really, really hate that purple fuzzy, singing...?" She stopped short of saying what she really wanted to ask. Her hands whirled about her head as she heard the children's songs that kept Trevor happy.

Maddy figured she had a rapport with the young mother now, and cut in when her description of the walks became too detailed.

"Do you have a good police presence around here?"

"What do you mean by 'police presence'?" She looked puzzled.

Maddy paused and thought for a moment. "Do you see a lot of police cruisers driving around here?"

"Lately, a lot, yeah! Some of us thought it was the house on the corner of Cochrane and Paardeburgh. You know, the one across the street from the park." The mother pointed up the street. "That's where I go and read for an hour or so and catch some fresh air. Trevor sleeps and I read. For all the time I'm there, cars come and go from that house. That's why we thought the police were driving by more often, but in all that time I sat at the park, I've never seen a cop car stop at the house. We all figured it was a crack house."

"So where do the police cars go?" Maddy asked as I stood silently.

"They just drive around slowly. Like slow, you know what I mean." She looked intense. "No one drives that slow."

"Did you ever see what the cop looked like? Was it the same cop driving each time?" My curiosity was on overdrive now.

"Nope. Never paid attention." She adjusted Trevor's hat to block the sun. "I just noticed we had more cops around and I liked it. Who's gonna complain unless you're a crook."

"Have you seen as many cops around since the little girl was killed?" Maddy asked the mother as she finger-waved at the baby in the stroller.

"Come to think of it, no! That's weird. Lots of cops driving around before, and since she was killed, nothing. What do you make of that?"

Maddy refocused her attention back to the mother. "That's what we want to find out."

Maddy and I thanked her for her time, and the mother continued on her walk with Trevor.

*****

Hours passed, and Galen was beginning to feel the effects of sitting too long. The table was covered in discarded coffee cups, food wrappers, crumpled sheets of paper, and open file folders.

Galen leaned back in his seat, his arms outstretched, and felt his back crack. He looked upwards at his watch; it was after six. He yawned, rubbed his eyes, and put his head down on the table, pushing his notepad to the centre. He was tired—mentally exhausted—and unprepared for this type of work.

Galen would normally be home by now, enjoying dinner with his wife and bitching about his job while she listened and pretended to care. It was a game they played. She would allow Galen to vent about his job as long as he went shopping with her, a tradition that had begun long before they were married and that continued to that day.

He grabbed his pager from the table, turned it on, and excused himself. He adjusted the heavy belt that weighed down on his pelvis as he walked down the hallway to his desk. Looking down at the display, he scanned the missed calls. Two unknown numbers and one from his wife. It had been hours since either Ethan or his wife had phoned.

By the time Galen got to his desk, his pager was vibrating in his hand. He looked at the display again. This time it was Ethan's home number. Still standing, he dialled Ethan's number and Maddy picked up the phone.

"Maddy? I thought I was calling Ethan. Oh, I see." He chuckled.

"You see nothing, copper." She was being playful. "Hang tight. You aren't going to like what we found out today." She handed the cordless phone to Ethan.

"Hey bud, busy?" Ethan sounded like he was calling about a barbeque.

"What've you got? Maddy said I wasn't going to like it."

"You aren't going to believe what we found."

11

I heard Galen fall down hard into his chair and roll back, hitting the wall behind him.

"You can't be serious! Jesus fucking Christ!" Galen spouted obscenities regularly, but only included religious overtones when he was really pissed off.

I had detailed everything we'd found out about the last two killings; something I felt the police should have done, but I didn't tell Galen that. Galen was completely silent as I went over the details of what Maddy and I had discovered at the two different locations.

Presented with all the circumstantial evidence, even a cop had to think twice about the possible suspect being another cop.

"Have you told anyone else about what you found out?"

"Nope, nothing to no one."

"I'm off shortly. You gonna be home?"

I turned to Maddy. "Galen's coming over. You sticking around?"

"Are you kidding? You couldn't drag me away."

I turned my attention back to Galen. "I guess we'll both be here. Have you eaten? I can pick something up before you get here."

"I can eat." The phone went dead.

Maddy had brought Chinese over the night before, and Galen and I had had pizza, so I decided on chicken. We went out and picked up a few chicken dinners, and kept them warm in the oven until Galen arrived.

It was after eight when Galen walked in without knocking. He never knocked. He looked tired. His uniform shirt was pulled over his belt, and his orange beard had started to show. Without saying a word, he walked to the fridge, bent low, and rummaged through its contents until he found the prize. He twisted the cap from the beer bottle and tossed it into the sink.

He fell into the couch and tilted the bottle back, then rolled the cold glass over his forehead. With his eyes closed, he asked to hear the details once again of what we had unearthed that day.

Galen sat upright and placed the beer bottle on the coffee table as

Maddy and I recounted the day's events again.

"Fuck, fuck, fuck." Galen stood and paced around the apartment. Having only recently met Galen, Maddy was unaware of Galen's habits. This was not good. Galen had a habit of swearing, and the more upset he was, the more he swore. If he spoke very little and walked about the room, he was very upset.

Galen walked past us several times, picked up the beer bottle, finished it, and went back to the kitchen. He ran the water in the sink, pulled a glass from the strainer, retrieved some ice cubes from the freezer, and drank two glasses of water, one after the other.

He came back to the living room, and sat down on the couch a little calmer than he was earlier.

"Even I have to admit; this doesn't look good on us. After telling the team investigating the child murders about the torn dresses, I was pulled in and asked to help out. We went over every detail of the case and came up with shit. No idea of who this guy could be. I don't think we were looking in the right place. Probably because we don't want to look at ourselves." He sat upright and placed his elbows on his knees. "Fuck! This sucks."

The sounds of glass exploding, plastic shattering, metal ripping, and then the repetitive sounds of a car alarm broke our conversation.

Galen jumped to his feet, ran to the balcony, and looked to the parking lot below.

"Son-of-a-bitch! Someone threw a TV out the window and it hit a car! That guy is going to be pissed when he sees his car."

*****

A kitchen towel was placed around her neck and twisted. He stood behind her, twisting the towel tighter and tighter around her neck until her trachea was constricted, blocking any air from entering or exiting her lungs. Her lungs burned, the pressure in her eyes increased, and her head felt as if it would explode.

The woman pawed at the towel at the front of her neck without results. She reached around and scratched at the assailant's hands, but they held the towel tight. She felt her nails dig in deep, and hot fluid oozing from the freshly opened wounds. Success! She continued to fight.

He loosened his grip. She took in a deep breath. Fresh energy to fight with, she thought. She let herself fall down hard to the kitchen floor. The towel loosened. On all fours, she took in another deep breath, her lungs filling with fresh air and new strength. Not knowing where he was or how close, she stood and ran for the apartment door.

She suddenly jerked back as her hair was pulled from behind. Her feet continued to run and she felt her hair being yanked from its roots. She saw that the deadbolt, chain, and door handle locks were all engaged. It would take too much time, and she knew that he was right behind her. Her feet pounded on the floor, planted, and changed direction, heading for the bedroom. She hoped he would have thought that she would only want to get out of the apartment as quickly as possible.

She slammed the bedroom door behind her and pushed in the lock button, but she knew it would not hold him for long. She reached for the cordless phone in its cradle. Her hands were shaking so badly that she had difficultly dialling 911. The phone rang once.

A loud crash echoed in the hall as he slammed into the hollow door with his shoulder. It splintered but held in place. She screamed loudly as the dispatcher answered her call.

"911. What is your emergency?"

She couldn't speak; the towel must have damaged her throat. She groaned, "Help." Her plea for assistance sounded like a squeak from a mouse. "Help." Again, she tried to impress upon the call-taker the extent of her distress. "Help."

Without hanging up, she tossed the phone onto the bed, stood behind the dresser, and pushed it hard until it began to slide on the carpet and crashed against the bedroom door. The operator could be heard yelling on the phone.

She lifted the television from the table in the corner of the bedroom and tossed it through the closed window. Glass shattered outwards and the television flew towards the parking lot. Moments later she heard glass shatter as the large cathode ray tube of the television exploded as it impacted the hood of a car. The car alarm began to sound. She hoped that the car was vacant when the television landed on it.

The assailant rammed the bedroom door again, and this time she saw the thin wood fracture inside and her assailant's fingers reach through the opening to pry more wood loose. She crawled on top of the dresser that was now holding the door firmly shut, grabbed a hair brush from the top of the dresser, and began to pound on the fingers poking through the opening.

As he pulled his hand away from the crack, she heard a loud scream of pain come from the other side of the door.

Hopping from the top of the dresser to the bed, she picked up the handset, cleared her throat, and tried to speak again.

"Still there?" She sounded like a child.

"Yes, the police are on the way. Do you need an ambulance?"

"Yes." It still hurt to speak.

"What's going on?"

"A guy attacked me."

"Are you safe?"

"Locked in the bedroom." Her throat burned with every word.

"Is the attacker still there?"

Holding the phone, she pressed her ear against the door, heard nothing, and told the call-taker as much.

"Stay in the room until the police arrive. I'll stay on the phone to confirm it's an officer on the other side of the door, and once the scene has been secured, you can come out."

She felt instant relief and let herself slide down to the floor. "Thank you," she whispered, her voice still muted.

*****

We all heard a loud scream, turned, and looked at each other.

"That sounded like someone in pain." Maddy ran to the door, opened it, and looked both ways down the hall. "Holy shit. There's a guy running down the hall."

Maddy stood in the doorway, pointing in the direction the stranger was running.

Galen bolted from the apartment and gave chase down the hall. He was gone before I could react. I ran to the door to see Galen in pursuit of the injured man. Galen was yelling at the man to stop, but he pushed his way through the stairwell door. Galen smashed through the door without hesitating.

"We should see what happened in the apartment," Maddy suggested.

"Good idea. Let me call 911 first. This all sounds a little wonky to me." I picked up the phone and stood next to Maddy.

The 911 call-taker answered and I identified myself, gave my paramedic ID, told her an off-duty police officer was chasing a man who had run from the apartment, and asked about the incident next door. It was confirmed that police and EMS had been dispatched to the address.

I hung up and kept the cordless phone with me as Maddy and I walked to the door next to mine. The apartment door was ajar, and Maddy and I positioned ourselves on either side. With my back against the wall, I reached around and rapped on the door. No reply. I knocked again, harder.

Still no answer. I pushed the door open and it creaked as it swung wide until it hit the inside wall. I motioned for Maddy to stay put as I slowly entered my neighbour's apartment.

The layout of her apartment was the reverse of mine. In the living room, all the lights were on, the curtains were open, and the television was off, but it appeared as though a scuffle had taken place. A lamp had been overturned, and the coffee table was pushed away from the sofa and rested up against the patio door. Magazines and small personal items had been tossed about. I picked up a magazine lying on the floor and noted the name on the subscription label.

Looking down the hallway, I knew it was a one-bedroom unit like mine, and the bedroom door was closed. The hollow core door was smashed inward, with splinters scattered on the floor. I called for Maddy.

I knocked on the door. "Nicole?" I spoke softly. No reply. "Nicole? My name is Ethan. I live next door. I'm a paramedic. Are you hurt?" Still no reply. I thought I heard a faint whimper coming from within the bedroom.

"I spoke to the police and they said they've dispatched a cruiser and an ambulance. My friend chased away your attacker." No reply.

Maddy placed her hand on my shoulder. "Hi…" She paused. I whispered her name. "Nicole, my name is Maddy. I'm Ethan's friend. Did you want to come out or me to come in?"

From the other side of the door, we heard scraping sounds, and then the door slowly opened. I stepped back and Nicole emerged. She was crying, and simply fell into Maddy's arms and began to sob uncontrollably. I walked out to the hallway as Maddy guided Nicole from the hallway to take a seat in the living room. Nicole began to talk to Maddy as she continued to cry.

I stood guard as other neighbours began to make their way from their apartments to the hall.

I knew most of them, and after a quick explanation that seemed to satisfy their curiosity, most of them went back into their apartments.

The door at the end of the hall opened and Galen strutted through, followed by two uniformed officers. I didn't know the two officers, but Galen was recounting his chase details, and I overheard that the man had disappeared once he exited the building.

The elevator bell sounded, indicating its arrival. The doors opened and two male medics wheeled their cot to the apartment.

"Ethan, what the hell are you doing here?" barked the medic pulling the foot end of the cot.

"I live there." I pointed. "We heard something coming from the apartment and came over to help. One woman inside. My friend, she's an ER nurse at the Civic, is inside with her. Give her a few minutes in case it's a sex assault or something, K?" They both nodded in agreement.

Galen had entered the apartment with the two officers while I was speaking to the medics. I peeked inside, was acknowledged by Galen and Maddy, and decided to wait in the hall.

The three of us waited, talking shop and trying to pick up anything from the conversation inside.

Galen came out. Sweat still glistened on his brow from the chase. He looked tired.

"Maddy's going to stay with her for a few more minutes. It's not rape, it's attempted murder. Guess what the guy tried to do?"

I shrugged my shoulders.

"Tie a belt around her neck and hang her up in the closet. Sound familiar?"

"The kid we attended to a few days ago."

"She fought back, made it to the kitchen. He caught her again, tried using a dishtowel or rag or something to finish the job. She beat him up and hid inside the bedroom. She threw the TV out the window to get attention, then called 911."

Maddy slowly walked out of the apartment with Nicole under her arm.

The medics lowered the cot, removed the equipment, and had Nicole sit on the stretcher. Both medics spoke softly and moved slowly as Nicole held Maddy's hand. Nicole looked exhausted as she sat on the cot. The medics hooked up the monitor, ran a set of baseline vitals, obtained her medical history, started an IV, and prepared to take her to the hospital. An officer stood beside the cot and asked the lead medic if he could accompany Nicole to the hospital in the ambulance, to which they both agreed.

The cot was raised; Nicole looked at Maddy, squeezed her hand firmly, and then let go. The medics pushed the cot to the elevator. The bell sounded, the doors slid open, and Nicole and the medics disappeared as the elevator closed.

"We just about done for the night?" Galen asked as he looked at Maddy and I.

I looked at Maddy and we both nodded in agreement. Maddy took my hand and pulled me into the apartment. She turned towards Galen.

"Have a good night, copper!"

12

The flower, heart, and rainbow cut-outs were pulled from the wall with the same care an art collector would use to remove a Picasso painting from its display. Standing at arm's length, fingers would find a loose edge and gently pull the material from the wall until the glue that held the cut-outs in place gave way.

Each piece was examined slowly as it was removed. The shapes were turned over, fingers were run delicately along the edges, mental notes were taken to remember each unique pattern and shape. They were all placed on the table in the centre of the room.

Tiny piles of floral material began to grow as each new piece was added. The sadness inside grew also with each piece that was removed from the wall.

Standing back, looking at the wall, there was sorrow in the bareness that remained. The glue had been rubbed clean, and the only evidence of the cut-outs that had once decorated the wall was now piled neatly on the table.

Eyes welled up with tears. The floral pattern treasures had to be destroyed in order to keep the secret safe. Too many people were looking for these tiny scraps of material and burning them was the only alternative to discovery.

Looking over the piles, a favourite was chosen and placed to the side. The rest of them, held carefully, were taken to the wood stove in the family room. It was a beautiful evening. The windows were open, and there was no need for a fire other than to eliminate the evidence.

The spring handle was turned and the heavy door creaked open on its hinges. The tiny scraps of material were placed on top of the kindling and logs inside the stove. To ensure the material would burn, rubbing alcohol was poured over the pile and lit.

The match flame came in contact with the alcohol vapours and the fire roared to life. The material edges curled, blackened, and broke away, falling to the bottom of the stove and joining the ashes resting below.

The stove door was closed and locked as the intensity of the fire grew. It was best not to look through the glass door panel as the treasures inside were being destroyed for the sake of safety.

The favourite piece, a heart made from red and orange flowers and green vines on a white material background, was picked up and carried to the bedroom. The police uniform peak cap was turned over and the tiny heart was reverently placed under the plastic lining inside the cap.

She stood in front of the mirror, placed the cap on her head, and looked at herself, confident that her secret would be safe inside her police cap. She then removed the cap and hung it carefully on the hook beside her police belt, and went to bed.

*****

He placed several used leather belts on the vendors' table at the flea market. The lady behind the table stood and placed the magazine she was reading beside the belts.

"That's quite a few belts ya got there."

He stood silently.

"These belts are all different sizes, ya know." She coiled each belt and placed them in a used plastic grocery bag.

"I know. I like the quality of the leather."

"Five dollars each. Ya got six belts. That's thirty bucks."

He placed thirty dollars on the table and picked up the bag. The lady scooped up the bills and noticed the fresh wounds on the back of the man's hand.

"Ya got some nasty cuts there on the back of your hand."

"Dog." He stuffed his injured hand into his pants pocket and walked away.

*****

Nicole lay in the hospital bed, sleeping with the help of medication added to her IV. Galen was outside her door, speaking to two other uniformed officers assigned to protect her until her attacker was arrested. There were polite nods from the two officers as they received instructions from the off-duty officer. It wasn't their first assignment to protect a victim, and it certainly wouldn't be their last. Galen emphasized the obvious, making sure the officers were aware of what he expected.

"Only one officer leaves the post at a time. You gotta take a piss, either hold it or use the john inside her room. She has a private bathroom. Stay on the same channel; you got fresh batteries for the portable radios at the beginning of your shift, right?"

The two officers nodded in agreement.

"Galen, seriously, between the two of us," one officer looked at the other, "we know what the fuck we're doing. No disrespect intended." The officer smirked at Galen.

"None taken. Between the two of you, huh? You two have what? A week and half experience. Fuck this up and I'll come down on you hard and fast." Galen shot them a look that indicated he knew exactly what hard and fast meant.

*****

Maddy walked into my bedroom wearing only a muscle shirt that barely went past her hips, and her loose hair hung down around her shoulders. Blindly, she reached to her right and turned off the overhead light. She pulled back the single, light bed sheet and climbed in bed to my right. From under the sheet, she pulled off her shirt and slid close to me.

"What a night. Playing cop is hard work. Galen can keep it. Any word from the copper on how the girl is doing?" she asked.

"None, but I expect I'll get a full and painfully long detailed report tomorrow," I told Maddy as her hand rubbed my chest. "I can tell Galen is pretty pissed. He has a tendency to take things personally, and when it comes to guys attacking girls, there is nothing worse." Maddy's hand whirled around my chest and then to my stomach, where her index finger circled my navel before she playfully stuck her finger deep inside. I doubled over, sitting up in bed and laughing as she continued to grab my stomach. She had me laughing so hard that I thought I would stop breathing when she finally stopped. I fell back into my pillow, tears streaming down my face.

"I thought... you said... cop work was hard?" I said between pants.

"I did. But it is also amazingly exciting." She slid one leg over me and kissed me. "You got your breath back yet?"

I didn't bother to answer, instead allowing actions to speak louder than words.

*****

The man slid the leather belt between the folds of the face cloth saturated in mink oil. He repeated the process of coating the leather several times until it was soft and the mink oil had fully penetrated the hide. The process was his way of relaxing after being so sloppy only a few hours prior. He had almost been caught, and he was furious with himself for taking risks that only a short while ago he never would have even considered taking. He had to stick to the methodology he had developed as a teen. He cleared his mind and went back to his new belt purchases.

Each finished belt was laid out on several layers of old newspaper. He didn't want the mink oil to stain his wood coffee table. The first few belts lay on the paper and bled a little mink oil onto it. As he lay the next belt down, his eyes caught an article stained dark with the oil. He paused and cocked his head sideways to read it. Part of the article was under one of the belts. With one hand he held the belt buckles, and with the other he pulled the top layer of the Ottawa Citizen free from under the belts.

He held the paper before him and read the headline:

"Another child found murdered. Few clues discovered."

He read the entire article, then read it again. He stood, left the two remaining belts that he hadn't oiled yet in the plastic bag from the flea market, and rushed to the guest bedroom where he kept his computer. He waited several minutes as he powered it up and the operating system whirled. Finally, he opened Explorer and typed in a search for more information on the dead children in Ottawa. Several thousand hits popped up on his screen. Stupid, he told himself. He refined the search to "murdered" children. The resulting list shortened to only a few hundred.

Scrolling down, he found articles relating to recent activity in Ottawa regarding several young girls killed in the city. His old CRT monitor flickered a few times, and he slapped the edge of the bulky frame until the picture stabilized. He had to squint to read the text. Instead of enlarging the image on the small twelve-inch screen—his eyesight wasn't what it used to be—he reasoned it would be easier to read if he printed each article that he thought was relevant to his search. He selected the articles and sent them to the print spool.

As the dot matrix printer clicked away, he tore the first pages off from the sheets still in the printer and trimmed the tractor feed strips off both edges. Then he tossed them into the wastebasket; the image topping each article was pixelated and grainy, and he was more interested in the articles anyway.

He noticed that each article from the Ottawa Citizen was written by a different reporter and had a distinctively different style to it. They knew that the killings were linked, but wondered if the investigative reporters had missed something. He finished reading what he had pulled from the printer, and continued to read each sheet as it finished printing. Each article was almost a carbon copy of the preceding one, told with a different voice. No new clues were found.

The articles only provided basic clues from each crime scene, either because the paper only reported what they knew or had been asked to keep certain details confidential, or because the police were completely inept. They kept referring to the killer of these little girls as "he" or "him," but the more he read, the more certain he became that the killer must certainly be a woman. He knew what he was: a taker of human life. He had come to terms with what he did to other people. And he reasoned that, based on what the paper was reporting and what he knew about the psychological makeup of what it took to take a life, the killer was most likely a woman. Only a woman, he reasoned, would take the life of a young girl. A man, sick as it may be, would most likely sexually assault the victim. He wondered if his unique skill set had somehow given him the ability to profile killers; if his brain had been wired differently, and he was able to analyze things to see what others couldn't.

"Idiots," he said aloud. "It's gotta be a woman." He sat back on the couch and locked his fingers behind his head. "I really have to meet this lady."

He felt an instant kinship with this woman, without knowing her, but because of what she did. He took the stack of papers he had printed, placed it in a cast iron pan, set it in the kitchen sink, soaked it with lighter fluid, and set it ablaze. He had pulled the batteries from all the smoke detectors in his entire house years earlier. Once the papers were nothing more than blackened ash, he ran the faucet into the pan, tilted it, let the ash slip into the sink, and watched it disappear down the drain. He then found the cleanser, scrubbed the bottom of the pan, and rinsed it well. He let the water run for several minutes to ensure that all the ash had made its way through the drain trap. He dried the pan, returned it to the cabinet, and cleaned up the kitchen before deciding it was time for bed.

All the belts were collected and hung in his closet along with his clothes. He had threaded the hanger hook through the belt buckles and hung each one on the rod in order of size, from smallest on the left to the largest on the right. If he had two belts of the same size, the black belt came first, and then the brown. He ran his hands across the collection of belts like fingers strumming a harp and felt the mink oil transfer from the leather to his fingertips. He ran his thumb across the oily fingertips, then closed his eyes and inhaled deeply. The oil left a delicate, mild smell in his nostrils.

Sometimes he hated himself for what he did and what he knew he wanted to continue doing. For years, the self-loathing tormented him, consumed him to the point where he had attempted suicide by hanging himself with a belt around his neck. He sat on the edge of the bed and remembered the event that had turned him into what he now was. Some memories fade, while others remain vivid; he could recall that day with distinct clarity.

His wife had gone to work for the day, as she always did, and he had kissed her goodbye as she left the house. He went to his job, and no one suspected the thoughts that whirled in his mind about what he wanted to do. When they broke for lunch, he took the company service van home, ate lunch, walked calmly to the basement, and selected the main beam that ran the length of the house. His beeper went off and startled him. He pulled it from his waist and looked at the number. His wife was calling. He calmly placed the beeper on the washer and it continued to vibrate on the white, baked metal surface. He stared at the beeper, not really thinking, just watching it move across the lid. The beeper stopped dancing on the washer and it broke his concentration.

He found a plastic step stool, placed it under the beam, and stood upon it. He pulled the black leather belt through his pant loops, slipped the leather noose around his neck, and felt the cool metal buckle on his throat.

The beeper started to dance again. He stepped down from the stool, picked up the beeper, and saw that his wife was calling again. He carefully placed it, still vibrating, back on the washing machine, and stepped back up onto the stool. His pants began to slip down and he laughed. He froze as he was pulling up his pants. If a simple thing like having his pants fall down could still make him laugh, surely there was a chance that this was a horrible idea. The beeper went silent, he pulled his pants up, and the moment passed. He felt the dark, ominous feeling come over him again.

Blindly, he checked the loop around his neck and felt the smooth leather as it wrapped from one side to another. He thought it felt like a collar, and wondered if the people who would come to find his body would think the same thing. Again, he chuckled, and again, the beeper came to life. He watched the beeper complete its dance and knew it was his wife. Not calling her back made him feel empty, but he had made up his mind.

He tossed the loose end of the belt over the beam and it failed to make its way to the other side, falling down around his head. He found the end of the belt, rolled the leather, and attempted to toss it over the beam. Again, the end of the belt failed to find the void between the beam and floor above. It came back down and poked him in the eye.

"Shit!" he screamed. His eye began to water as he laughed loud and hard. His pants fell down around his ankles. Reaching down to pull up his pants, he fell forward off the plastic stool and onto the concrete floor. He struck his forehead and rolled onto his side. As he lay on the floor, he began to laugh so loudly that his belly started to hurt. The laughing eventually subsided, his heavy breathing turned to soft panting, and the stars he saw in the eye that had been poked with the belt disappeared.

He lay on his back; the cool concrete felt good. He stared up at the wood beams above and wondered if this was something that was meant to be. He stuck a few fingers inside the belt that was still around his neck and loosened its grip. He continued to stare at the beams. The dark thoughts didn't seem to have control over him the way they did earlier, but that wasn't anything new. His moods continually fluctuated in ways he knew weren't normal. People get depressed, he told himself, but not like this. He often thought about what it would be like to die, but until today, he was unable to own up to the inevitable decision and kill himself.

The decision had been made to shut out the demons that came to be a part of him. Now that he had attempted to end his life, he knew it was the right thing to do.

He wasn't laughing anymore. Determined, he stood, pulled up his pants, stepped on the stool, and jumped as he fed the length of leather over the beam. Grabbing the loose end of the belt, he tied it to the loop around his neck and kicked the stool out from under his feet.

Immediately, he had a change of heart and realized that he no longer wanted to die. His throat had closed tightly around his trachea from the tension being applied by the leather belt. He tried to inhale, but his lungs were in a vacuum. His fingers dug at the leather collar around his neck, but he couldn't find a way to free himself. He tried to touch the floor with the tips of his toes, and was only inches away. His feet kicked in the air, trying to find a foothold to brace against so he could free himself. He was too far away from the washer and dryer. He began to see stars again as hypoxia started to take effect. He was using the remaining oxygen in his system faster than normal, and knew he only had a few moments to act.

He looked up, and decided to grab hold of the beam that the belt was wrapped around and pull himself up. With both hands grasping the beam firmly, he pulled, the tension on the belt loosened, and he was able to take a breath. He tried to hold himself up with one hand and untie the leather knot, but as soon as one hand let go of the beam, his weight pulled him down and the leather snapped tightly around his neck.

It felt as if his eyes would pop out of his head at any moment. Once again, he took hold of the beam and pulled himself up, but this time he reached over the beam, hooked his elbow, and locked his hands together. He took in a deep breath but was only able to take in a small amount of air through the trachea that was in spasm.

The beeper started to vibrate on the washing machine yet again.

He knew now that he didn't want to die and would do anything to stay alive. His grip began to weaken, and he slipped down and felt the leather dig into his neck again. He tried to hoist his weight up so he could anchor himself around the wooden beam, but the energy needed to keep himself up was too great, and his constricted trachea wasn't letting in all the oxygen he needed.

His fingers began to burn and, one by one, they opened until they released their grip. He slid down; his right arm stuck at the elbow between the beam and the floor above was the only thing keeping him from death. He thought the bones in his arm started to crack from his body weight pulling down. Muscle began to tear; if bones could fracture slowly, surely this is what it felt like, he reasoned. The pain was intense. If he blacked out from the pain, his arm would relax and he would die. If he pulled his arm free, he was hoping his weight would break the belt, or at least that he would have a few moments to fight to save his life.

He jerked his arm, ripping the skin on a jagged nail from above. Blood began to flow freely from the wound. He fell, but the belt held his weight and jerked him to a sudden stop. He felt the belt tighten around his neck. Reaching up, he clawed at the belt, trying to free himself. Spinning in the air, his weight turned his body to allow him to see his wife standing at the doorway—still, unmoving.

"It's about time you did something, you spineless bastard. You should've done this years ago. I hope it's a horrible way to die." The contempt in her eyes was undeniable.

"I'll come back in a few minutes. Make sure you're dead, then I'll call 911 and play the grieving widow." She turned and walked away.

Stunned, he let his arms fall to his side. In the last few moments of his life, he had realized that he was taking the easy way out and giving his wife exactly what she wanted. It was at that moment he knew for certain that he didn't want to die. He only had enough left inside him for one last attempt. Looking up, he grabbed the beam with both hands, and pulled himself up high against the ceiling. He curled himself up in a tight ball, and then let himself drop. The sudden second stop would either fracture his neck or the leather would give way and break.

The belt snapped when his weight pulled the leather tight. He fell to the concrete below, slipped the leather from around his neck, and inhaled deeply. He was panting as he ran from the basement and up the stairs, and he caught up to his wife just as she was about to leave the house.

He grabbed her by the arm and spun her around.

"You fucking bitch."

He kneed her in the groin. She coughed and doubled over. With one end of the shortened leather belt in each hand, he encircled her neck, and, in the front, twisted the belt together. Immediately, her eyes widened, and her nails dug deeply into his hands and arms. Nothing fazed him. His purpose was singular. He was determined. His intent, deadly.

For several minutes, she struggled as she fought to catch her breath. As she was losing her life, he was finding his. Eventually, she stopped fighting. Her arms dropped to her sides. The veins in her eyes burst from the increased pressure as the belt was constricted around her neck, and he stared into them until she was no longer able to see him back. Her legs lost the ability to hold her upright, and he supported her entire weight. He released both ends of the belt and let her drop to the floor with a heavy thud. The belt had dug deeply into the skin and left a narrow furrow around her neck. He chuckled when he made out tiny bumps in her neck where the sizing holes in the leather had been.

He looked down at his hands; one was blood stained, but both had grooves in the webbing between the thumb and index finger and across the palm, from the belt as it had dug in. The blood from the open wound on his forearm continued to drip down his arm and onto the floor.

"I guess if I'd had a better belt, I'd still be dangling."

He kicked the lifeless body in the stomach to see if there was a reaction. Nothing!

A large patch dressing was applied to his forearm to stem the flow of blood. That's when he realized the house needed to be cleaned from top to bottom. He wanted nothing of his old life to cross into the new. Carl Ryan ceased to exist from that moment on. He didn't care about any personal belongings still in the house. He would create a life. From that moment, the old Carl Ryan no longer existed.

The man formerly known as Carl Ryan stripped naked, slid under the single cotton sheet on his bed, and fell into a deep sleep.

13

I woke up the next morning to the smell of coffee brewing. The bedroom was still dark; only a sliver of light broke through the cheap curtains that hung over the window.

I pulled up my boxers I'd left on the floor the night before and walked into the kitchen, expecting to find Maddy there. Instead, I found a note taped to the fridge:

"Gone home to feed the cat and do some running around. Call me later. K. Thanks for last night. xxoo"

I poured my coffee and carefully retrieved the Ottawa Sun from outside the front door of my apartment by cracking the door, sticking out my arm, and patting the floor, trying to find the paper.

"Left, left, got it."

I recognized the voice, pulled the newspaper inside, and left the door open.

"A little early for you, isn't it?" I asked him.

Galen walked in holding his extra-large coffee and a bag. "Usually, yeah, but I got home late and couldn't sleep. Wife kicked me outta bed a couple hours ago." He tossed the bag to me and told me it was two plain bagels, and to toast them. He would wait at the table until they were ready.

As he'd claimed, inside the bag I found two untoasted plain bagels and half a dozen pats of butter.

"How's the girl from last night?" I called out from the kitchen.

"Under guard by two snot-nosed rookies with barely a week's experience between them. She saw nothing. I mean zilch, nada. Pulled some tissue from under her nails. It's gonna take fucking months to get anything on it," Galen yelled out. I toasted the first bagel, presented it to Galen with most of the butter, and went back into the kitchen. "Did a little search before popping by. Turns out, there've been almost a dozen belt-related deaths under mysterious circumstances in the last few years. That doesn't count the fuck ups where a murder may've be classified as a suicide." Pause. "Hey, you got any more butter? I thought I bought six for mine. I figured you would've had some margarine or shit here for yourself." He started to butter his bagel.

"Do you know how many accidental deaths there are by guys getting their ya-ya's while they hang themselves by belts?" he went on.

"No," I yelled, "how many?"

"Fucking lots. What's wrong with the old fashioned way?"

"Old fashioned way of what? Getting your ya-ya's off or killing yourself?" I questioned with a snarky tone.

"Fuck off."

I was silent as I sat down at the table with my bagel and fresh coffee, tossed him the last two butters, and started to eat.

"You coulda put on some clothes first. Christ." Galen spat out little pieces of chewed bagel as he made fun of me. He spun a stack of stapled papers across the table. "What I could pull off the system before coming over." He spread the last two butters on his bagel and took another bite. With the food puffing out his right cheek, he went on.

"Check out the first one. It's the oldest one I could find on CPIC with a belt used to strangle someone and left on scene. I talked to one of the detectives who said that a belt is usually used when the attack is not premeditated. The attacker makes a last minute decision, whips out his belt, and uses it to strangle the victim. And it's usually a guy. It takes a lot of strength and time to strangle someone. And, they usually take the belt back. These are the ones where the belt was left behind." He tapped the top sheet and left a butter stain where he touched the paper.

"What am I looking for?" I asked.

"Read it, Goddammit."

As I finished my bagel and coffee, I read the first report detailing an unsolved homicide in Kingston, Ontario, from 1995. It was initially thought that the death was a result of a break and enter. There was no sign of forced entry, however; nothing taken from the home, and the husband couldn't be located afterwards or since. The ligature was a partial belt found still secured around her neck.

The husband remained the strongest suspect since he disappeared the same day his wife was found dead. The house turned out to be a forensic technician's nightmare. The wife cut hair at home on the weekends, so police found several dozen different hair samples, as well as cat hair from their three house cats.

Canvassing the neighbours, it was learned that the husband and wife seldom argued or were seen arguing before she was found dead. But they were also extremely private and didn't socialize much. Of course, Kingston Police had to investigate all possible angles, and one of them was that the husband was abducted and not the killer at all.

After several months, all the leads had dried up. It never was determined if the husband was actually a victim or the perpetrator of the crime. Carl Ryan had never been seen again. It was assumed that, if he was the one responsible for his wife's death, he had probably committed suicide.

I flipped through the remaining case files, looking for any similarities between the first one and the others that Galen had printed off. The one thing that stuck out was the size of the belts. Each belt was a different size; most of them were larger, over size forty. Only the first one was a smaller size. The two pieces, when assembled, were a size thirty-four.

Reading further, all the reports claimed that the belts were of full grain leather, and only the first belt was made of bonded leather. Bonded leather, I discovered, is leather fibres that have been glued and forced together under tremendous pressure. It has the look and appearance of regular leather, but lacks the tensile strength.

"That's why the first belt broke. It was cheaper leather. If it was the husband, and he realized why the belt broke, he evolved and needed a better product to make sure the belt didn't fail in a moment of panic." Galen was still chewing, and touched his index finger to his nose as he spoke.

"You have any plans today?" Galen went on as he took another bite.

"Plans?"

"I'm going to Kingston. I called their HQ and they're expecting me in a few hours."

I thought about what Maddy had said in her note. I was torn between staying behind to call her later or going with Galen. I opted to call her now.

"I'm calling Maddy."

"What? For permission?" Galen finished his coffee.

I smirked and walked to the phone.

"And get dressed for Christ's sake. God, I could lose my lunch if I didn't have a strong stomach."

For a moment I thought about pulling down my pants and mooning him, but sanity prevailed. I closed the bedroom door and started getting dressed while I waited for Maddy to pick up the phone.

"Hello." Her voice was almost musical.

"Busy?" I balanced the phone between my shoulder and my ear, lifted one leg to slide it into my jeans, and fell on the bed.

"What are you doing?" Maddy asked as she heard me grunt.

"Getting dressed for a road trip to Kingston with Galen. We found a few leads that we want to follow up there."

"Pick me up or should I meet you at your place?" She sounded excited.

"Meet me here. That'll give me time to shower."

I yelled at Galen that I was going to grab a quick shower without telling him that Maddy was going to join us. Our relationship was still new, and I wasn't sure if Galen was ready to accept Maddy into our fold.

By the time I was out of the shower, Maddy and Galen were sitting at my dining room table chatting like old friends. I could only assume that Galen was OK with Maddy joining us. I walked into the room with a towel over my head as I dried my hair. Maddy stood and grabbed a cooler filled with bottled water and food Galen had prepared for the trip while I was in the shower.

"Come on, get dressed, we're waiting for you. We should've been on the road by now." Maddy was pulling Galen by the hand, and was giddy and smiling. Oddly, so was Galen.

I didn't finish drying my hair; instead, I pulled a shirt off its hanger as it spun and fell off the rod to the floor.

*****

Two hours later, Galen pulled his minivan into the Kingston police station parking lot on Ontario Street. I exited the vehicle, twisted my back, and heard it crack. Gazing south, Maddy and I stood beside each other, looking out on to Lake Ontario as the ferry was pulling away from the docks on the way to Wolfe Island. The ferry engines were at full throttle as the propellers churned up the waters, and the stacks were blowing grey smoke into the air.

"We should do that sometime," Maddy stated.

"It's a plan."

Galen's eyebrows were raised, and he shook his head gently from side to side in disgust. I thought I overheard him say, "Kids," under his breath as he pulled open the front door and waited for us to catch up. Galen spoke to the desk clerk, who already had a note that we were to meet Detective Crawford. Galen showed his Ottawa Police identification and vouched for our presence. We were asked to take a seat and wait while the detective was summoned.

In only a few moments, the security door opened and a tall man entered. His hair was cut short—military style—and stood straight up. He was dressed in a sharp dark suit, light blue shirt, and bold red tie. His shirt looked to be a few sizes too small, as the top button squeezed his neck and created jowls that normally he wouldn't have had. I wasn't sure if the redness in his face was due to the glow of the tie or the tightness of his shirt.

He extended his right hand and smiled broadly as he welcomed Galen. "So…" His voice trailed off. "You're looking into one of my cold cases, are you?" Detective Crawford spoke with his teeth clenched; his jaw never opened. Only his lips moved.

Galen stood, and shook his hand firmly. "We are. I don't remember reading your name on the detective's report."

"I wasn't a detective back then when I had a lot more hair." I looked at his hair; he had a thicker head of hair than I did. "I was on patrol when the call came in and I found the body. All you would see is my badge number and signature. When you called it in, the front desk checked the case file and passed your message on to me. I thought I'd meet you myself and see if we can shed some new light on this case."

Detective Crawford gestured, inviting us past the security door and into the station. We walked down a long, brightly lit hall to the banks of elevators where he pressed the down arrow button. The doors opened and we all entered, and then stood in silence as I looked at the numbers going down from "M" to "B2."

"All cold cases are kept in the basement with the archived files. It's sad, really. We just don't have the resources to pursue cases that aren't going anywhere."

An almost indistinguishable "ding" told us we had arrived. The elevator doors slid apart and Detective Crawford turned right. The basement was in stark contrast to the main floor. The hall was dark and smelled musty, and the walls were painted a battleship grey. He unlocked a door with a plastic sign stuck to it that indicated what was inside: "Archive Room."

He offered us a seat at an old wooden table that had probably been destined for the garbage, but was saved and given another lease on life. I was afraid that I would end up with slivers in every finger and my elbows by day's end. The antique foldout metal chairs were most certainly salvaged along with the table. One creaked when Galen sat down, and Maddy cast me a look of fright, thinking that Galen would fall flat on his ass.

Detective Crawford returned with a single banker's box with the case file written across it in large black bold letters and the name "RYAN." He let it slam on the wooden table. I got the same look from Maddy.

"This, unfortunately, is all we have, which amounts to diddly squat. Four months of investigative work gave us this." He pulled out a plastic Ziploc bag containing two parts of a leather belt and a single red four-inch binder. All the notes had been three-hole-punched, inserted into the binder, and categorized by tabs. Both items were placed on the table. Detective Crawford set both hands on his hips.

"After the fourth month, we had zilch. Mr. Ryan didn't show up on any store videos, his credit cards were never used again, and his bank account was never accessed after that day. We had no leads, no tips, nothing. The file sat on the corner of the detective's desk until he was re-assigned. It got put into the cold case files and forgotten. Frankly, we don't have the money or the resources to pursue this case. When you called," he looked at Galen, "I was shocked. I was certain it was the husband who killed his wife and then jumped into Lake Ontario. That's why we never heard from him again."

Galen placed the papers he had printed off earlier in the day on his desk.

"I can only imagine a few of these are not related, but check these out. Way too similar to your case, with one odd twist. Ethan," he motioned to me, "separated the cases where the belts were of high quality. It seems with the first case, the husband—we will assume it was the husband who killed his wife—had a cheap, bonded leather belt. It broke, so he upgraded to a better quality leather. This pile," he slid the few cases across the splintered desk, "are the ones I'm sure are related."

Galen stood to emphasize his argument. "I've never taken any psych classes, but I know people. I bet this guy had issues, major fucking issues. Killing his wife was an accident. Your report claims the wife came home because she was worried about her husband. Whether she caught him with another woman, another man, his pants around his ankles, snorting coke, who the fuck knows, who the fuck cares, he flipped for some reason and chocked the living shit outta her. He got his jollies outta it. It set him off; he finally found his purpose, his joie de vivre if you will. Odd; most of the people who commit multiple murders don't stray away from a comfort zone. They lead normal lives, work, contribute to society, and some are even married. I bet that, because Carl's first victim was his wife, he had to leave. So, he defies what we know about most multiple-victim killers. He's random; he has no territory, no victim preferences. I'll bet he's a day labourer, working for cash, no questions, no cheques."

Detective Crawford looked at him, "Joie de vivre? Really?"

"What? I'm from fucking Ottawa; I'm cultured," Galen smirked. "It's half French, half politicians, for Christ's sake. I've picked up some French along the way but neutral in my politic. Anywho, my guess is he hasn't disappeared. He took on a few new aliases, and when he gets stressed, he uses a belt because it's comfortable. When things get hot, he moves on. We had one death just recently, and these two stopped an attempt on a girl last night."

"Good work. And that's why they're here?"

"No. Ethan is a paramedic who was at the first suicide slash"—for effect, Galen used his index finger to cut through the air— "murder. It was murder, plain and simple. And last night, the attack was botched because the girl was brave and fought back. And, I've saved the best for last." He pulled a vial from his pocket. "We have DNA from under her nails. She took the proverbial pound of flesh, if you will. If Kingston can't afford to test a few samples found at your crime scene, Ottawa can. Besides, if it turns out to be true, we just proved the bastard hubby is still alive."

"Well, you three can go through the file, find what you need, note what pages you want copied, and I'll arrange for a few samples of the scene DNA to be handed over after the necessary paperwork is completed." Detective Crawford was smiling.

Galen stood and handed the binder to Detective Crawford. Shocked, Detective Crawford asked why he was being handed the binder.

"There's not a lot here. Instead of spending hours reading in this basement, how about just copy the whole thing and we can be on our way." Galen always was more "matter of fact."

Detective Crawford agreed, took the binder, and motioned for us to follow him back upstairs to the lobby.

As we walked to the elevator, Detective Crawford stopped short and Maddy bumped into him. She stepped back, and with her head down, she chuckled and grabbed my hand.

"Sorry about that, Detective," she offered.

The detective seemed completely oblivious to the accidental bump, "Completely forgot to mention: I arranged a visit of the Ryan house. The new owners are fine with you guys stopping by if you want."

The three of us looked at each other and nodded in agreement.

Thirty minutes later, we pulled up in front of a small, post-war bungalow. It had a white exterior, and paint peeled from the trim around the door and windows. The concrete front porch was cracked, and large portions were missing from the corners and steps. The car parked in the driveway was a brand new Ford. I guessed the car was probably worth more than the house.

Detective Crawford exited the Kingston PD SUV, walked up to the front door, and knocked. The door opened, a couple stood in the doorway, and the three of them spoke for a few moments. Detective Crawford turned, pointed at us, and then waved us in.

As the three of us walked up to the front of the house, the young couple was more than happy to invite us in. A few feet into the living room, they stopped, making us all stand in a group in the front foyer. There was an awkward silence as we wondered why they had invited us into the house only to have us all stand in a group at the front door. The Cargill's reminded me of a couple lost in time—most definitely the 1970s. Mr. Cargill was thin and tall, with stringy long hair down to his shoulders. He had a prominent widow's peak and streaks of grey throughout hair that was all tied back in a ponytail. All that was missing was a tie-dyed shirt and sandals.

"Right there." The husband pointed down at my feet.

There was confusion as we looked at each other, wondering what he meant.

"That's where she was killed. Right there. She died right there, and we swear her spirit is still here." The husband had a huge grin on his face, as if he was happy about the deadly history of the house.

Detective Crawford broke the uncomfortable tension in the room. He pushed through us and past the homeowners, farther into the house.

"Mr. and Mrs. Cargill, this is Officer Hoese with the Ottawa Police and his friends, who are helping him with the case that may have started in this house with the previous owners."

Galen reached between Maddy and myself and extended his hand. Both Mr. and Mrs. Cargill shook it with vigour. Mrs. Cargill, a wisp of a thing, had a broad smile that showed nothing but beautiful white teeth.

"I have this gift, I can feel the spirits, and as soon as we walked into this house I could feel the pull." Mrs. Cargill was more than happy to share the story.

"The pull?" Maddy asked.

"The spirit world sometimes pulls at me if there's an unsettled soul. In this case, the murder of Mrs. Ryan, was it? When we were looking at buying the house, the real estate agent was a little apprehensive..."

"Apprehensive, my ass," Mr. Cargill cut in. "She was downright scared shitless about even bringing up the whole murder thing. So we kept yakking away and got the price down way freaking below what it should have gone for. Besides, the bank owned the house and they just wanted to wash their hands of it. So we kept the offer price low and they buckled because they knew selling it was gonna be a pain."

Mrs. Cargill cut her husband off. "Actually, I wanted the house as soon as I found out about the murder. I'm more complete when the spirit world is close."

Through clenched teeth, Detective Crawford coughed, "Anyway, let's move on. Is it still OK to show them the basement?"

"Sure, follow me." The Cargill's were more than happy to play hosts to the police, Maddy, and myself. They seemed to truly enjoy the fact that someone was killed in the house. We followed them through the kitchen and down a few steps, turned, and went into the basement.

Mrs. Cargill spun in circles around under the beam with her arms out wide. "This is where I feel the karma is really intense for Mr. Ryan." She stopped spinning, and wobbled for a moment. "It was only after a few months after we moved in did we find this spot. I think something happened right here." Mrs. Cargill pointed to her feet. That was when I noticed that both Cargill's were barefoot. I wasn't surprised.

While everyone was looking down at Mrs. Cargill's feet, I looked up to the floor joists under the main floor and noticed something. Without asking permission, I located an old chrome chair with a split in the vinyl, dragged it across the concrete floor, and gently pushed Mrs. Cargill aside. I stepped up and examined the wood.

"Detective, what is the width of the belt that was used to strangle Mrs. Ryan?"

"One and a half inches. Why?"

I rubbed the wood beam and felt a section with my fingertips. "There's a smooth section on the two edges of the wood, and it runs across the top, too. And betting dollars to donuts, it's one and a half inches wide." I stepped down from the chair and Galen almost knocked me over to get up on it. It creaked under his weight.

Galen felt the wood beam. "Son of a fucking bitch. You're right." Without hesitation, Galen pulled the leather belt loose from his pants and wrapped it around a different section of the beam.

"You better not drop your trousers while you're up on the chair, copper," Maddy advised.

Galen ignored Maddy and wrapped one end of his belt around his hand. Then he grabbed the buckle end and hopped from the chair, sending it flipping over to the floor. Galen swung and dangled from the belt, and only let go of the buckle end when he felt his pants start to loosen from around his waist. His feet landed hard on the concrete floor, and he quickly held onto his pants to prevent them from falling down around his ankles.

He hurriedly threaded his belt through his pant loops, righted the chair, and inspected the wood beam. He carefully ran his fingers along the rough-grained wood, then stopped when he found the exact duplicate marks I had found only a few moments earlier.

"You're absolutely, fucking dead bang on, bud. The leather compressed the soft pine down and flattened it out. So what the fuck happened here with the Ryan's? Did he try to hang his wife, or hang himself, or what?" Galen was excited by what he had found. "Maybe next time we should have a fucking psychic as part of our investigative team."

*****

Carl Ryan drove randomly down Ottawa city streets, trying to wrap his mind around the concept of the killer he was certain was a woman. He asked himself that very question over and over again: "Why do I know this is a woman? It has to be. Who else could it be?" He had absolutely no certain way of knowing it was a woman other than a gut feeling that told him he was right.

Earlier in the day, he had studied everything he could find online on the seemingly random killings of young girls. Maybe the reporters were too stupid to know that the killings weren't random; they were planned, methodical. A lot like the way he worked. In a short time, he had come to admire this stranger. A woman he didn't know, but he wanted to meet. The only problem that remained was finding her.

*****

Detective Crawford drove us back to the Kingston police department. We thanked him, and picked up our copy of the case file and sample of DNA. All the paperwork was signed by Galen before he took possession of the banker's box of material. Before getting into the car, Maddy asked to use a bathroom and pointed to the Tim Horton's across the street.

A few minutes later, we were all sitting at a table in the donut shop with three fresh coffees in front of us.

"How cliché is this? They actually put a Tim Horton's donut shop across the street from the police station." Galen was already on his second old-fashioned plain donut when he made the obvious comment we were all thinking.

Maddy wasn't paying attention. She had now proved to be the analytical one of the group. Her coffee still had the lid on it, and remained unopened.

She was scanning the scene report, forensics reports, and all the other details of the case. Galen and I were chatting and sipping our drinks.

With her head still down, Maddy exclaimed, "Listen to this: it says Carl Ryan had no history of any psychological problems, no problems at work, was socially active, liked to hang out with his friends. His former employer says he was just a normal guy and was a good worker right up until he disappeared."

Maddy finally looked up from the copies of the police report Detective Crawford had given us. "Why would someone so normal end up killing his wife? Well, supposedly killing his wife, anyway."

With his mouth half full, Galen countered, "If I had a bitch of a wife who nagged me, pestered me, and generally pissed me off for years, I'd probably kill her, too. I wonder if that counts as mental anguish."

"Hey! That's not nice, copper." Maddy's tone was unmistakable.

"I'm just saying."

"Well, don't say. K?"

Galen knew he was beaten. Best to leave things be. Instead, he just smirked at Maddy, and she winked back. I could tell those two were going to be good friends for a long time.

Maddy continued to read the police reports while Galen and I discussed the attack at my apartment building the night before. We hashed over the same details we had discussed on the way down to Kingston. Nothing new was said; nothing new was discovered. Every few minutes, Maddy would look up from the files, shake her head, and go back to reading.

It was early evening by the time Galen dropped us off at my apartment building. Maddy stretched, thanked Galen for the day, yawned, grabbed my hand, and led the way up to my place. There wasn't even a question of if she would stay over or not. I turned back to Galen and he was smiling broadly.

*****

Carl Ryan sat alone at a table for two. The table was located against the wall near the front of the restaurant. He didn't try to hide or conceal his presence. He finished his meal, and then ordered a second beer and dessert. He had a newspaper laid out on the table before him, and he scanned the headlines, finding the occasional article to read and then flipped the pages every few minutes. For the past hour, Carl had scanned the restaurant, looking for just the right patron. Like a lion hunting its prey, Carl was able to weed out the weakest of the pack. He had developed his own profiling system based on posture, facial appearance, and physical characteristics. His methodology was his own, non-scientific, but he had been perfecting it for years. And his last attempt had been a failure. He had almost been caught. His last two attacks had been similar. Both in apartment buildings. It was something new and exciting for him, but the thought of being caught frightened him to his core.

Carl picked out the weakest of the herd and kept his eye on the lone male sitting at the bar on the elevated section off the main dining room.

The man was slumped forward against the bar, head down, chin on his chest. His left arm was propped against the bar, and the other hand held onto the tall glass of beer the entire time. The contents of the glass barely moved for most of the night. Occasionally, the man would look up at the television on the wall, take in whatever was on, tilt the glass, and take a sip of the draft. The man's posture was more indicative of depression than that of a person who's had too much to drink. Carl noticed the length of the man's legs. The man at the bar was only partially sitting on the stool, but his right leg dangled at his side and his foot was flat on the tile floor.

If this guy isn't drunk, he could easily outrun me with those long legs, he thought. I'll have to work around that and take that advantage away from him.

Carl continued to watch the man as he sipped his beer and maintained the same depressive posture. The depressed man only took a few more sips, then he gestured to the bartender that he was done, dropped a ten-dollar bill on the counter, and walked towards the washroom.

Carl recognized his opportunity and waved for the server. He made hand gestures in the air as if he was writing up the bill, indicating he was ready to leave. Carl kept his eye on the hallway where the man had disappeared. Looking above the doorway, Carl noticed the universal sign for the bathroom. He knew where the depressed man had gone.

The server presented Carl with the bill and a polite smile to entice a larger tip. "Cash or credit?" she asked.

Carl flipped open the vinyl folder, glanced at the bill, and laid out two twenties.

"That should cover everything nicely. Keep the change." He handed the folder back to her as he stood, grabbed his nylon jacket from the seat, and walked out the door.

Strolling to the parking lot, he slipped on his jacket, dropped to one knee, and pretended to tie his shoe as he kept an eye on the front door of the restaurant. A couple walked past him holding hands. Their conversation was soft, muted, and meant only to be heard by themselves. The girl let out a giggle, pulled her hand from his, and slapped him.

Probably some comment about what he wants her to do to him tonight, Carl thought.

As the couple turned the bend in the sidewalk, the depressed man walked out of the main door and held it open for the couple, who thanked him. He didn't reply. Instead, he let the door go and made his way towards Carl. Carl stood, corrected his jacket, and pretended to fumble with his keys. The depressed man and Carl were now walking side by side towards the parking lot. The depressed man paid no attention to the stranger at his side. Carl noticed the man's strides were almost twice that of his own.

The depressed man walked straight. Carl turned right and walked down the next aisle. He kept his eye on the tall, lanky, depressed man as he stopped at a car, pulled the keys from his pocket, and unlocked the door. Carl darted between the parked cars and waited for his moment.

The man sat down and closed the driver's door. He paused, held the keys in his hand, and stared straight ahead. A sharp rap on his window broke his attention.

The man turned to see Carl smiling at him. Carl mumbled something indistinguishable. The man shook his head and shrugged his shoulders. "What?" he screamed.

"Keys," Carl yelled.

The window rolled down half way.

"I must've dropped my keys after I left the restaurant. Did you see them or hear them hit the ground?" Carl asked.

"No." The man started to roll up the window.

"Do you have a flashlight I could borrow?" Carl's voice was barely audible.

"What?"

Carl made the motion to roll the window down. The depressed man again cautiously lowered the window half way, but his attention was on the window, not on the man outside. Carl reached in, grabbed the man by the hair, and jerked his head towards the window. His head caught the edge of the glass, which opened a large gash on his scalp.

Again, before the man could react, Carl repeatedly slammed his head against the window until the stranger couldn't defend himself. Blood and loose hair stained the window. Streaks of red flowed down the glass. Carl continued to smash the man's head until he felt his body go limp. It was only then that Carl released his grip on the man's hair. The unconscious man slumped forward and his head rested on the steering wheel. Carl looked around the parking lot and made certain no one was around the see what he had done. Carl looked down at his hand. He was holding onto a handful of the man's hair. He shook his hand and the loose hair blew away in the evening breeze.

Carl pulled the nylon sleeve of his jacket over his hand, opened the door, leaned in, and pushed the unconscious man towards the passenger seat. He picked up his long, lanky legs and forced them over the console. The man was a heap on the passenger seat. Blood continued to ooze from his wound. Even in the darkness, the light shimmered off the slow-moving blood as it escaped from the wound.

Carl covered his left hand with the jacket sleeve again, grabbed the window crank, and rolled the window all the way down until the glass was inside the door. A few hairs stuck to the rubber seal where the glass disappeared, but Carl was comfortable that most of the evidence was hidden.

With both hands covered by his nylon jacket sleeves, he sat in the driver's seat and realized he couldn't touch the gas or brake pedal. He made a mental note of where the edge of the seat met the console, and then released the seat lock lever and pulled the seat forward far enough so he could drive the car. He knew better than to adjust the side and rear view mirrors.

The key was already in the ignition. With his fingers still covered by the nylon sleeve, he turned the key and brought the engine to life. Carl shifted the car to "D," pulled out of the parking lot, and headed for a secluded area of town with an industrial parking lot he knew wasn't used at night.

*****

Maddy came out of the shower with her wet hair slicked back and a towel wrapped high around her body. I was sloughing on the sofa with my feet crossed on the coffee table. The television was on with the volume muted, and my eyes were barely open as I drifted in and out of consciousness. I felt Maddy drop onto the sofa beside me, bringing me back from the edge of sleep. With my eyes closed, she flipped her wet hair, sending drops of water cascading down my face. She lifted my shirt and kissed my stomach. The damp hair and her lips tickling my stomach woke me up. I laughed and squirmed as she continued to tickle me. She pulled back, and then straddled my lap. No words were spoken. I simply stared at Maddy sitting on my lap with that white towel acting as a sexy night gown.

Maddy held my face with her hands, leaned in close, and kissed me hard.

My hands moved to rest on her smooth, warm, wet thighs and squeezed them softly. She pulled back, untied the towel, and let it fall to the floor.

"You should've joined me in the shower," she offered.

"If only I'd known the offer was open."

"My shower door is always open for you." Maddy leaned in again and kissed me.

14

The bedroom was completely dark when I woke up to the sound of the phone ringing in the living room. I tossed the covers off and heard Maddy moan and roll over to my right. I had forgotten she was even there. I wasn't used to having someone share the bed. It was only as I was running down the hall that I realized I wasn't wearing anything. Sitting on the sofa, I picked up the phone, and before I could speak I heard Galen talking to someone else.

"Hey! Hey! Galen!"

"Hang tight." His voice was distant as he held the phone away and continued a conversation with someone else. I was able to make out a few words: "body," "car," "dead." My curiosity was piqued. As I sat there on the sofa in the darkness, I saw the time displayed in red on my VCR: 6:14.

"Christ." I wanted to go back to bed. Rubbing the sleep from my eyes, I could feel that my body needed more time in bed. I switched the phone to my other hand, reached for a pillow, and covered my lap with it. Looking around the room, I saw Maddy's towel from last night lying on the floor under the coffee table. Straightening my right leg, I curled my toes, latched onto the terrycloth towel, and pulled it in closer. The pillow was replaced with the towel and positioned behind my head. Just as my head rested on the pillow and my eyes closed, I heard Galen's voice yell my name.

"What?" I yelled back.

"You working today?" Galen asked.

"No. Tomorrow day shift. Why?"

"I figured you'd still be sleeping. Get dressed and get your fucking ass down to Triole Street."

"Where?"

"Do you know where Shore and Triole Streets are off St. Laurent Boulevard?"

"Where?"

"Do you know where the Red Lobster is on St. Laurent?"

"Yeah."

"Just north of Red Lobster. Turn east on Shore and then north on Triole."

"K, bright guy. Where on Triole?" I asked sarcastically.

"Look for all the flashing cop cars, genius." Galen chuckled. "Oh, and wake Maddy. She should be here, too."

"How did you know…" My voice trailed off. "Forget it. I'll," I paused and corrected myself, "we'll be right there."

When I hung up the phone, I stood to go back to the bedroom to wake Maddy, only to find her already leaning against the corner wall to the living room. She was rubbing her eyes like I'd been only moments earlier.

"What's going on?" she asked.

"That was Galen. He wants us both to meet him at some crime scene."

Maddy perked up before I got another word out. "Well, what're you waiting for? Let's get dressed and shove off."

"Think we have time for a shower?" Maddy knew what I meant.

"You had your chance last night and blew it. Come on, we're wasting daylight." She reached down and pulled me up from the sofa by my hand.

"Really?"

"Really!"

*****

I turned north on Triole Street and knew exactly what Galen was talking about. Triole is an industrial cul-de-sac on the east end of Ottawa, with used car dealers and repair shops on either side of the street. At the very end of the street, police cruisers were lined up bumper to bumper, engines running and lights flashing. The lights did little good as the morning sun was rising high in the east in the cloudless sky, and was more intense than the roof lights on the cruisers.

Yellow police crime scene tape was strung across the road between two wooden utility poles. A lone male police officer stood guard on the far side of the tape. He looked like a man who had mastered the art of sleeping while standing. His peak cap was down low, his eyes were closed, and he remained motionless as we approached. Maddy noticed the man's odd stance and looked over at me as she sipped her coffee in its travel mug.

The officer remained motionless as I put my car in park, opened the door, and walked over to him. On cue, his eyes opened and he straightened his back, pushed his cap up, yawned, and turned towards me.

"Finishing the night shift?" I asked politely.

"Flipping nights. I hate them with a passion." He shrugged his shoulders back. "Can I help you?" I heard his back crack when he shrugged.

"Officer Hoese called us to the scene."

The officer took a few steps away from me and keyed the mic attached to his vest. I heard mumbled voices. The radio crackled a few times. His head nodded, he looked back, nodded again, and walked back towards me. He pointed up towards the crime scene where I could park my car behind one of the other cruisers and report directly to Officer Hoese. I thanked him and went back to my car.

"I'm not really sure what to expect. You ready for this?" I asked Maddy.

"Excited is more like it." She was beaming.

The officer held the scene tape up and I drove under it, then parked as instructed. Galen met us as we exited my car.

"Hey copper. Long time no see." Maddy leaned in and kissed Galen on the cheek.

"Not in uniform, sweetie." He wiped his cheek to wash off her kiss. "This way." He turned and walked away. Maddy and I silently followed him around a repair garage to the back of the parking lot where there was a dozen or so cars in various stages of disrepair.

"What've we got?" I asked.

Without looking back, Galen took his cap off and laid it on one of the police vehicles as we passed.

"Christ, I'm sweating so much, I may just die out here." He pulled his orange hair back, then wiped his hand on his pants. "Between this stupid vest and hat, I'm gonna loose ten pounds in water."

With the sun coming up over the building, the temperature was rising, but it certainly wasn't hot out.

It suddenly became evident which vehicle we were here to see. A group of men and women in uniform were each doing their own thing around the car.

"So why are we here, bud?" I asked as we stepped from the road to the dirt parking lot.

"I told the 'LT' that you discovered the guy hanging in the closet, and almost caught the guy when he attacked the girl in your building, and might be able to help out. He was more than a little hesitant, but he called your shift supervisor who vouched for you, Ethan, and called the Civic ER to confirm your position there, Maddy."

Galen placed his hand on my back to guide me to where he wanted us. "Anyway, a security guard on road patrol pulled in here a few hours ago to grab a little sleep and found this guy in the car. When I heard he had a belt around his neck, I jumped the call and got permission to bring you in. Don't show me up or embarrass me. K?"

"Was EMS called in to confirm death?" I asked.

"We know dead, and this guy is dead. No need. Besides, the ME has already come and gone," Galen replied.

We passed a collapsible table with disposable medical gear laid out for the police to use. Galen grabbed a pair of nitrile gloves from the box marked "X-Large," Maddy followed suit and pulled a pair of small, and I donned a pair of medium.

No one seemed to question two civilians on scene as we approached the older model car. All four doors of the car were open, as was the trunk. Maddy kept her distance behind me. As a paramedic, I was more familiar with evidence and crime scene protocols. Each step was calculated and planned, and I moved slowly as we got closer to the car. I heard Galen make introductions to his colleagues. I waved in acknowledgement. I took a quick glance in the trunk as I passed and saw that it was empty. Either everything had been taken as evidence, or it was empty to begin with.

As I stood beside the open driver's door, I squatted like a baseball catcher to get a better view of the inside of the car.

Inside was a tall, thin young man. He was sitting upright, with his head back against the head rest and his seatbelt still fastened. It looked like he had simply fallen asleep if not for the dried blood in his hair around his left ear and the leather belt wrapped tightly around his neck.

"Whatcha got, Medic Boy?" Maddy whispered in my ear.

Pointing to the dried blood in his hair, I whispered back, "Look there. The blood is pretty thick. The hair is matted but I can't see the laceration. Looks serious. I think there's a section of hair that was yanked out or he's going bald in patches. Could be certain meds, cancer, chemo maybe? Don't think the blood loss was significant enough to be cause of death. You?"

"You mean dead before the belt choked the life outta him? Nah. The blood loss is substantial but not life-threatening. What do ya make of the belt?" Maddy asked.

"Looks like a good quality two-inch black leather belt. Let's see; if I was a right-handed attacker, I'd wrap the buckle end around the right side of the guy." I was acting out the movements as I spoke. "Assuming I was in the back seat or the attack came from behind." I tilted my head and tried to see the buckle end behind the dead man's neck. "Yup, buckle on the right. So I'm guessing right-handed. Be great if I could move the body."

Maddy stood up and yelled out, "Hey, copper. Can we move the body and check the car?" Her outburst was meant for Galen, but every police officer responded to the "copper" comment.

Galen looked at the lead investigator, who nodded in agreement. Galen gave me the thumbs up.

I nodded in acknowledgement.

I reached in, touched the man's head, and spread the blood-matted hair. I searched between the hairs to find the laceration, and oddly, it was near the bottom of the area of dried blood. There was a five-centimetre laceration that was still wide open. There were other smaller lacerations surrounding the one main wound. I could see the white bone gleaming from between the two sides of the skin. I placed my thumb in the centre of the wound and pressed hard. The skull remained firm. My guess was that the wound did not cause a skull fracture.

"Look here." I pointed to the area of the lacerations, and with my index finger made a circle where the dried blood matted the hair. "If this guy was standing or sitting when he got cut, the blood would flow down. Instead, the area where the blood matted the hair is towards the upper section of his head. His head was pointing down after he was cut and started bleeding."

"Makes sense. Look." Maddy pulled his left ear. "There's no blood at all in the left ear." Maddy ran her fingers through the man's hair. She pulled her gloved hand out and looked at it. There was no blood transfer from his head or hair onto the glove. "Been more than six hours, I'd say. I've never seen wet blood in someone's hair in the ER for more than a few hours unless it's an active bleed. And this guy's hair is crusty with dried blood."

I put his head back against the headrest. I opened the dead man's eyes and examined them. "Busted blood vessels in his eyes. He was alive when he was choked. Petechial hemorrhage."

Maddy pointed to the man's neck directly above and below the belt. "There was a lot of anger when he was being choked. Look how far that belt dug into his neck. The bastard yanked hard to dig that deep into the skin." The area of skin above and below the belt was swollen and raised, making it appear like the belt was lower than the skin.

I performed a quick body assessment on the dead man the way I would an unconscious trauma patient. Running my hands flat against the man's body while applying gentle pressure, I was checking the skeletal system for inconsistencies, broken or displaced bones, any wet areas indicating possible bleeding or discharge of urine, and bumps or swelling where there shouldn't be. When I felt his back and buttocks, I failed to notice a wallet. To determine his identity, that would be one of the first things the police would search for. I patted down his front pockets. His left front pocket had change, I assumed; they felt like coins and clanked when I pinched and moved them. Nothing rested in the right front pocket.

When I ran my hands down one leg and then the other, I noticed that both his feet were about where they should be to comfortably control the gas and brake pedals. A quick look at the seat track showed that the seat had been moved.

"The seat's been moved." I pointed to the track.

"How do you know?" Maddy asked.

"Look at the outer edge of the track where the seat locks in place. There's a section of about eight to ten inches where the seat has been moved back and forth along the track. That section is free of dust. It would take time to accumulate more dust." I pointed to the edge of the locking track almost at floor level.

"Coincidence. That could've been anytime in the last week or so," Maddy countered.

"True. But one thing Galen taught me is that there is no such thing as coincidence in crime."

Maddy stood up, walked around to the passenger side of the car, and peered in through the open door. She looked through from the passenger side to the driver's side.

"Hey Galen,"—this time she knew better than to use "copper"— "why is the driver's window down?"

Galen looked at the lead investigator who answered, "That's the way we found it."

Maddy glanced at the temperature control settings, and the horizontal slider was positioned half way between hot and cold. "Odd," Maddy whispered to herself. She examined the climate control. The older model car had no air conditioning and the temperature was set to blow warm air; the fan was at 3. "Chilly night last night; why roll the window down?" She inspected the passenger side of the cab and found nothing out of the ordinary except for an extremely small blood smear on the right edge of the passenger seat. The black interior made it almost indistinguishable.

"Ethan," Maddy called out. "If the guy was lying on the seat, would his head be about here?" She was pointing approximately half way up the right side bolster of the passenger seat.

"Seems about right. Why?"

"There's a tiny, and I mean tiny, itsy-bitsy smear of blood right here. Well, it could be blood. It's dry on black vinyl. For all I know, it could be ice cream." Maddy looked at the height of the man, and had a puzzled look on her face.

Maddy walked around to the driver's side again and almost pushed me out of the way. She closed the driver's door, and then opened it again. She reached down and used the crank to raise the window. It became apparent what she was looking at. She rolled the window back down.

"Galen," she called out.

Galen walked over and stood by the rear driver's side tire. "What?"

"Did they figure out how he got that cut on his head?" Maddy questioned Galen.

"They figure he was hit from behind. Why?"

"I think he was attacked while sitting in the car and had his head smashed against the window."

"And why would you say that?"

For effect, Maddy thought actions would speak louder than words. She cranked the window and watched Galen's eyes open wide as the window revealed the secret it had held while hiding inside the door.

"Fuck. That's great." Galen called out to the lieutenant to join us. He turned to Maddy. "Roll the window down."

As the LT was walking over to the car, he yawned and turned his neck, and I heard it crack. He looked tired and had a serious case of bed head. The lieutenant was a short man by police standards; not an imposing presence at all. His light summer suit was wrinkled as if he had been sleeping in it, and he wore leather closed-toe sandals without socks.

"LT, I know you really extended yourself when I asked if these guys could take a look at the crime scene." Galen was not himself. He seemed almost like he was speaking to his father. He couldn't make eye contact and spoke softly. Not his usual mannerism. "But seriously, these two are truly observant and look at things a little differently."

"The ME and scene techs went over the car and the vic. We collected everything we needed. I figured it couldn't hurt. Besides, Ethan, right?" The Lieutenant extended his hand. We shook. "I think we've actually met on some crime scenes when you were on duty." He tuned to Maddy. "Charles Lezcars. And you are?" He straightened himself up slightly when he introduced himself.

"His girlfriend." Maddy pointed to me with her head and extended her hand. Lieutenant Lezcars laughed out loud and turned to Galen. "I like them already." He turned his attention back to us. "Whatcha got?"

Galen decided he should do the talking. "Did the techs figure out how he got that nasty cut on his head?"

Lieutenant Lezcars opened his notepad and flipped through the pages without looking up.

"Nothing. They can't find the weapon or figure out what caused that wound. We'll have to wait until he goes on the table. Why?"

On cue, Maddy rolled up the window to reveal the dried blood and stands of hair stuck to it. Without hesitation, Maddy gave her interpretation of the events.

"K, I'm not sure if the bad guy was in the passenger seat or outside the car, but the laceration fits to where the glass would be if the window was rolled down a bit and his head repeatedly hit against the edge of the glass. The head wound is definitely not the immediate cause of death.

"The belt used is indicative of the type used in the other deaths. The way the belt was wrapped around his neck and the way the end was pulled, the guy was most likely in the back seat.

"We found some of the greasy dust along the seat track that showed the driver's seat had been moved very recently. And, there's a smudge of something on the far side of the passenger seat, most likely blood. I think the dead guy was lying on the passenger seat while the other guy was driving."

"K, is that all? Cause we found the smudge, as you put it, and we did notice the seat had been moved. But the window, shit, that's good. We probably would've found that at the police garage," the lieutenant went on to explain.

Galen intervened. "Probably, yeah, but they found it now, LT. Our techs should've found it but they didn't. And believe me when I tell you, they know more about the belt killer than most of us right now."

Lieutenant Lezcars placed his hands on his hips and took a stance. "And why, exactly, would these two know more about the belt killer than us?"

"Because they're smart and they know how to read people. Trust me, LT, when I tell you these two can help us." Galen was adamant.

Lieutenant Lezcars turned and walked away. "Just don't let them muck out our investigation, Hoese, cause if they do, your ass is mine."

"My wife might say otherwise, LT," Galen laughed.

"That went better than I thought," I said as I tried to break the tension. Turning to Maddy, I added, "I think you handled yourself pretty freaking well with him."

"Thanks." She hip-bumped me, making me lose my balance and stumble sideways.

"Now that he's gone, what do you really think happened?" Galen asked.

I looked at Maddy, and she passed the torch on to me.

"K, what do I think happened? Here's my take. The guy was sitting in his car; the window was part way down. His attacker surprised him, reached in, grabbed his hair, and slammed his head against the window repeatedly to render him unconscious."

"Why that way instead of the attacker being in the passenger side?" Galen looked puzzled. "Could he not have been in the passenger seat and pushed him into the window?"

"Think of the mechanics involved to push someone hard enough over and over again having to reach over, as opposed to grabbing him by the hair and yanking him a few inches into the window," I countered.

"Point taken."

I continued, "The guy was probably unconscious, then pushed or pulled over to the passenger seat. Then the attacker drives him here before he wakes up, props him in the driver's seat, and strangles him."

Galen nodded then asked, "OK, why?"

"I have no idea."

Maddy cut in on the conversation. "Does it matter why he did it? Do you think he even knows why he does it? I think it's probably some kind of weird primeval instinct that forces him to do it, or the guy is just a fucking whack job. Personally, I'm going with the whack job theory. If this really is our boy from Kingston, he's gone to the dark side and there's no way back."

We were so engrossed in the examination and speculation of what had happened that we failed to see the small van pull up and two men dressed in Tyvek suits and nitrile gloves ready themselves to remove the body for transport to the Ottawa General Hospital for an autopsy.

Galen saw the white suits approach and pulled Maddy and I aside to give them access to the car and the body. I watched as they set up the stretcher near the back of the car and opened a large, purple plastic body bag.

Before we arrived, the first set of crime techs had already collected most of the evidence needed including any hair and fibre samples, fingerprinted the deceased, swabbed as many surfaces as possible, and taken more pictures of the car, its contents, and the body than are taken at your average wedding.

One of the techs that arrived carefully placed each one of the deceased's hands in a brown paper bag and taped the opening closed to prevent the bags from falling off. The bags would collect evidence that may fall from the deceased's hands during transport. They labelled the bags "Hand Right" and "Hand Left." Because of the unusual way in which the man was killed, one of the techs entered through the passenger side and sat in the back seat. From the front seat, the tech held his head on either side while the guy in the back carefully removed the belt from around his neck and placed it into another paper evidence bag.

Before long, the tall lanky dead man was in the plastic body bag and all the evidence bags were meticulously given to the first set of crime scene techs. Signatures were exchanged on various forms to accept or pass along evidence from one person to another, and then cruisers started to drive off, leaving fewer police behind.

By this time, Galen, Maddy, and I were standing by my car going over the circumstances of the man's death.

"Do you think he had to kill again because you stopped him at your apartment building the other night?" Galen asked of us.

Maddy decided to give her opinion. "If killing is like sex for this guy, you need to get your fill before you're satisfied for a while. If he needs to kill a few people the way he killed his wife, get his jollies, then for, I don't know, a few weeks, a few months, he's almost normal. He most certainly would need a job, makes some friends, and then moves on before the things come crashing down. He's probably a very smart guy."

"Are you sure you don't have a psych degree?" I leaned in close and kissed her.

"Baby, you do not want to know what I think about you," she told me.

"Christ, I'm gonna toss my breakfast." Galen puffed out his cheeks.

"Hey copper, I think you're pretty cool. Can I kiss you while you're in uniform?" Maddy didn't wait for permission; she leaned in and gave him a soft kiss on the cheek.

*****

Sheila Tomlinson knelt down and pressed out her own skirt over her lap before fastening the front buttons on her daughter's dress. It wasn't that her daughter couldn't do it; Sheila enjoyed this little task. When Sheila was at eye level with her daughter, she thought of the times when her own mother had done the same with her. Now that Sheila had her own daughter, she relished the time they spent together.

Tabitha would squirm when her mother fussed with her clothes or hair, and wanted to dress herself. She was becoming her own little person, and would test her independence whenever she could. Sheila would smile and know that, shortly, all this would be a thing of the past. She did up the top button at the front of the dress and Tabitha immediately undid it.

"Ma, why do I have to wear a dress?" she asked.

"Because you're a beautiful little girl and beautiful little girls wear dresses." The argument had no logic, but she was having a conversation with a nine-year-old, who was soon to be ten. "Besides, you look beautiful in this dress. It's always been my fav, and you'll be too big to wear it next summer."

"I hate flowers. I hate this dress. Everyone else wears pants and T's to play. Why can't I wear T's? And you always get mad when I get my dress dirty." Tabitha's reasoning made more sense than did her mother's argument.

"Well, maybe the other girls aren't as pretty as you." Another poor argument.

"Ma, there are lots of prettier girls. Dresses don't make me prettier. You just think I'm prettier because you're my Ma."

Sheila pulled Tabitha's hair down and placed it on her shoulders. "Go play. Are you going to the park to meet Ashley and Monica?" The park was only four houses down the street, and Tabitha had been walking there by herself since the summer prior.

"I'm going to Ashley's first so I can put on a pair of her pants and a T, then we'll go to the park. I don't wanna look like a dork."

Sheila knew better than to argue the point with Tabitha. They had the same discussion every few days, but Tabitha was turning into her own person No matter how hard she tried, Sheila couldn't turn her daughter into a smaller, younger version of herself. Sheila stood, kissed her daughter on the top of the head, and sent her on her way.

*****

Maddy and I left Galen and the few remaining police officers at the crime scene. There was little else for us to do. We stopped at Denny's for a quick breakfast, and then Maddy decided she needed a nap. We weren't far from her apartment and made our way to her place. Breakfast and the drive were uncomfortably quiet. I think the impact of seeing the body in the car was finally sinking in.

As an ER nurse, Maddy was used to seeing dead or seriously injured patients, but seldom will nurses see a patient before paramedics take them to the hospital. Wounds are dressed, fractures splinted, IV's started, meds given, cardiac monitors attached; a small portion of their job is done before the patient even arrives in the ER. It's like gift wrapping the injured and presenting the ER staff with the patient. Paramedics spend a lot of scene time stabilizing and prepping patients for transport. Then off comes the wrapping. The ER staff start to cut off the dressings to see what's underneath, exposing the wound or the injury, removing the cervical collar, and taking them off the back board. Even then, the ER staff are in a well-lit, temperature controlled environment. They aren't subjected to extreme weather, snow, rain, winds, or upset family members with the benefit of security around.

Without saying anything, Maddy walked directly to the bedroom, closed the blinds, pulled the drapes to make the room as dark as possible, and curled up on the bed. Shift workers often have their bedrooms fitted with multiple layers of devices to shut out daylight when they need sleep after a night shift.

I wasn't that tired and decided to let her sleep. I didn't want to impose, and wanted her to get some rest and deal with the incident without my interference. I went to the living room, fell into the sofa, placed a pillow behind my head, and closed my eyes.

A sharp tug on my left arm brought me back from the brink of sleep. Maddy was pulling me into the bedroom. Not a word was said. She crawled into bed, curled up on her right side, wrapped my left arm around herself, and fell asleep.

*****

Galen sat in his cruiser. The seat was pushed all the way back, and a metal clipboard was propped up against the steering wheel. He was the last cruiser on scene. Even though the last of the scene tape had come down, the body had been taken away, and the victim's car loaded on a flatbed and towed to the police compound, Galen was still busy filling out redundant forms that asked the same questions in only slightly dissimilar ways. The questions were designed to elicit a possibly altered response. Either that, or to make you think in a different way to remember an important detail of which you otherwise wouldn't have thought. Galen preferred to think it was just a way to piss off the front line officers.

He pulled the coffee cup from the drink holder. Galen knew his drink was ice cold as soon as he touched it, but he'd started his shift at four in the morning and was too tired to care. He tilted the cup back, and as soon as the cold coffee touched his lips, he spit the liquid back into the cup.

Christ. It's as cold as ice. Who the fuck drinks cold coffee? he thought as he emptied the coffee onto the dirt parking lot through the open window and replaced the paper cup in the cup holder.

As Galen finished his paperwork, he cursed his decision not to bring his thermos of coffee that morning. His wife had set the timer on the coffee maker so it was ready when he woke up; Galen had just been too lazy to make it before leaving. The radio continued to squawk. He tuned it all out and only listened for his vehicle number.

*****

"Ottawa, put us 10-7 scene. Christ, can you get the 10-2s here. There's a freaking mob out here."

Paramedic Andy Clark knew swearing on the radio was totally against protocol, but whenever he—or anyone, for that matter—got a call for a child, the adrenaline started to pump. It takes a lot for an experienced paramedic to get excited, and Andy had been around a long time. When the call came in for a possible child VSA, Andy and his partner Kyle—a new graduate who still wore his stethoscope around his neck all day long—felt their stomachs go sour. Andy really hated his job sometimes.

"That's 10-4, 4299. 10-2s have already been dispatched and should be there any moment," the female dispatcher replied.

As soon as Andy booked 10-8 in service to the call, Kyle immediately donned a pair of gloves, adjusted the stethoscope around his neck, and applied his seatbelt. Andy silently thought the seatbelt would never fit around all the gear the new kid had on his belt. Andy carried a glove holder on his belt, and that was it. Newbie, he thought to himself and shook his head in disbelief. Kyle squirmed and almost had a smile on his face, anticipating the call.

"You know it's a call for a possible dead kid, right?" Andy pointed out.

"Yeah." Kyle remained unfazed.

"Well, don't look so fucking happy. K," Andy told him.

Andy slowed his speed and hit the air horn a few times to get the crowd that was preventing him from parking close to the curb dispersed. The crowd parted and Andy knew why there were so many people watching. Two adult males were performing CPR on a young child. The man doing compressions had his back to the ambulance. The second man performing ventilations was facing the first man. He had one hand pinching the dead girl's nostrils and the second hand was on her chin. His hands were stained red with blood.

Andy and Kyle exited the vehicle and ran to the back of the truck. Andy's training told him that you never, ever run on a call. If anyone sees you running, it could instil panic in the bystanders. All the rules were suspended when Andy saw the sight of the lifeless young child on the ground.

Most of the equipment was already strapped to the cot before he and Kyle pulled it out. The carriage fell and the wheels smashed against the pavement. Kyle reached behind and unlocked the swing arm from the floor bolt as Andy was pulling on the cot. Once freed, the two of them took a few quick strides and lowered the cot beside the young patient. Even though Andy was driving on this call, he was the senior medic, and all of Kyle's excitement was now replaced with fear. He had never had a patient this young before.

Andy went straight the patient, placed his gloved hand on the back of the man doing compressions, and could feel the dampness through the glove.

"How're you holding up?" Andy asked. He looked down to see a young girl. Her age didn't matter. All that mattered was that at this very moment, she wasn't alive. Bright red blood covered her face and neck and ran down her white shirt. The ground beside her was saturated with blood, and the knees of the man doing compressions were also covered in blood. She had lost most of her blood in only a few minutes until the pressure dropped so low it couldn't sustain life. The young girl would have fallen unconscious before she died.

The left side of her throat had been cut. Not a cut, this is more of a slash, Andy thought as he looked down. He could see the trachea and knew that if the laceration was that bad, the carotid had been severed as well. All fear and anxiety left Andy. This was business now.

The man nodded that he was all right, but he truly looked scared and tired. Sweat dripped freely from his brow and the end of his nose. His eyes were wide, his mouth open, and he was panting. Andy knew CPR was an exhaustive exercise, but stopping for a short time to replace him was "not indicated" at this point.

Andy looked directly at the man providing ventilations. "Keep it up for a minute longer," he instructed. With his right index and middle fingers, Andy felt for a carotid pulse on the right side of the neck. For just a fleeting moment, seeing his fingers on the girl's neck reminded him how on TV, actors always check for a pulse behind the ear. One of his pet peeves. There was no pulse in the young girl's carotid; he hadn't expected one. Deep down, experience told him it was already too late.

"Did anyone see what happened?" Andy asked the crowd.

Heads shook; no one replied. He was waiting for the mother to come over, distraught and just plain getting in his way. Andy hoped she wouldn't show up until after they left. It would be easier, not only for him, but for the mother as well.

Andy heard the police siren in the background come to an abrupt end, and noticed two police officers walking towards him. One of the officers was already speaking into his shoulder mic. Andy hoped he was asking for more officers on scene. Both officers already had their nitrile gloves on, ready to help.

Kyle arrived and knelt on the grass with the young girl's head between his knees. He took over ventilations from the man covered in blood, who simply fell backwards on the grass and covered his eyes with the forearm that was still blood-free.

CPR was exhausting but easy. Kyle knew that providing an effective airway was much more difficult. He placed the Ambu Bag, a manual device used for artificial respiration, over the girl's face, wrapped his hand around the mask and jaw, and squeezed the bag once. Air was forced from the PVC bag down her trachea and into her lungs, and immediately blood was forced back up and coated the inside of the mask. Blood dripped down the sides of the mask and across the young girl's face to the grass below. Kyle pulled the BVM away from the girl's face, pulled the hand-powered suction unit from the bag, and went to suction the bright red blood from her mouth. He opened her mouth to insert the suction tip as the bystander performed a hard downward compression. Blood sprayed upwards and splashed Kyle in the face.

Dropping all the equipment, Kyle fell backwards. He wiped his eyes with his hands and spat out blood-tinged sputum. Kyle pulled off his nitrile gloves and continued to wipe his eyes with the back of his clean hands. Reaching inside the bag, he pulled out a one litre bag of IV solution, ripped off the end where the line attaches, and began to rinse his face with the sterile solution.

"You OK?" Andy yelled at Kyle. Silently, Kyle waved back, indicating he wanted Andy to help the young girl.

Andy pointed at two bystanders and in a stern, authoritative voice, barked out an order.

"You and you, give him a hand." He pointed to Kyle.

The two police officers who had just arrived on scene saw the commotion and offered their assistance. One officer took over CPR, so Andy moved to the airway and asked for the other officer to hand him the trauma kit.

Andy pulled a face shield from the bag to protect himself and attempted to clear the patient's airway. Little could be done. Andy kept suctioning the airway, but with each compression, the airway would refill with blood.

Andy knew this was a load and go situation. He quickly grabbed the largest abdominal dressings in the trauma kit, ripped open the packaging with his teeth, and slapped it over the large laceration on the girl's neck.

"You OK to go soon?" Andy asked his partner.

"I'll be ready when you are." Kyle was lying on his back while the two bystanders drained IV solution over his face to clear the blood from his eyes, nose, and mouth.

Andy knew he should've called for backup. He knew she should have a collar applied, and be placed on a backboard to have the cardiac monitor attached. Fuck it, he thought, too late now. He made sure the dressings were secure on her neck while he told one of the officers to clear all the gear from the cot.

"Ottawa, 4299." Andy didn't wait for them to acknowledge. "Do you have a supervisor on the way?"

"10-4 4299. ETA five minutes."

"10-4." That was five minutes too long.

Once the cot was clear, he instructed the police officer doing compressions how to help him lift the patient from the ground to the cot with the minimum of movement. One the count of three, the patient was lifted from the grass to the cot and the second police officer took over compression.

"You ready to move?" Andy asked Kyle.

"As ready as I'll ever be." Kyle was still having his eyes rinsed and spitting out the atrocious taste of IV solution.

"You and I are in the back." Andy looked at the officer who had just stopped doing compressions. "You're driving." Andy knew this wasn't protocol, but under the circumstances, he was out of options: Kyle was unable to drive or care for the patient, one officer was needed for CPR, and Andy would manage the airway, so someone had to drive the rig. Since the supervisor was still a few minutes out, Andy elected to leave now.

*****

I felt a hand on my shoulder, slowly shaking me from my late morning nap. There was confusion as I opened my eyes. My mind didn't register my surroundings and I bolted upright. Maddy jumped back, startled.

"Geez, warn a girl before you do that." She was laughing at me. No doubt the look of confusion on my face made her laugh. I felt my heart racing; thumping in my chest. I think I was more frightened than Maddy was.

The room was now bright, and I finally made the connection as to where I was. Maddy must've woken up first, and opened the blinds before waking me.

"I didn't think I was that tired." I slapped the bed. "Comfy mattress."

"Yeah, sure. Like the mattress made a difference. You know you snore when you're tired, right?"

"Must be the pillow. I never snore."

Maddy laughed loudly as she exited the bedroom.

"Galen's on the phone. He wants to talk to you."

"Again? Did he say want he wanted?" I questioned.

"I may be a lot of things for you, but your secretary is not one of them. Oh, and clean the drool off the side of your face before you come out," she said as she wiped her right cheek and tossed the cordless phone to the bed. It bounced and landed on my lap.

Picking up the cordless phone, I wiped both my cheeks and felt nothing. She'd got me.

"Hey bud, what's up?"

"Busy?" Galen asked.

"Nope."

"Wanna be?"

"Why?"

Maddy returned to the bedroom and stood at the door, leaning against the frame. She was swinging the car keys around her index finger. *My God, she looks gorgeous standing there*, I marvelled. I was lost in the moment and forgot I had my best friend on the phone. It was at that very instant that I realized I was totally and madly in love with this woman. I was staring in disbelief at a girl who I'd only met a short while ago, and she had already totally and completely taken over my life.

This annoying voice on the phone pulled me back from my fantasy.

"Have you heard a word I've said?" Galen sounded upset.

"Sorry, bud. This phone has a terrible connection. Say it again."

"The LT said I could call you in again. EMS just took a little girl to the hospital. We doubt very much she'll survive. Wanna guess what she was wearing?"

I wasn't in the mood for guessing games. "Where are you?" My voice was stern and direct. I was now angry—no, more than angry. A chill ran through my body and I leapt from the bed. Maddy sensed my mood and walked ahead of me down the hall without saying a word.

"Got it. We'll be right there." I wanted to slam down the receiver. *I hate fucking technology.* Looking at Maddy's cordless phone, I realized I had to move a slider switch to the right to hang up. It lost all potency when I wasn't able to slam the receiver into the cradle.

"You're driving," I instructed Maddy.

Less than fifteen minutes later we arrived at yet another scene reminiscent of the one we were at earlier in the day. We parked about half a block from where the police had sectioned off the corner of the neighbourhood. It was a carbon copy from that morning—yellow police scene tape, cruisers idling with their roof lights activated—but the mood was decidedly more sombre.

Lieutenant Lezcars turned towards us as Maddy and I walked towards the scene. He waved us through and another uniformed officer raised the tape, granting us access to the restricted area. Off to the right, a crowd of onlookers was standing on the opposite side of the scene tape. Their arms were crossed in front of themselves in a form of self-comfort that is used when someone else isn't around to provide the feeling of reassurance. Others had their hands covering their mouths in disbelief at the events that had occurred on their street.

To the left, I assumed the same evidence technicians were repeating their actions from that morning. Hair samples, fibres, and fingerprints were being collected and tagged. Only a few feet from where the men and women in white Tyvek were doing their jobs, I saw what was obviously the area where I would've been if I had been working and assigned this call. Some dressing wrappers and a pair of light blue nitrile gloves with stains of red were lying in the grass where the medics had treated the young girl. The grass where I assumed the girl had been lying was stained dark. Only one thing does that, and it takes a lot of fluid to leave a dark stain that size.

Lieutenant Lezcars walked over to greet us. Although his hair was no longer a tangled mess, he was showing signs of stress and aggravation. He extended his hand to both Maddy and I, and we shook it without saying a word. He turned and removed his suit jacket, tossed it on the hood of a cruiser, and then walked towards the area where the attack had taken place earlier. He tugged on his tie to loosen it, and then placed both hands on his hips.

"She was found by her two friends. It was supposed to be a play date. A fucking play date. Instead, she winds up dead. Christ, I don't think she was much older than ten years old."

I didn't want to interrupt him. Lieutenant Lezcars needed the time to allow his emotions to settle in. He continued to look across the crime scene and was lost in thought. A gentle tug on my arm pulled me back.

Galen was standing behind me and indicated with a slight head movement that he wanted me to follow him.

We stood beside what I thought was his cruiser and Galen said in a hushed tone, "The girl didn't make it."

Not wanting to show any reaction to what I had just heard—something that the bystanders could pick up on—I stood before Galen, stone-faced.

"Why was there blood on the scene?" I whispered. Maddy was busy looking at the people behind the scene tape.

"I'm not sure. Why do you ask?" Galen leaned in close.

"The three of us studied each and every child killing case and not once was the girl cut or had a bleed. Why now? What was different?"

Galen held up his index finger to indicate he would be right back. I stopped him.

"What was she wearing?"

Galen flipped open his notepad and read out softly, "Pink lace-up low-cut sneakers, faded jeans, white T with a floral band around the neck." He closed the notebook. "It's our guy."

"Was her shirt ripped? Did the guy take a souvenir?"

"I don't know. I wasn't here when the call came in, and by the time I arrived, your guys were working on her. It was fast. The first cops on scene said that when the paramedics showed up she still had a pulse, but they were concerned with the laceration and the breathing. So they did a load and go. It's our guy," Galen argued vehemently.

"Really, why? Each and every previous attack, the girls were wearing a floral dress. The dress was ripped and a swatch taken. And not one of the girls was cut," Maddy interjected.

"Maybe he was interrupted, wise-ass," Galen offered in explanation to Maddy. "Sorry, hon. I'm used to calling your hubby names. It just slipped out. Sorry."

I decided to offer my interpretation of the events. "The one and only time he gets interrupted is the one time the girl is not wearing a dress, and is the one time she gets a cut. And the lieutenant said she was about ten. All the other girls were much younger. Makes zero sense." I made a circle with my index finger and thumb to emphasize my point.

"Fuck. You're probably right. Hang on." Galen walked towards the lieutenant and whispered into his ear. Lieutenant Lezcars looked over at me and then turned back to Galen, and the two of them approached us silently. The lieutenant with his wrinkled suit and sandals reminded me of what Columbo might've looked like as a young detective before the wrinkled raincoat.

"Whatya got?" the LT asked us.

"I worked on one of the young girls killed by the Flower Collector. It was the last victim, I believe, before this girl," I told him.

"You call this guy the 'Flower Collector'? Seriously?" The lieutenant was not impressed. "The press will have a fucking field day if they hear we named this asshole. Who baptized this fucker with 'Flower Collector'?" The LT air-quoted "Flower Collector."

My voice was subdued. "I did."

A female uniformed officer and another detective approached quietly behind Galen and Lieutenant Lezcars. Galen nodded to Erin Rodda and Detective Nardone from the group assembled to catch the "Flower Collector." She acknowledged Galen with a silent nod.

"Hey, don't get me wrong. I like it. Just don't let the press hear us talking about it. Giving a name to this bastard personalizes the killer. Usually the press will give a name to the perp to sensationalize the news for ratings. Myself, I'd rather just shoot the pricks and let them rot in hell."

Erin waited for a break in the conversation before speaking. "I spoke to the mother at the hospital before coming here. She's aware that her daughter," Erin flipped her notepad open, "Monica Fisher, aged ten, passed away. If you guys want anyone to talk to, I have one of the other girl's mother here." Erin pointed to a woman behind the yellow tape, who was clutching her daughter tightly.

"Sure," the lieutenant agreed.

Erin pointed to the woman and waved her over. A heavy set middle-aged woman lifted the yellow tape for her daughter, and the two of them walked hand in hand to the group. The young girl was still crying; her eyes were red and swollen and her nose was running. Sheila stopped before Lieutenant Lezcars, who remained silent. Erin read the lieutenant's face and broke the silence.

"L.T., this is Sheila Tomlinson and her daughter Tabitha. Sheila. This is Lieutenant Lezcars. He was the first detective on scene. If it's been determined that Monica's death is related to the other girls who were," Erin paused, "hurt, then the team assigned to track down the person responsible will take over."

Sheila pulled Tabitha in tightly next to her. "You mean those other little girls who died. This might be because of the same person." Sheila began to well up and the tears flowed freely. "You think what Monica was wearing is the reason she was attacked." Tabitha started to cry loudly as she pulled herself in tighter to her mother's leg until they became one.

Detective Nardone broke in. "We can't speculate right now, and we wouldn't want to even guess as to who may have done this or what the motives are."

"And you are?" Sheila asked.

"Detective Nardone." He offered his hand. Sheila didn't return his greeting. He pulled his hand back. "I'm in charge of trying to find out who hurt these girls." Detective Nardone waved towards the area where Monica had been lying earlier.

Sheila blurted out, "Hurt! These girls weren't hurt. They were killed. Don't try to humanize what happened. Be honest for Christ's sake."

Tabitha hid behind her mother and I could see her body arch up and down in sync with her sobbing. Maddy noticed it as well and crouched down. She leaned in close to Tabitha and whispered, "Are you scared?"

Tabitha peeked out from behind her mother and wiped her nose with the back of her hand. Sheila's hand slid down. She placed it softly on Tabitha's head and stroked her hair. Tabitha nodded her head in agreement.

"You know something; I'm pretty scared myself and I'm a grown-up," Maddy said softly.

"Why are you scared?" Tabitha inquired.

"Because I don't like bad people. Bad people scare me and you know what?"

Tabitha shook her head from side to side.

"It's perfectly OK to be scared and afraid of bad people. In fact, it's OK to be on your toes and make sure you don't get into trouble." Maddy paused for a few moments. "Do you think you can tell me what happened?"

Tabitha nodded in agreement. Maddy sat down on the grass and patted the area beside her. Tabitha let go of her mother and sat down facing Maddy. For several minutes, Maddy just smiled at the little girl as she composed herself before she told her story.

Lieutenant Lezcars and Detective Nardone saw what was happening and motioned for everyone to give the two girls sitting on the lawn some room. Galen and I stood away from the detectives and other police officers, and I watched in amazement at how easily Maddy was able to develop a rapport with this little girl in such a short time.

Galen leaned in close to me and whispered in my ear, "She's pretty fucking amazing. If you don't marry her, I will."

I smiled and didn't offer a response. I was too busy staring at Maddy as the two of them began to quietly discuss the events of the morning.

"…and then I got changed out of my dress and put on a pair of Ashley's jeans and this T." Tabitha tugged at the shirt she was wearing. "Monica was outside waiting because I was taking too long getting changed. Ashley and me were trying on different clothes, and Monica got pissy with me. Is it my fault she died? Is she dead because Ashley and me were inside and she was alone outside?"

Maddy's voice as calm and reassuring. "Absolutely not. Monica was hurt by a bad person. Monica decided on her own to leave the house. You can't blame yourself. You have no control over what the bad person did any more than you could control what Monica did."

Tabitha paused to contemplate what Maddy was saying, her young mind having trouble processing what was happening. I watched over Maddy's shoulder as Tabitha wiped her runny nose again with the back of her hand.

"Is Monica's mom gonna be mad at me?"

"No one is mad at you," Maddy replied. Her voice had a calming effect on the little girl. "You have to be strong for Monica's mommy now. She lost her little girl and you and Ashley need to be there for her and help her through this."

Tabitha didn't reply; instead she looked up at her mother, who was now crying softly, hugging herself, and nodding in agreement.

*****

A block up the street from the crime scene, a small two-door car sat in the convenience store parking lot. The lone male occupant sat in the driver's seat, sipped his Dr. Pepper, and nibbled on potato chips. A map book was open and lay visible on the dash. The car radio was on and set to a soft rock station.

Looking passed the map book, he could see Galen, Maddy, and Ethan at the crime scene. Maddy was sitting down with a little girl. He put a handful of salty chips in his mouth, which was followed by a mouthful of pop. When the bag was finished, he tapped it, causing all the loose salt and crumbs to fall to the bottom. He tilted the bag back and let the contents of the foil chip bag slide into this mouth. His lips tingled from the extra salt. He licked the salt from the corners of his mouth and looked inside the bag: empty. He crumpled it into a ball and tossed it outside. Shaking the can, he found it empty, but tried to salvage another sip from it. He crushed the can and threw that to the ground as well.

"Hey, asshole. There's a garbage can two feet from your car." The young man was walking past the car, and had seen him pitch the garbage out of the window.

"Pick it up yourself if you care that much." He started the car, backed it out of the parking spot, and drove away. The young man walked over, picked up the can and crumpled-up chip bag, and put them in the large metal trash can.

15

Tom, Galen, Maddy, and I sat around the table at the restaurant. We had intended to have a quiet dinner but no one felt like eating. Maddy and I had brought Tom up to speed on the events of the day. The restaurant was full; the sound of conversations, china plates clanking against each other, and laughter filled the space. Servers balanced trays of food at shoulder height between the tables and around chairs. Occasionally, a glass would fall to the floor from a server's tray, sending shards flying. The sound of breaking glass would cause an immediate round of applause from the patrons and the server would bow in appreciation.

Four glasses of beer sat on the table, the pitcher was still half full, and the plate of nachos was untouched. I rolled the glass of beer between my hands and let the condensation cool down my palms. Regardless of the circumstances or who killed the little girl Monica, Tom and I had dealt with death in the past; it's a common element of our job. However, the death of a young child affects every medic a little differently. Especially when that death was caused by a senseless act of violence. Tom, Maddy, and I had barely touched our drinks; Galen was already on his second glass of beer.

Under the table, Maddy kept swinging her knee back and forth and gently hitting my leg. She never let on as to what she was doing above the table. She held onto her glass with both hands and stared into her beer.

The young female server came over to the table, pulled the plate of cold nachos from before us, and replaced it with a large plate of steaming hot wings with various dipping sauces on the side.

"Compliments of a customer," the server said.

Galen stood and looked around, scanning the room. "Who?" His voice was stern and direct.

"What's going on?" Tom questioned Galen.

"The guy sitting right over there." The server pointed to an empty table in the corner. "He was a few minutes ago." She sounded confused. "If you're concerned about the safety of the food, I can guarantee the customer didn't touch the plate. He ordered the food, paid cash, and was still sitting there when I walked out of the kitchen with your plate of wings."

"What did he look like?" Galen demanded.

Everyone started talking over each other, no one paying attention to what the others were saying.

"What's going on?" Maddy jumped in.

"Just a guy. I don't know." The server was beginning to sound nervous. "I just brought the wings."

"Get your manager." Galen gave a direct order, his voice gruff as he left the table to walk around the restaurant. The server stood, unmoving, not sure exactly what was beginning to unfold before her. "Move your ass, girl," Galen barked.

"Galen, be nice," Maddy broke in.

"She's on break right now." The server was almost crying.

"Get her anyway."

"Galen, please, be nice."

"What's going on?" Tom asked again.

"It was him."

"Him, who him?" I broke in.

"The belt guy. Him," Galen shot back.

Tom jumped to his feet and bolted from the restaurant. Through the window I saw him stop in the parking lot, looking for anyone in their car or driving away. Tom spun around, looked back into the restaurant, and saw me watching him. He put up his arms in desperation.

The server was still standing at our table, watching Galen as he walked around the upper section of the restaurant before moving to the lower section. He turned to see that the server was still standing with us and hadn't yet left to retrieve the manager. Many of the patrons had stopped what they were doing and begun to listen to our conversation, or watch as Galen inspected every inch of the restaurant. He paused at the table where the man who had ordered the wings for our table had sat, and began to look at the ceiling.

"This table?" he asked the server. She nodded in agreement and began to walk to Galen. "Do those cameras work?" Galen was pointing at the cameras that were affixed around the dining room and bar of the restaurant. "Where are his dishes? Did he eat?"

"No, umm, yes, I don't know." The server had a look of confusion on her face. "He had a beer or two. That's it."

"Where're the glasses?"

"They must have been picked up already and taken to the kitchen to be cleaned. Why?"

Looking defeated, Tom sat back down at our table.

The server stood beside Galen and asked him to calm down so as not to upset the other guests. Galen ignored her and positioned himself behind the chair where the mysterious man had been sitting. He crouched down and looked up high at ceiling level around the restaurant. As Galen was examining the dining room, a well-dressed woman in clichéd restaurant formal attire arrived and stood before him. Her short jet-black hair stood in contrast to her crisp white shirt, but matched her pressed black skirt and nylons. She held an air of authority, and attempted to convey that in the way she stood. Her arms were down by her sides, exhibiting an open demeanour, and not crossed in front of her in a confrontational manner. She nodded at the server who gratefully left the table.

"Sir." Her voice was that of someone who was well versed and highly skilled in dealing with unruly customers. "Can I help you?" She stood on the opposite side of the table, across from Galen. I chuckled to myself when I saw the woman dealing with Galen in this manner. If it had been a man talking to him in that way, Galen may have just hauled off and sucker-punched him.

"Do those cameras work?" Galen asked as he pointed at the cameras that were affixed to various spots around the restaurant.

"And you are?" Her voice was monotone, her stare unwavering.

Galen reached into his back pocket and pulled out his wallet. He went to flip it over to show the manager his police badge, but realized he didn't have his identification with him. "Shit." He patted down the front pockets of his jeans and found what he was looking for. Galen pulled out his business card from the police department and handed it to the manager. The card was folded, creased, and a little dirty. She studied the card while Galen held it before her.

"Follow me," she instructed. Galen looked at the card, noticed its condition, and let it fall to the ground.

*****

Without saying another word, Galen moved from around the table and followed the manager down a hallway that led through the kitchen to the offices. Without looking back, the manager spoke softly.

"Those are dummy cameras in the lounge area; the real ones are hidden, and there're more real ones than fake ones. Customers try to do stupid things like steal cutlery and shit like that, or 'dine and dash' when they think they're out of view of the cameras. Bunch of dumb fucks." Business formal disappeared when she was out of view of the customers.

Galen started to chuckle as he walked behind the manager down the hall to her office. He kept his eyes on the back part of her skirt as it wiggled from side to side. The skirt turned right and Galen followed. She sat down behind her desk, and motioned to Galen to take a seat as she spun around and turned on a bank of monitors on the wall. Behind her desk, six monitors were divided into four small black and white sections. Every part of the restaurant was displayed, with several sections of the dinning area overlapping from screenshot onto the next.

"The fake cameras are located in areas that the customers can easily see. The real ones are hidden. And as you can see, they overlap to show the entire restaurant." Galen stood, walked around the manager's desk, and leaned over her shoulder to see the monitors.

"Can I recommend a Tic Tac if you're gonna get this close?"

Galen ignored her and continued to look at the monitors.

"Can you go back and see the section the guy was in?" Galen asked as he continued to scan the monitors.

Without replying, the manager scrolled the mouse over the "rewind" button and the tape began to play backwards. Customers and servers walked about in reverse. Galen was surprised that he found an act as mundane as walking in reverse so comical. He had a broad smile on his face until he saw what he'd come for.

"Stop!" he yelled.

The manager recoiled and covered her right ear. "You don't have to yell. Christ, my ear is ringing."

"Sorry. Can you zoom in on that guy?" Galen pointed at the screen. A lone male sat at the table, looking off in the distance towards the area where Galen sat with Ethan, Tom, and Maddy.

"Nope, but I can print out a screen shot if you want."

"You can do that?"

She nodded, and a gentle whirl could be heard as the printer warmed up. A minute later, a sheet of paper rolled out of the thin slot on the top of the large laser printer. Galen snatched the paper from the tray and felt the warmth of the sheet as he glared at the black and white image of the man sitting at the table. He immediately recognized the face, and left the office without saying a word.

"You're most welcome. Fucking jerk." The manager turned off the monitors and went back to work.

*****

Tom and I sat at the table finishing off the wings as Galen bounded up the two steps from the main dining room to where we were sitting. I was still nibbling on a piece of chicken when Galen stood before us and tried to catch his breath.

"Where's Maddy?" he asked as he waved the piece of paper in the air.

"Washroom. What's up?" Tom pointed at the paper being waved about with a chicken wing.

"Proof of life." Galen pulled out a chair and sat down. He grabbed one of the glasses of beer and tilted it back, finishing whatever was left in the glass.

"You know that was my glass." Tom pointed again with the same wing. I was still busy eating while watching my two friends banter back and forth.

"I don't give a shit." Galen turned to me. "Did you get a good look at Carl Ryan in the file?"

I nodded, my mouth still full of chicken.

Galen placed the printout from the security feed a few inches from my face. I leaned back and swallowed hard. I wiped my hands and pulled the sheet from Galen's fist.

"Holy shit." I was looking at a grainy image of a man who could've been the older brother of the younger Carl Ryan I'd seen in the folder. My greasy fingers left reddish fingerprints on the printout. "Is this really Carl Ryan?"

"I'd bet his life on it." Galen poked Tom in the ribs. Tom swiped at Galen's hand, shooing it away. Galen took possession of the printout again and laid it on the table.

"The guy who killed the kid in the closet?" Tom asked.

"Looks like him. You sure?" I asked Galen.

Galen nodded enthusiastically.

"I thought you said he was probably dead?" Tom asked Galen.

"We thought he might be. No one has seen him in years," I offered. "And he was here. What was he doing? Following us?"

"He musta been. How else would he know we were here?" Galen theorized.

"Who's been following us?" Maddy had returned from the washroom. One look at the printout in front of Galen prompted instant recognition. "Holy fuck. That's him. That's Ryan." Maddy picked up the printout. "I'd bet my life on it."

Tom used a fresh chicken wing to point at Galen and Maddy. "Seems you and Galen are pretty sure that's Ryan. You're both betting lives on it. Could be a bad omen if you're wrong."

Maddy and Galen looked at each other with trepidation.

*****

The man formally known as Carl Ryan sat in a fast food restaurant finishing his combo meal. He finished the burger, and the thought that his diet was not exactly healthy went through his mind. When he'd been married, he'd been forbidden to eat junk food; no burgers, no hotdogs, no candy, nothing that was considered unhealthy. There were a few fries left; he wasn't hungry any longer, but couldn't get the image of his wife nagging him about not wanting to finish his raw vegetables out of his head. She had always served them cold without butter and without dip. He pulled the fries from the red cardboard box and finished them. He wet his finger, ran it around the rim of the red box, and licked his finger clean. He had been forbidden salt when he was married, so now he craved it daily.

A woman carried her tray over and sat at the table next to him. She nodded to him and Carl acknowledged her. He took a sip from his straw and went about his business.

"Your work is good but sloppy." The woman at the next table took a bite of her fish burger, then a sip of her drink.

Carl ignored her.

"I saw you there today. Rookie mistake. Staying around the scene and watching." Her voice was calm, steady, and barely audible.

Carl felt his pulse race and an instant sense of nausea course through him. His limbs felt like lead, and even though he had the urge to run, he had serious doubt that he could've made it to the side doors before collapsing. It took all of his strength simply to reply, "Excuse me?"

"You stuck around to watch after you killed the little girl today. Amateurish. Then that stunt at the restaurant. Are you nuts? They probably have you on video surveillance. You're showboating, and if you keep that up, you'll get caught for sure."

Whoever she was, she knew everything. Carl had to act as if he had nothing to hide.

"Not sure what you're talking about, but I'm leaving now." He gathered up his garbage on his tray and attempted to stand. His legs almost buckled beneath him but he managed to rise. Sweat began to roll down his forehead and his hands were clammy.

"Sit down." She took another bite of her sandwich. With her mouth full, she continued. "You spent too much time sitting in the parking lot watching the scene, and I copied your plate number and the description of your car. After that, it was easy to track you down. If you're gonna go around and be a copycat killer, you should at least steal a few cars to cover your tracks." She took another bite.

"I don't know what the fuck you're talking a…" Carl's voice trailed off. "You?"

She bowed her head, took a sip from her cup, and pulled a few fries from the red box.

"I've been looking for you. I tried to find you. I just knew it was a woman. It had to be a woman." Carl was now elated, and all sense of urgency to disappear was gone. "Really, you saw me? So, you were at the scene too. Wasn't that foolish of you, also?" He chuckled a bit. "I didn't see you there."

"Be more observant next time."

"Yeah, I'm getting a bit cocky. It was a bit stupid of me, wasn't it? I mean, to go back and follow that cop to the restaurant? If you found me this easily, I should get outta town."

"No one is looking for you. The cops are clueless. They still don't have any idea who you are." She took a few more fries. "What made you decide to copy me?"

"For one, I wanted to draw you out. And, I wanted to confuse the cops and keep them busy with another one of your," he paused, "trophies." Carl smiled; he no longer felt threatened. "I figured if they were running around like freaking headless chickens, they would be too busy to follow up on my other exploits."

She almost choked, but held back. She had assumed he was a copycat killer, but he had all but admitted he had killed before. She had the upper hand.

"Good point. Ottawa is pretty small to have this many homicides all at the same time. They'll have to add additional resources, and I doubt they can handle the workload without fucking it up." She had to push him. "But why copy me? You coulda just done someone else in a different way and let them fumble about." A customer walked past and she stopped speaking.

Carl took the opportunity to move to her table. He left his tray behind.

Without looking at him, she whispered, "Bring your tray over. You're inviting the lobby cleaner to come over and pick up your shit, and they may overhear us. If you have your tray in front of you, they won't come over to pick it up." Carl reached across, grabbed his tray, and placed it in front of him.

"I wanted to meet you, so I copied you. Figured it was the best way. Didn't think it would happen so soon." Carl was now able to speak more softly. "I figured the police wouldn't be able to tie the two latest homicides to me."

She took a few fries from her own red box and a sip of pop. She was getting a better idea of who exactly this man was.

"I can understand." Suddenly, it hit her. The words screamed inside her head: Wait, what did he say? He said, "the two latest." Could it be the two homicides from earlier today? If so, he was the one who had killed the man in the car. She now knew exactly who he was.

She decided to change the direction of the conversation. "Why me? And why now?" She took the last bite of the sandwich and wiped her mouth with a napkin, then took a sip from her cup.

"Dunno, kindred spirits, all for one, who knows. I saw something on the TV and I just had to meet you. I tried looking around town, tracking you down, and looky here, you find me. Do you ever meet someone and something clicks? No real reason, you can't even define it, but there was something, something strong that made me want to meet you." He paused and looked at the woman across the table whom he'd met only a moment ago but had come to idolize. She had a soft smile, and a kind face. "Well, that's what happened. I had to meet you." He waited for her to smile back or show any emotion, but she sat stone cold. "Anyway, that's why I did what I did."

She felt a sense of pride but was also slightly afraid of this man. Before entering the restaurant, she had placed a small calibre handgun in her purse and arranged a few tissues over the piece to conceal it. She was afraid, not stupid.

She looked across the table and studied the features of the man who in some weird way was the same as her.

"Thank you, I guess. In a way, I understand. Two corrupt souls, lost in ways the normal world will never know or understand. So…" She paused, pulled the last of the fries from the red box, took a sip of her drink, and asked, "Care to tell me how you got started?"

"Really? You want to hear about me? All I want is to hear about you." Carl looked at the strange woman to whom he already felt closer than the woman he'd married. "K, well, I was married, once, don't think I'll get married again…" His words trailed off, lost in the sounds of bells and alarms, conversations from other customers sitting in booths and teenagers talking about whatever teenagers talk about late in the evening. Cars drove up with their headlights on, bathing them both in their glow.

To anyone walking past, the words between the man and woman sitting in the fast food restaurant were benign. To an outsider, it appeared that the two were on a first date, getting to know each other. They sat at the same table, on opposite corners, both fixated on the stories told by the other. They knew they were different; driven by some urges they couldn't explain. They didn't want to know the reasons they had these needs. To find another person inflicted with the same condition was karma, fate, Zen. She wasn't physically attracted to the man—he was cute, she thought—but she felt a bond; the type of connection two alcoholics discover when they meet to discuss their recovery.

Carl had always wanted to open up to someone, and he felt that this was perhaps the one person who may understand what he was going through.

"It was my wife that brought out the real me. The feelings inside me, something exploded, you know, right here," he pointed to his stomach, "all of a sudden I felt something real. It's hard to explain, I was alive for the first time." He wanted to reach out and touch her hand but held back. "What about you?"

She smiled at Carl; she had never told anyone why she had this desire to do what she did.

"When I was younger, I dunno, maybe five or six, there was a bunch of us playing, and this one girl, funny thing is, I don't remember any of their names now, anyway, she was really annoying the rest of us. You know how that happens in a group. She really wasn't doing anything bad, she just wanted to belong.

"So this one girl, she was bigger than the rest of us, a girl's version of a bully, everything had to be her way, she tormented this annoying little twerp.

"After a few hours, most of us had gone home, but the next day, this bully took us to see something.

"Off in the woods, this little twerp was dead. She was lying on the ground, twigs and leaves around her. Her eyes were open, and they had this glazed look. It looked the same as the type of glaze you find on donuts. You know, that cloudy hazy sugar glaze. To this day, I still see those marks around her neck. You could actually make out the handprints that wrapped around her neck. And the colour of her skin was all weird, not white or pale, more greyish.

"She was wearing this white dress. It was so pretty, white, red roses all over, I think. Sleeveless, with this circular neckline." She made a sweeping motion under her own neck to show how it would've looked. "This bully kicked the dead girl and threatened us. If we ever told, we would end up the same way. To this day, you're the first person I ever told this story to. She was never caught. It really affected me. I never realized how much until just now."

The conversation continued, tales shared, laughter from both at stories old and new, and for a few hours, they were normal people. Judgement wasn't passed; they both suffered from the same affliction. Neither of them noticed the restaurant had been empty for almost an hour. The lights had been dimmed slightly and the young man working the lobby shift had cleaned most of the tables and windows. The large waste bins had been pulled from their storage containers, wiped down, and filled with disinfectant, and were left in the open air to dry. The staff behind the counter had removed their mandatory hairnets and hats, and began preparing to close for the night.

As the man and woman continued to talk, the lobby cleaner walked past and interrupted them to collect their trays. They slid their trays to the edge so he could remove them. He smiled politely and went on his way.

"Do you think he heard what we were talking about?" The man looked over his shoulder as the lobby cleaner walked. The woman kept her eye on him. The lobby cleaner went back to work as if he had heard nothing. He didn't look back, or attempt to steal another look at the couple still sitting alone in the restaurant.

"Nothing to worry about. He doesn't look nervous, hasn't looked back. We should go, anyway." She looked at her watch. "It's already after midnight. We've been here over three hours. We gotta go."

"K." The man stood up and offered his hand to help her up.

She looked at him, snickered, thought twice about taking his hand, then accepted, rose to her feet, and released his hand. She was pleasantly surprised at how she felt when she touched his hand. It was a schoolgirl response—a shiver, a rapid pulse, a little tingle—not the type of reaction for an adult. She led the way and walked out with the man at her heels. They ignored the night staff wishing them a good night and left the restaurant. They stopped just outside the door, each one not knowing where the other was going to walk.

There was uncomfortable laughter between the two, and then silence.

"I'm going this way." She pointed in the opposite direction of where she actually needed to go.

"That way." He pointed in the other direction. "Can I see you again?"

As she opened her purse, the gun-metal grey of her handgun glistened as the overhead parking lot light shone off it. She quickly covered it with the loose tissues. She took out the receipt from the fast food meal she had just finished and found a pen. She jotted down her personal Nokia cellphone number; it was the only secure number she could trust.

"Leave a message and I'll get back to you." She didn't tell him it was her cellphone number.

The man looked at the number, carefully folded the paper, and placed it in his shirt pocket. Several scenarios ran though his mind at that moment: lean in to kiss her on the cheek (*too forward*, he thought), offer to shake hands (*too formal*), simply walk away (*too cocky*), or offer his number (*too presumptuous*). Instead, as he stood there wondering what to do, she stepped in closer and gently kissed his cheek, then turned and walked away.

"Wait, your name?" Carl called out. "I don't know your name." He held his arms out to the side, almost pleading with her for that little bit of personal information he desired.

"Next time." She didn't turn around. "I'll look forward to your call. Don't make me wait too long."

16

Early the following morning there was a barely audible knock at the apartment door that almost went unheard by Maddy. If she had been in bed instead of being in the washroom, she wouldn't have heard the knocking. She finished, washed her hands, grabbed the robe from the back of the bathroom door, and went the living room. Peering through the peephole, she recognized the face of the man standing in the hallway.

"One sec."

Quickly, Maddy ran to the bedroom, picked up the cordless phone, and dialled Ethan's home number. She was hoping he hadn't left for work yet.

"Morning." The familiar voice was breathless and sounded rushed.

"Ethan. Maddy. Can you stop by my place right now please?"

"Be right there." Ethan knew Maddy didn't sound like herself. He hung up the phone and called Tom.

Maddy quickly pulled the clothes she had worn the previous evening from the hamper, dressed, and went to the front door to unlock it. Maddy clutched the phone tightly and placed her thumb on the "9," just to be prepared.

"Come in." She waited until her guest walked past her, left the door slightly ajar, and then walked quickly to the kitchen table, taking the chair closest the apartment door. The phone stayed hidden under the tablecloth. Her guest stood at the sofa, waiting for Maddy to change her mind and join him.

Maddy turned in her chair. "What do you want, Robbie? You know you aren't even supposed to come anywhere near me."

Robbie fell into the sofa and patted the cushion next to him. "Come 'er."

"What do you want?" Maddy's tone was firm and she raised her voice slightly, both to show her displeasure at Robbie being at her apartment and to let her neighbours know what was going on.

Robbie stood, walked over to the kitchen table, and, as he passed

Maddy, placed his hand on her shoulder and gave it a gentle squeeze. Maddy pulled her shoulder away in disgust.

"What do you want?" she said through clenched teeth.

"I saw you on the news last night. I was worried. What are you doing standing with the police on the news?" Robbie took his seat and cradled his chin in both hands. "So what's going on with you? You seemed pretty chummy with one of the guys on TV. Ya were standing pretty close to that one guy. He looked like a fag to me. You hanging out with fags now?"

"Robbie, you aren't even supposed to see me, let alone come close to me. Remember that little thing called a 'court order'? Who I hang around with, their sexual orientation, anything I do," Maddy's voice rose, "is none of your fucking business."

"I just wanted to make sure you were OK."

"You don't have any right to worry about me. You should leave right now. I don't want you here. I don't need you and I certainly don't want you fucking with my head anymore. You got that?"

Robbie remained unfazed by Maddy's sudden burst of rage. He simply smiled back at her. It was the one thing that always infuriated Maddy when she had dated Robbie. Whenever they argued, the more upset Maddy became, the calmer Robbie would be. It was his way of showing he was in control. Robbie would smile at her with that smirk she had come to hate.

"Can I get a coffee? You remember how I like my coffee, don't you?"

Maddy remained in her seat. "What… do… you… want?"

"Coffee, triple, triple. Surely you remember that, don't you, my little sweet pea?" The toothy grin remained cupped in his hands. Things hadn't changed; Maddy still wanted to smash out that toothy grin with a hammer.

Maddy stood and walked backwards from the table to the kitchen while keeping the phone hidden as best she could. She placed the phone on the kitchen counter, filled the kettle with water, and plugged it in. From the cabinet, she pulled out the only teacup she had with flowers and vines imprinted on the side. It was her passive aggressive way of emasculating her ex-boyfriend. They remained silent as the water boiled, and then she slowly prepared Robbie's coffee, waiting for Ethan to arrive. She carried the cup to the table and placed it before him. His hands still cradled his face.

Robbie picked up the cup and blew across the top to cool it down. He took a sip. "Perfect, sweet pea. You always knew how to make my coffee. Cute cup. Not much here. You wanna start making me a second cup. This won't last long."

"I'll give you a couple of bucks so you can buy yourself another coffee when you leave. What do you want?" Maddy regained her composure but her thumb remained firm on the number 9 button.

"Tell me why you are hanging around with that gay-looking guy I saw you standing close to when you were on TV last night. Tell me what's going on and I'll leave."

Maddy sighed deeply. "It's none of your business." She pointed towards the door. "Leave now."

Robbie tapped the table to his right. "Come 'er, sweet pea. Keep me company."

Maddy stood her ground. There was an excruciatingly long silence as the two stared at each other; neither one wanted to be the first to break role. Maddy felt her heart beating in her chest. She heard footsteps approaching quickly from the hall. She prayed she had stalled long enough.

The already-opened door creaked slowly wider and Ethan walked into the apartment. His face was red, and sweat dripped from his brow. Instead of waiting for the elevator, Ethan had run from the lobby to the eighth floor. He silently walked into the apartment and placed himself between Maddy and the man sitting at the table. Ethan's chest heaved as he fought to catch his breath.

Ethan looked at Robbie sitting across the table with a cold, steel gaze that left nothing to the imagination. Robbie took a sip from the cup and placed it on the table, and then stood up. The size difference was apparent immediately to Ethan. Robbie stood a few inches taller and had at least forty pounds over him. Robbie walked slowly around the table and planted himself a few feet from Ethan.

"You're one of them fags I saw on TV last night, aren't you?" Robbie stood with his hands resting on his hips.

"And I'm the other one." Robbie turned to see Tom standing in the doorway. The two men were approximately the same size and weight, but Tom was solid muscle, not fat like Robbie. Tom took a few steps into the apartment. "And believe me when I tell you, you don't wanna mess with me." Tom had a gentle smirk on his face. He knew that the stranger standing in Maddy's living room wouldn't put up much of a fight.

Robbie looked at Maddy, who was standing beside Ethan and Tom at the door. Robbie laughed loudly and knew he was beaten. Before he could leave, Maddy spoke up.

"I'll be calling those cops you saw me with on TV and telling them you violated your court order to stay away from me."

Robbie's smiled disappeared quickly. He glared at Maddy.

"I'm gone. Don't worry about me, I won't be back."

Robbie bumped into Tom as he walked out of the apartment in an attempt to intimidate him, but Tom's solid mass refused to budge, and Robbie bounced off Tom into the doorframe. He paused momentarily, looked back at Maddy, and left in embarrassment.

Tom entered the apartment, then closed and locked the door. Maddy took in a deep breath and fell into Ethan. She hugged him with all the energy she had left, then turned to Tom and offered the same hug.

"You two made it over fast."

"Your call sounded urgent. I didn't need much more than that." Ethan knew better than to question Maddy about the circumstances of what had just happened; instead, he asked Tom to call Galen and relay what had just transpired.

Ethan led Maddy to the sofa and sat her down, then positioned himself beside her. She curled up on the cushion with her legs beneath her and her head resting on Ethan's shoulder. He could hear Tom speaking on the phone in the kitchen. As Ethan stroked Maddy's hair, she closed her eyes, took in a deep breath, and let her body relax. She felt a huge relief in having someone she could trust again.

Tom motioned to Ethan as he covered the mouthpiece on the phone. Ethen waited for a moment, slid his arm out from behind Maddy, whispered into her ear, and then stood to join Tom.

"What's up?" he asked in hushed tones.

Tom leaned in close to Ethan. "Galen says he can't stop by but he's sending another patrol car to take a report and will talk to the ex."

"Do you think I should leave her?" Ethan asked his friend.

"She's got a strong will. You stay and she might think you see her as being weak, you leave when she needs you and she might see you as being insensitive."

Ethan looked at Maddy as she straightened herself on the sofa. "I'll ask her." He made his way back and sat beside her. "Would you like me to stay with you for the rest of the day? I'll call in sick."

Maddy turned and looked Ethan in the eyes. "Don't you dare call in sick. I'm not some pathetic little woman who needs a man to care for her." She had a stern look on her face and her voice was unwavering. "But I think it's sweet you want to take care of me. Go. Leave. Play ambulance driver with your friend." She leaned in close so Tom couldn't hear. "I want you back here right after you finish your shift."

Ethan stood. "Lock your door and keep your cellphone close by. I'll see you later."

*****

Galen had been pulled from road duty, and sat in the same boardroom with the same group of detectives who had been investigating the murders of young girls. Papers passed between work areas, evidence was placed on the white board, and quiet discussions went on between small groups of officers. Only Galen remained silent. He found it hard to concentrate on the matters before him. Fumbling with papers, he pretended to be working but his mind was on the events of the previous day. He tapped his pen on the table and looked around the room. He wanted to be back out on the road where he felt comfortable; here, he felt like he had little to offer.

Glancing up at the white board, the evidence from the previous day made it almost certain the young girl who had died the day before was a copycat killing. He had known that for certain yesterday; today, they had to weigh the evidence, and avoid jumping to assumptions. Too much politics, he thought.

"Hey, what's got you down?" Erin leaned in close over Galen's right shoulder. Galen turned to his right, found nothing, then spun his head quickly to the left and saw Erin laughing.

"You're such a child," Galen barked.

Erin was laughing as she took her seat beside Galen.

"You're in a good mood," he exclaimed.

"I had a good night," she replied.

"Are we interrupting your social life, you two?" Detective Nardone barked.

Erin coughed, "Not at all, sir," and swung her knee under the table to bump Galen's knee. Galen closed his eyes and shook his head.

"K. Back to the board, guys." Detective Nardone tapped the white board with his black marker. "Did everyone get this morning's handouts? Galen went over the evidence with me and I have to agree, the latest death is eerily similar, but there are just way too many variables this time. We can consider a copycat, or the unsub purposely changed his or her routine to throw us off." Detective Nardone started to pace back and forth across the front of the conference room. "No idea is too farfetched. We need ideas, folks, so let's start spit balling and get the juices flowing."

Erin leaned in close to Galen. "If he starts clapping his hands to get 'my juice flowing,'" she air quoted, "I think I'm gonna puke."

"You have something to add, Uni?" Nardone barked from the front.

"Sir, I was just telling Galen, you have too many inconsistencies between the girls. The first victims were almost, well, I don't know, embraced if you will by the unsub; there was care involved. The latest vic was brutalized. Whoever did this didn't have all the details, didn't know what the MO was. It's a bad copycat." Erin stood and walked to the white board. "Look at the first vics; yes, they were strangled, but no other sign of violence of any other nature was found on them. I'd lay dollars to donuts that the unsub for the first killings was a woman. The latest one was done by a guy. It was sloppy, lazy, rushed."

Nardone and the other detectives nodded in agreement. He thanked Erin for her perspective as she returned to her seat.

Hours later, Erin and Galen were standing outside the police station on the sidewalk. They had both just ordered hotdogs from the street vendor and were adding condiments before sitting on the curb between parked cars. Erin pulled the tab on her can of pop and washed down a mouthful of hotdog with Coke. Galen watched Erin finish her meal in three quick bites, then wipe her mouth with the back of her arm. She chugged down the rest of the Coke and let out an "Ahhhh" as she leaned back and braced herself with her arms behind her. Galen stared in amazement.

"What?" she asked.

"Nothing. Just, um, did you even taste the dog? You inhaled it."

"Grew up in foster care. I bounced around from home to home, had so many brothers and sisters—well, if you can call them brothers and sisters—that if I didn't eat fast, I didn't eat."

Galen took a bite and spoke while he chewed. "Sorry to hear."

"Don't sweat it, it wasn't as bad as a lot of people make it out to be. I always had a roof over my head, a bed to sleep in, food on the table, and clothes on my back. Bouncing around from family to family, I never stuck around long enough to get close to anyone. I learnt a long time ago that relationships are disposable. Don't get attached, don't get hurt."

Galen took a sip of Diet Coke and a small bite from the end of the bun. "That sounds like a sad way to live."

"Not at all. I've never been hurt, my emotions are intact, and I don't let anyone get too close."

Galen leaned over and bumped her left shoulder with his right. "I'm the opposite; I love being in love. I have a great wife; when I first met her, she was the most beautiful woman I'd ever seen. Still is. She had long wavy black hair, it's cut short now, but she's stunningly gorgeous with a bod to die for, smart, a helluva lot smarter than me. I can't imagine her not being around."

"See. My point. You can't imagine her not being around. If she left you or, heaven forbid, died, you'd be devastated. I have my friends, but if I never see any of them again, I'd be OK with that. I rely on myself, I don't get hurt, and no one hurts me. I think you sound needy. Is that what you want, to be needy?"

"Being in love and expressing your feelings and wanting to hear those words back isn't needy, it helps make you feel complete, whole. The best part of my day is when she tells me she loves me or misses me."

"Needy. You're needy."

"Erin, I feel sorry for you. I feel more complete having someone to share things with."

"Don't feel sorry for me, I may have found someone to share things with." Erin stood up. "I'm getting another hot dog. You want another, it's on me."

"If you're buying, I'm eating."

*****

My head bounced off the passenger window as Tom cut across multiple lanes of traffic and jerked the wheel sharply to the left.

"Did that wake you out of dream land? You know we have a Code 4 right?"

"Yeah, I know." I was rubbing my head as Tom was laughing at my pain. "Whatta we got again?"

Tom reached down and turned the knob that controls the siren tone. He changed the tone from "Wail" to "Yelp" in an attempt to get the attention of drivers that refused to give way.

"Move you fuckhead," he screamed at the cars in front, and laid on the horn. The sound of the siren mixed in with the horn did nothing for the pain that reverberated in my head.

"Possible suicide on a farm just outside city limits."

"Shit. Seriously?" I had no desire to see whatever it was we were going to. If it was a suicide, I hoped it was pills and nothing, well, icky.

Sitting upright, I tightened my seatbelt, donned a pair of gloves, and passed a pair to Tom who was still busy navigating traffic. He pulled from a paved street onto a dirt side road and floored the accelerator. The ambulance engine revved, the rear tires spun in the gravel, and the back end of the ambulance swerved left and then right. Tom corrected the steering wheel, righting the rig, and we sped forward.

Glancing at the trip sheet, I remembered I had jotted down the address before I fell asleep. "We're looking for 614 County Road 43. Did dispatch say if the 10-2's were on scene yet?"

Tom shook his head from side to side. He hadn't reduced his speed when we'd moved from asphalt to gravel, and he concentrated on keeping the rig out of the ditch. His attention was fixed on the road ahead and not on answering my questions. I looked at the house numbers on the blue signs at the ends of the driveways, even on the right, odd on the left. I kept my eyes on the houses on the right. We were in the high six hundreds, and every few houses I would call out the number so that Tom knew we were getting close.

"620–618–slow down, 616 614."

Tom blew past the house and slammed on the brakes, and the tires slid in the gravel. He slapped the lever into reverse and checked the side mirrors, and I heard the whine of the engine as we backed up.

Looking down the drive, I didn't notice any police cruisers, but a lone figure walked down the side of the yard looking sombre. Not a good sign. Tom drove the rig slowly towards the man wearing the plaid flannel jacket and thread-worn ball cap. He stopped the rig and the man walked slowly to the driver's window.

"Don't hurry." It was obvious the man had been crying before we arrived. His eyes were red and swollen. He pointed to the back of the property. "He's 'round the back on the right."

"Any safety issues we should concern ourselves with?" Tom asked politely.

The man just shook his head and walked towards the house.

Tom booked us on scene and told dispatch that the police hadn't arrived yet. We each grabbed a portable radio, instinctively knowing we didn't have to bring any equipment. Should we have waited for the police to arrive? Possibly. As a team, Tom and I had arrived first before the police on at least a few dozen suicides.

As I exited the vehicle, I looked behind me, to the side, and ahead. I wasn't sure what to expect and didn't want to be surprised. We didn't speak and walked slowly, scanning the property as we got farther from the rig. Evergreens lined the property to the right. On the left, the house was a single-level wood-clad home painted in a mosaic of colours—probably in whatever colours were left over from various paint jobs. The wooden screen door was partially open, and for some reason known only to the homeowner, a cinder block painted yellow was beside the screen door. The man who had met us only a few moments earlier was nowhere to be seen.

Tom was ten or fifteen feet to my left as we walked farther up the driveway, past the house, and towards the multiple shacks that dotted the property. I could see the front end of a tractor parked behind one of the sheds. I wasn't surprised to see household appliances half-covered in long grass. At one point, I surmised, he was going to "fix 'em up and get 'em going again" or sell them for scrap. Whatever the reason, an old fridge sat there, tilted slightly and resting in soft mud, the door ripped off years earlier. Inside, it was apparent that some animal had decided it would make a good home. A nest of twigs and leaves kept something warm on colder nights.

What should have taken less than sixty seconds took several minutes as we kept our senses on high alert, and each step was calculated and planned. A voice yelled out from behind us, "He's off to the right." I turned and saw the man who had greeted us when we'd first pulled in. He was pointing to the right, indicating where to go. Obviously, he wasn't getting anywhere close to where he wanted us to be.

I was beside a clapboard structure; the wood looked like it had been milled around the turn of the last century. I was the first to turn to the right as I passed the corner of the antique shed and saw the redness in the dirt. A barn cat was licking at the red liquid; it looked up when I turned the corner and darted off into the field.

"Hey." I caught Tom's attention.

Where the cat had been, there was a small puddle, not a pool, of blood, with a bulky soft tissue mass on the edge. The patient's head was off to the side of the small puddle. Without walking farther straight out instead of cutting the corner, I wouldn't have been able to see any more of the scene. A few steps farther and I noticed the shed was a three-sided structure with the back wide open to the sky.

The man's body lay on its right side. The cause of the man's injury was evident. A double-barrelled shotgun lay on the ground beside him. Cliché, I thought. Why is it always a double-barrelled shotgun? It's a farm, after all, I reasoned. They use shotguns in the country, I think. I really wasn't sure.

I stopped a few feet from the body. A full assessment to determine if the patient was still alive wasn't needed. I could tell from where I stood and didn't need to go any closer. The right portion of the man's skull was missing and that mass in the puddle was most likely whatever was left of his brain. Taking in the details of the scene, I couldn't imagine ever getting to that point in my life where I would choose this way out.

There was a wooden milking stool still upright in the centre of the work area that I imagined he'd been sitting on as he mulled over his options before deciding to pull the trigger. A depression in the soft earth shaped very much like the stock of the shotgun was by the man's feet. Looking up, I saw that the tin roof had new holes from the buckshot that had blasted through the skull yet still had the velocity to travel through the tin. Tiny bits of red matter were stuck to the underside of the tin roof, validating my theory. I looked at the far wall of the work area, and more red matter was sprayed on that vicinity as well. The top right portion of the skull was missing, blown off in a second as the man's thumb pressed the trigger and the hammer struck the shell. If I had wanted to, I could've seen his face; it was intact. All I had to do was kneel down and look at ground level. Curiosity said yes, reason said no. Reason won out.

"Cancer." The voice of the man who had met us at the road could be heard. "He was old, lived alone, and was scared. Sonofabitch, I'd be scared too. He was eighty, I think, maybe eighty-one. Could you imagine dying alone of cancer in the house you were born in. Never married. No kids. Lived here his whole life. His father farmed the land when the city was nowhere as close as it is now."

The man's whole life was summed up in one paragraph: born on the farm, worked his whole life, alone, died where he wanted to, on his own terms. Is that what life is? A series of bad one-liners that can sum up your life in ten seconds or less?

I decided I wanted to see his face; to remember the man for who he was, not how he died. I walked around, knelt low, and gazed at his face, refusing to look at the wound about his brow. I saw the face of old man, skin weathered, wrinkled; he looked wise, grandfatherly. The kind of face you look up to when you're a kid, holding your grandfather's hand, feeling safe and secure.

I wanted to drive back to Ottawa, find Maddy, hold her, and tell her how much I care; that whatever happens, I could never tell her that I love her too many times. I didn't want to end up like that man, old, deciding how and when to die, alone.

"Life sucks."

"What's that?" Tom asked.

"Huh?"

"You said something. 'Life sucks.'"

"Yeah. It does." I stood and started to walk back to the truck. Two police officers walked towards me, and I silently thumbed directions to the body, smiled politely at them as we passed, opened the passenger door to the rig, and sat down. It seldom happens. I try not to let it happen. Every now and then, a call managed to penetrate my shield and gets to me. There's no reason why one call gets to me and another does, this one did.

Grabbing the zip pack, I retrieved the form I needed to document this call. The green and white form sat on the zip pack, blank. I stared down at the form, waiting for something to come to me. I knew Tom would be speaking with the police, finding name, birthdate, meds, medical history. Guys like this old farmer would be lucky to see a doctor once or twice in their lives if they got sick.

The driver's door opened, and Tom climbed in and silently handed me a sheet of paper with his call notes jotted down. He didn't say anything. Not a lot of things bother me about this job, but every now and then, something happens that changes everything.

I scanned the note Tom gave me, using the information to start filling in my form, and cranked up the radio for some background noise. Pen scratched paper, blank sections started to get filled in, and the events of the patient's last day were sanitized and compartmentalized into pre-determined boxes approved by some random government committee.

"Let me know when you want to leave." Tom's voice showed signs of stress too. "I can go any time."

"You OK?" I didn't look up from my form.

"He looks like my grandfather. A lot. 'Course, any old man with a wrinkled face could be my grandfather." Tom paused, staring out the windshield. "You know what, I cleared with the 10-2's. Let's go get a coffee and a fucking donut. I'll even buy."

*****

Carl sat on the white plastic lawn chair, his crossed feet propped up on an overturned pail. He sipped his Dr. Pepper, then put his head back and stared up at the stars through the sections of the night sky not covered by darker sections he assumed were clouds.

He heard feet rustle in dew-moistened grass that was crushed by white sneakers. The wearer made no attempt at a stealthy approach. She sat down in the same type of chair as Carl's, noticed the cooler, and plunged her hand into the ice water. She rustled through the freezing water in the cooler and pulled out a can of Diet Coke. She dropped the can back into the frigid liquid, and her hand swirled around, found another can, and pulled a beer from the cooler. She placed the can on the arm of the chair, shook the water free from her hand, and then pulled back the top and tilted the can back.

The two of them sat on a small wooden deck at the back of a rental home. The backyard was tree-lined on all three sides with overgrown cedar shrubs that should've been trimmed the previous decade. The remote location of the house and the overgrown backyard were two of the reasons

Carl Ryan rented it.

"Aren't you a little old for a Dr. Pepper? I mean, even this late at night? Doesn't it taste like cough syrup?"

"You have your drink, I have mine." Carl proclaimed his love for the drink with a loud belch, then laughed. "Sorry, love the taste. Hate the bubbles."

"Classy," she said before releasing her own version of a beer belch.

Without looking at each other, they laughed softly, drank from their cans, and gazed into the night sky.

"Can I ask you a personal question?" Carl didn't bother to look to his right.

"Sure. What's up?"

"Do you trust me?" he asked.

"Loaded question. We've both got shit on each other that could end it for both of us. On the other hand, I know a hell of a lot more about you than you know about me. That gives me the upper hand."

Carl's gaze didn't deviate from the sky. "And," he took a sip from his can, "I'm good with that."

"You are? Why? I find that odd. I mean, you obviously hate women. You killed your wife. You killed more women than men. Do you think of just women as disposable, or both sexes?"

"I'm not gonna argue with that." He belched. "I honestly don't remember much about what happened with my wife, I just know I felt something different after; elated, thrilled. It was something amazing; something new inside me was growing. I wasn't the same person afterwards."

There was silence for a few minutes as the two of them looked into the night sky and sipped their drinks.

She leaned across the arms of the two chairs and extended her hand.

"Erin. Pleased to meet you."

Foolish mistake, he thought, grasped her hand firmly, and smiled.

"Pleased to meet you, Erin."

Erin sat back in her chair. "I've got an idea. Care to hear it?"

Carl crushed his Pepper can, tossed it into the cooler, and found another can of his favourite drink. He pulled back on the lid and downed half the can.

"You bet."

*****

Erin was straddling Carl, her body covered in sweat, her hair wet and her bangs sticking to her forehead. She brushed her hair back with both hands then slid her hands over her bare breast, down her stomach, and over her thighs until they met Carl's chest. She placed her hands firmly on his shoulders, leaned forward, and began slowly rotating and grinding her pelvis, feeling Carl inside her. Carl dug the back of his head into the pillow, let out a soft moan, moved his hands up to Erin's waist, and held tightly.

Carl moaned softly, barely audibly, and as the moment approached he opened his eyes to watch Erin when it happened. She knew it was close; she lowered herself, began to lick the sweat from his neck, ran her tongue to his chest, and then bit and held onto the soft tissue of the left side of his chest. Carl screamed in pain. Erin dug her teeth in deeper, shook her head from side to side, and then released her grip and pulled back.

"What the fuck was that?" he yelled.

Erin was laughing, her lips covered in blood. She ran her tongue over her lips to wipe away the moisture and laughed again. Her finger ran around the edge of her lips, cleaning whatever blood still remained, and then she slid her finger into her mouth and sucked on it.

"Mmmmm."

Her eyes were closed, her body quivered slightly, and Carl could feel moisture ooze onto his crotch from inside Erin. She seemed to derive more pleasure from the violence than from sex, or simply needed that little bit extra to help get her over the edge.

Erin fell over onto her back, laughing and panting at the same time.

Carl jumped from the bed and ran to the bathroom. Blood dripped freely from his new wound.

"Jesus Christ. What the hell was that?" he screamed at her.

Erin continued to laugh and giggle. He pulled the towel from the rack and pressed it against his chest to stem the bleeding. He twisted in pain as the towel soaked up the blood. Carl pulled the towel away to reveal a perfect impression of Erin's bite mark on his chest. Any deeper and she could've taken a mouthful of flesh.

From the bed, Erin called out, "I want you to do something for me tomorrow."

"What? Get a fucking tetanus shot?" Erin laughed again. What a fucking psychotic bitch, Carl thought.

"No. We need to play a little game. You up for it?"

"Does it involve me losing another pound of flesh?"

"Nope. Remember, I had an idea. It's something right up your alley. We can do it tomorrow night."

"As long as the bitch doesn't bite me again," he whispered to himself.

17

Donna Hargreaves untied her apron and tossed it into the hamper. She grabbed a clean towel from the kitchen and wiped her forehead, then reached up under her T-shirt and dried her armpits. She lobbed the towel into the hamper.

"Two points, or is that three from this distance?"

"You're, like, three feet away," the cook said.

Donna held up five fingers. "Five. Five feet. Besides, I get extra points for style." Then she blew him a kiss.

"Not sticking around to help clean up or joining us for a few drinks?" he asked.

"Nope. Dining room's all clean. Ready for the Saturday morning rush. I have tons of homework to do. No social life for me." Donna pulled her backpack off the hook at the back of the kitchen and slung it over her shoulder. She waved to the kitchen manager and the cook, and left the restaurant for the short walk home.

Donna stepped outside, stood silently, titled her head back, took in a deep breath, and felt the warm night air fill her lungs. She extended her arms and let the light breeze flow over her T-shirt. As she inhaled, the smell of cigarette smoke made her cough. She turned to see a man leaning against the building, smoking a cigarette.

"Sorry, waiting for my bus." He offered the pack of cigarettes to her. "Want one?"

Donna smiled politely and shook her head from side to side. "Don't smoke." She didn't recognize him as one of her customers from the restaurant.

"Do the buses still run this late at night? I've been here for half an hour and I haven't seen one come by yet." He dropped his butt and put it out with the sole of his shoe.

"Don't know. I always walk." She turned to leave. "Have a good night."

"Damn. Maybe I should start walking, too."

Donna paid no attention to the short man as she briskly started her walk home. She noticed the man was following her, but his pace was much slower, and her long stride quickly added distance between the two of them. Just to be sure, she reached into her purse, found her keys, placed the long, metal key to her apartment locker between her fingers, and made a fist. She kept her fist in her purse, just in case. Let the short little bastard try something, she thought.

Donna listened to the footfalls behind her; the cadence remained constant. She casually looked behind and noticed the short man was smoking another cigarette—coughing—and the distance between the two had grown since she had left the restaurant.

Arriving at the entrance to her building, Donna quickly scanned the area around her. Feeling safe, she inserted the key, entered the front foyer, unlocked the second door, and walked to the elevator. She finally felt comfortable enough to let her guard down.

The doors opened, and Donna smiled politely to the woman with the shopping cart who exited the elevator before she entered. She stepped in, turned, pressed the button for the fourteenth floor, and watched the doors close before her. She glanced up at the large red display as the numbers slowly increased until the bell rang at her floor.

As the woman with the shopping cart exited the elevator, she noticed a man stumbling with his keys, attempting to get them in the lock in the outside door. He inserted a key and turned up, but tried pushing the door instead of pulling it outwards. Another night of drinking the devil's brew, she thought.

She opened the inner lobby door, reached across, and pushed the release for the outer door. The man pulled his key from the lock, fell forward, regained his balance, straightened up, and thanked the lady for letting him in.

"My wife is gonna kill me," he offered as they passed.

She waved her hand in front of her face to help defuse the odour of alcohol. "Praise the lord," she muttered, and watched him walk slowly to the elevator. She let the door close behind her as she walked to the parking lot.

The man stood at the elevator, watching the numbers increase until they stopped at the fourteenth floor. He reached into his pocket, pushed a piece of gum through the foil, and popped it into his mouth to help rid himself of the foul stench of the rum. A quick gargle of liquor right before he'd gotten to the door had helped push the performance over the edge.

When the door opened on the fourteenth floor, he paused, and looked right then left. Fifty-fifty either way. He went right, silently walking heel to toe down the hall. He paused at each door, pressing his ear against them to listen for any noise inside each apartment. Hearing nothing, he went to the next door. Half way down the hall, he heard noise coming from inside. He waited for a few moments, and then with a gloved hand, turned the door handle with the patience and skill of a diamond cutter. When the handle was fully cranked, he put his shoulder to the door and pushed carefully to see if it met with any resistance from a chain lock. There wasn't any light breaking through the crack. Nothing!

He opened the door gently, anticipating that she would scream or slam on him. He could feel each beat of his heart. His breathing was laboured; he attempted to control his rate but the anticipation was more than he had imagined. Inside his gloves, his hands were wet. He thought his gloves would fall off if he didn't pay attention. The entire apartment was dark as he quietly closed the door and locked it.

He waited for several minutes for his eyes to adjust, and slowly pulled the leather belt from around his trousers. He wrapped the long end around his right palm and held the buckle in his left. Once his vision had become accustomed to the lack of light, he scanned the apartment for the layout of the furniture and the rooms. Waiting to hear any sign that the occupant of the apartment was asleep, he took his first step. Again, each step was planned, methodical. His teeth were clenched tightly, the pressure building in his temporal mandibular joints.

The wall was to his left; he was certain the first door on his right was the bedroom. The bathroom was directly ahead of him. At the door he paused, looked inside, and again waited for his eyes to adjust. She had left the curtain open, and moonlight burst into the room adding an eerie silver glow. He could see her perfectly. It was the same girl he had followed home from the restaurant.

He loosened the leather belt from around his hand, fed one end through the buckle, and made his way to the bedside. He extended his arms until they were just above her head, waited for the right moment, and then struck. He slid the belt around her neck, brought his hand together, and pulled the long end of the belt, closing the loop around her neck.

Donna woke up in a panic. She didn't know what had happened, only that the air trapped in her lungs had nowhere to escape, and she was unable to bring in any new air. She dug at whatever it was around her neck, her legs kicking wildly at the bedsheets, wrapping them around her legs. The pressure in her lungs was building fast; she needed to breath. Donna tried to sit up, but the weight of the attacker was forced down on her. She knew she was at the edge of the bed and formed a defense.

Donna rolled to her left, falling to the floor and sending the attacker tumbling on top of her. His grip on the belt failed as he went sprawling. Donna reached up and dug her fingers under the belt, loosening its grip around her neck, and took in a breath. With her lungs full of fresh air, she found strength to kick the person on top of her. Donna tried to pull the belt from around her neck, but the pin found a hole and the belt locked in place. She tried to scream, but the belt had damaged her larynx and what came out was inaudible. Forgetting about the attacker, she clawed and pulled at the belt. This distraction gave the man time to regroup and take a run at her, pushing her into the wall. He found the end of the belt and, using it like a whip, leaned back and flung her against the wall a second time.

Donna's head hit the doorframe, sending her reeling to the floor. Stars burst in her mind. Her brain needed to reboot to get control of the situation. As things started to come back into focus, the pressure around her neck increased, stopping her breathing again. He forced her onto her stomach, placed his knee in the small of her back, and pulled tightly on the belt. She felt the carpet under her face and kicked wildly into the air, then reached up, clawing and scratching anything she could touch. She reached back, took hold of the attacker's hand, and dug her nails in deep.

Donna continued to swing her arms and kick, but the intensity was now gone. There was almost nothing left. Her mouth opened and closed like a goldfish out of water. Her body wanted air—needed air—but the belt prevented the exchange of oxygen. In less than five minutes, Donna lay on the floor, unmoving. The man released his grip on the end of the leather belt and let it fall to rest on her back. Placing his hand on her back, he checked to see if she was breathing. There was no movement.

*****

The phone rang early Saturday morning. I opened my eyes to see a fracture of sunlight bursting through the curtains, cutting across the bedroom like a laser beam. Blindly reaching for the phone, I elbowed Maddy in the ribs. She stirred, moaned, and rolled over. I had forgotten she was still in my bed. It was nice to have someone lying next to me. The phone rang again.

"You gonna answer that?" Maddy's voice was muffled and tired.

To avoid disturbing her, I hopped out of bed, ran to the living room, and picked up the receiver. Before I could say anything, the caller said my name and then paused. Galen was out of breath, his voice quivering.

"You OK?" I asked. I could hear him breathing heavily.

"I shoulda waited until I caught my breath. Sorry." He took in a deep breath. "Phew. Sorry. That's better. Had to walk up fourteen flights of stairs. Elevator's been sealed off. Found another one today. This time, the girl didn't make it and they left the belt."

"What girl?" I panicked, thinking it was the girl who had survived the attack from the other night.

Galen knew whom I meant. "It wasn't Nicole. It was another. The chief is having a fit. He called everyone in. And I mean everyone; we all got called in from the belt murder investigations, and the OPP and RCMP have been called in. He even wants to call in the FBI. And he wants your ass down here now."

"Me? Why me?"

"How the fuck should I know? He pulled me aside, got in my face, yelled at me for ten fucking minutes, and said to get that, and I quote, 'fucking skinny assed ambulance driver down here.'"

"He knows it's my day off, right?" I waited for Galen's comment, but I knew I was pushing my luck. "Give me the address."

Less than an hour later, I walked up the fourteen flights of stairs, doubled over at the landing, and understood why Galen had been out of breath when he'd called. Still looking at the floor, I recognized the shoes as they approached.

"Outta shape?" Galen asked.

"I hate stairs." I straightened up. "Why's the elevator locked down?"

"Prints and DNA. Camera in there, too. In case she took the elevator. She probably took the stairs; I would. Techs just started in there and the other one is out of service."

"K. So what's going on?"

Without saying a word, Galen turned on his heels and walked down the hall. I followed slowly behind as I tried to catch my breath. As we went down the hall, I could see apartment doors open and eyes peering through, attempting to see the story that was unfolding in the hall. Down the corridor, an apartment door was being guarded by two uniformed police officers, each one larger than Tom. As we got closer to the guarded apartment, I stopped at the door that was slightly ajar, directly across and just down from the crime scene. A set of wrinkled eyes with grey eyebrows watched my every move. I stopped walking, leaned against the wall, and pulled out a sheet of paper, pretending to look over something I had to review. It was actually the piece of paper I had used to scribble down the address.

"Hey," I whispered, looking down at the sheet of paper.

"What?" the old lady's eyes whispered back.

"Did you see what happened?"

"You a cop?"

"Do I look like a cop?" Our conversation was barely audible.

"You all look like cops."

"Did you see what happened?"

"I heard what happened, then opened my door and saw someone running down the hall."

"Did you tell the cops?"

"No way. I'm not getting involved."

I stuffed the sheet of paper back in my pocket. "Galen, this lady said I could use her bathroom. I'll be right out."

The old eyes cast me a surprised look, then, slowly, the door opened, inviting me in. The apartment was dark, the curtains remained drawn, clutter was minimal, but the smell of old person hung in the air. It's difficult to describe the scent that only comes from reclusive old people who seldom leave their homes. It's a combination of stale air, mould, decaying food on the counter, and body odour. It's a smell that is mildly offensive, memorable, and unique to the age demographic.

The door closed quietly behind me. It took several seconds for my eyes to adjust to the dim lights in the room. The old lady walked over to the far end of the sofa, reached up under a lampshade, and turned on a light instead of opening the curtains. Perhaps for safety, she kept her distance, standing behind the lamp. I thought she would be dressed in some moth-eaten sweater, antique dress, and loose stockings, but she was well dressed in black slacks and a white shirt with a string of fake pearls around her neck. She remained silent as I scanned the apartment. For whatever reason, all small one-bedroom units look similar to me, and not unlike my own. We even had our furniture is approximately the same locations. I envisioned this lady could be me in another fifty years.

"You just gonna stand there?" Her voice was still soft, slightly above a whisper. "You wanna sit?"

Except for the age and style of the furniture, the old lady and I placed our furniture in almost the same spots. I sat, crossed my legs, and waited for her to start talking. Instead, she walked past me into the kitchen, grabbed two cans of Pepsi from the fridge and handed one to me, and then sat on the far end of the sofa. It was still early in the morning but I couldn't refuse the drink. I ran my finger around the lip of the can, popped the lid, and took a big gulp. She took a small sip from her can and placed it on the end table.

There was an uncomfortable silence that went on far too long. I finished half my can before she spoke.

"Mind my manner, but you're the first man in my apartment in almost twenty years. Not used to haven' company. 'Specially male company. You gonna ask me what you want to know or do I hafta guess?"

I chuckled inside and held my drink with both hands. "Did you see anything this morning? I mean from the apartment across the hall."

"You said you weren't a cop. If you're not a cop, why the interest?" She cast me a quizzical look of mistrust.

"I'm a…" I paused. I didn't want to tell her my real job. "I work for the city. I help out when they need my, what would you call it, my unique perspective from a medical angle."

She pointed with head towards me. "Doctor?"

"Nope." I tried to relate. "You watch Quincy?" I was referring to the television show where the main character was a coroner who worked on cases involving suspicious deaths. She nodded.

"I'm like Quincy. Except not a doctor."

She pondered what I had just said, and then the story began to unfold.

"I was sitting here," she pointed to where she was currently sitting, "watching the news. Have to stay current, you know." I nodded in agreement. "Well, I heard this bang. Not like a gunshot. Not that I've ever heard a gunshot, or a car backfiring. You don't hear that much anymore with those fancy cars today. But in my day, cars backfired all the time. Anyway, I heard this loud bang, like a thud, didn't think anything of it, then it happened again. BANG!" She slammed her fist into her palm. "So's I jump up and run to my door. And I do what you saw me doing, you know, peeking out the open door. So's anyway, I'm looking out and the door opens and the oddest thing happened." She just stopped.

"Yes."

"Well, that door the police are guarding opens up. This girl comes running out of the apartment right past me. Don't think she saw me. She was looking straight down the hall. She came bursting outta that cute girl's apartment across the hall. Donna's such a sweetie, comes over every now and then. You know, just to chat and make sure I'm OK. Such a darling. From all the hoopla out in the hall, I fear she's dead, isn't she?"

"A girl? You said you saw a girl."

"Yup. A girl. That's the funny thing. She was dressed like a guy. She had on a guy's pants and shirt. A really bad wig. Too big for her. And a ball cap pulled down low. But it wasn't the girl across the hall; I know her, and the one dressed like a man was much shorter." She took a sip from her Pepsi and cocked her head to reinforce her point.

"If the cap was low on her face, how do you know it was a girl?"

"I'm old, not stupid. She was about my height. And when she ran past, I could see the smooth complexion of a young woman. Men don't have smooth skin like that and she was pretty. Full lips and blonde hair that snuck out under that God-awful wig. And men don't have stuff pushing out the shirt the way this girl did. I mean, if I was a bit younger, she would be a darling," she said coyly with a broad smile. I laughed.

"Would you recognize her again?" I asked.

"I doubt it. Saw her for but a moment as she ran past and my eyes aren't that trustworthy. I can see fine but she had on that wig and cap." She took another sip. "You drink up. You hardly touched your Pepsi." I obliged, took another sip, and held my can with both hands.

"You seem confident she was, well, a she."

"I know my women. I never fancied the company of men."

"OK." I was lost for words.

"Are you shocked, young man, that a woman in her seventies would say that?"

"Not at all." I was, but I didn't want to make her feel uncomfortable.

"When I was younger, much younger," she giggled, (I never would have thought of her as a giggler) "my boyfriend left for the war. There were a lot of lonely women left behind. That's when I found out who I really was. My boyfriend never made it back from Europe. Bless his soul. Kept my secret to myself for years. As you get older, you realize that some secrets are not worth keeping and sharing is much better than being alone."

I gulped down what pop remained in the can, stood, and offered her my hand.

"Thanks, my dear. For the pop and the information. I've learned a lot today."

She cradled my hand in both of hers. "If you have someone, I mean someone you truly care about, tell her. Or him."

The door closed behind me with a gentle click. Galen stood at the entrance to the crime scene, waiting for me. He motioned for me to join him, and then slipped past the two hulking officers standing guard. I followed him into the living room. It was a mirror image of the apartment I had just left. Instead of the bedroom down the hall and to the right, this one had the bedroom to the left.

I waited silently while Galen stood with the officers. Feeling uncomfortable and out of place, I stuffed my hands in my pant pocket and rocked back and forth on my feet. Looking around the living room, I failed to see a body or anything to give away where the body may have been. From my left, several crime scene technicians in their white Tyvek suits appeared from the bedroom, carrying brown paper bags that had the tops rolled down. They were secured with red plastic adhesive tape and were labelled "Evidence" in contrasting white.

Leaning back to get a better view of the action, I noticed that none of the bags looked large enough to carry anything of substance. They were, however, large enough to carry a leather belt.

A hand grabbing my arm and pulling me down the hall threw me off balance from my stance.

"Where're we going?" I asked Galen.

Galen dragged me into the bedroom and stopped when we were only feet from the body.

The girl lay before me, prone. She had short, dyed-blonde hair with her natural roots starting to show. A black leather belt was secured around the girl's neck like a bad style accessory; the strap was fed through the buckle and dangled down her back to rest on the floor, the same way all the other victims had been. There was a deep, trenched indentation around her neck to indicate the force that had been used to strangle the victim. She was tiny; not in stature but in frame. She looked to be about five foot eight, maybe five foot nine, but maybe a hundred pounds soaking wet.

I checked the area first before I knelt beside her. Using my index finger to guide my eyes, I followed the belt around the neck to the buckle. Without looking, I held my hand up and simply said "Glove." Someone—most likely Galen—placed a light blue, powder-free nitrile glove in my hand. I slipped it on so that I would be able to touch the leather garret. Using my index finger again, I lifted the tail end of the leather belt that came forth from the buckle to see the skin hidden beneath. There was bruising where the buckle had dug into the base of the neck as the belt had been tightened and pulled down to choke the victim.

The victim's head was turned towards me. I pulled a few strands of her hair away from her face and looked into her bloodshot eyes. Tiny blood vessels had burst from the increased pressure from the strangulation, an effect called petechiae. She was a pretty girl, young, too small to fight off an attack from behind. Her left hand rested beside her face. Under her nails, skin and blood was visible. Evidence. We had skin samples from Nicole, the victim who had survived; the police would compare DNA from the two samples. From my crouched position, I scanned the room and found the cause of the two "bangs" the older lady across the hall had described. The cracked drywall showed the effects of a scuffle.

Behind me a sour, gravelly voice barked out orders, causing everyone to leave the room. When I stood and turned around, Galen was standing beside a younger man wearing a wrinkled suit and leather sandals: L Lezcars.

"I was told by Officer Hoese the chief called you in. The last thing I want is you to fuck up this investigation. I understand you've been to a few of these," his fingers swirled around the room like he was stirring a pot, "scenes and you know your way around. Where's that girlfriend of yours?"

"Not here today." I wanted to keep my response short.

I really didn't know this man whom I'd only met once before but for a small man, he had an imposing presence. The sweat started to form under my arms and down my back. My pulse quickened and my heart started to pound in my chest. I was nervous and started to ramble.

"The perp was a girl, not the one we know who's committed the other related crimes. She was shorter than the vic. You can tell by the indent on the back of the neck where she had to pull the belt down when it was tightened and they struggled. The new dents in the wall are most likely a result of the fight as the victim tried to break free." I pointed to the two cracks in the drywall on the opposite sides of the bedroom. "The belt is consistent with the type used in the past: good quality leather, used, no way to track the sales, various sizes but always a bit on the large size." I continued to ramble.

Lieutenant Lezcars paused for a few moments, looked at Galen, and then back to me. His voice was now calm.

"I've already looked at the surveillance tape from the security office. The camera in the lobby shows what looks like a man running out the front door."

I looked at Galen, silently asking permission to speak my mind. Through telepathy, I was certain Galen granted me permission.

"We're almost certain that Carl Ryan is the one responsible for the other belt murders. In the past, he hasn't been caught on any surveillance cameras. We know his physical appearance from the attempted murder in my apartment building, and he is much taller than the person you saw on the tape. Carl Ryan is smart—plans out his attacks—and I seriously doubt he would have made so many errors in one incident."

Lieutenant Lezcars asked, "If you didn't see the surveillance tape, how did you know what the person leaving the scene looked like?"

Before I could answer, Galen spoke on my behalf.

"This is why I keep him around, L.T."

"Unless you're psychic, you're just full of bullshit. Somehow you managed to see that surveillance tape already and you're just trying to make yourself look good aren't you." Lieutenant Lezcars laughed. "You sonofabitch." He pointed a finger at me and laughed. He extended his hand without saying another word, shook my hand with a firm grip, and then turned on his heels and walked out of the room.

"He must like you. He never shakes hands with anyone. Like, no one." Galen looked impressed. "You gotta tell me how you knew that stuff."

I whispered, "Paramedic intuition."

Galen and I exited the bedroom and walked to the living room. The man in white was speaking with a group of men and a woman. Galen excused himself and went to join them. I decided to wait out in the hall.

Several minutes later, Galen and the woman came out to speak with me.

"Ethan, this is Erin."

"Hi." I extended my hand to greet her, but she just glared at me.

Erin turned to Galen. "Sorry, I'm late. Personal issues to deal with." She then turned her attention to me. "Everyone was impressed by your observations and conclusions, Ethan. The guys canvassed the whole floor and didn't get anything. Amazing how you got that description so fast. You bullshitting us or just bold faced fat fucking liar?"

Stunned by what Erin had just said, I looked at Galen.

"What the fuck, Erin? Come with me." Galen grabbed her by the shoulder and spun her around. "Now."

The two of them walked down to the end of the hall, turned, and faced each other. Fingers pointed and voices raised as the two police officers confronted each other, defending their unique perspectives when it came to my involvement. The other officers turned and watched as Galen and Erin continued arguing.

One of the portable radios a uniformed officer was wearing started to squawk, but was barely audible over the screaming. My attention turned from Galen and Erin as the officer moved his ear closer to the mic clipped to his epaulette. He turned up the volume on the radio but it did little good. He raised his arm and told everyone to be quiet.

©"Another kid was just found. Mother said she was gone for less than a few minutes." The officer brought everyone up-to-speed on the call that had almost gone unheard because of the argument.

Erin broke away from Galen without saying another word, stormed past me, and purposely bumped into me, knocking me off balance. She hit the panic bar on the stairwell door, pushing it hard enough to send it crashing into the wall. I heard her footfalls as she bolted down the stairs.

I turned to Galen who stood motionless in the hall. He looked furious for multiple reasons, his jaw clenched tightly as he walked by.

"Go home," he said without looking at me. He made his way to the stairwell, pushed the door open, and disappeared. After the door closed, I looked at the other uniformed officers in the hall who now avoided eye contact with me. The old lady's door was open, and her eye peeked through between the jam and the door. Her index finger curled back, inviting me back into the apartment. After waiting for a few moments until everyone had gone back to their jobs, I slipped back into the apartment. The door closed behind me.

It was still dark and the smell remained, but I had become accustomed to it. From behind me, I heard the old lady say, "It's her."

18

I spun around. "What?" I grabbed her by the shoulders and repeated myself: "What?"

"The girl who just ran past in the hall. I watched the whole thing. My door was open. I saw her earlier today. The one who was dressed like a man. That was her."

"How?" I was at a loss for words.

"Honey, you don't forget a chest like that and her face. She ran past my apartment exactly the same way that she did earlier, and I recognized her complexion. That's her. I know it."

I released my grip on her, took a step back, and put my hand to my forehead.

"Holy fuck." My head was spinning. The whole situation had just become more convoluted than I could even comprehend. I turned back to the old lady. "You're sure. It's the same girl?"

"I'm old, but I'm not senile. Yet. Her face, her chest, but it was the way she ran. Just too many things the same for it not to be her."

I held her again and looked her in the eyes. "Don't tell anyone what you've just told me. No one. You got that? I'm serious. No one. Don't tell the cops, the newspapers—no one. I want to keep you safe." I released my grip. She rubbed her shoulders where I had held her tightly.

I paced around the apartment, trying to arrange the events in my mind. Every time I thought I had a grasp on the situation, I thought of something else that distorted my earlier train of thought. Then I realized something horrific.

"Do you have a sister, brother you can live with?"

"Why?"

"I'm scared she may have seen you. And if she did, she may come back for you." I paused and paced the apartment again. "No. Not family. A friend. Someone outside the city." I was stammering like a child.

She walked over to me and held me by the shoulders the way I had been holding her earlier.

"Honey, I'm old. I'm a lesbian. I'm sick. No one is going to believe me that I recognized her because I thought she was attractive and I recalled some of her features. What kind of proof is that?"

She made a valid point. "I'm not concerned about what the police will think. I don't want her to come back and…" I cocked my head to the side and couldn't bring myself to say it out loud.

She smiled at me and touched my face. "You're worried about me," she said in surprise.

"I am." I amazed myself. "Please. Go somewhere and don't tell me. I'll give you my home number and you can call me in a few days. Do you have money for a cab?" I pulled cash from my front pocket, unfolded two twenties, and stuffed them in her hand.

"I'll pack a bag. Do you want another Pepsi?"

I laughed loudly. "Please. That would be nice."

*****

I went straight from the crime scene back to my building. As I went through the lobby, I scanned the area around the ceilings and corners for CCTV cameras. Sure, I have to use a key to get in past the front foyer, but is the building I live in secure? I wondered. I couldn't spot one single camera in the common area or after the locked doors, or even pointing at the mailboxes in the lobby. As I stood at the elevator, I looked to my right then left down the halls and didn't see a camera at either end. Could it be the building doesn't have any cameras? And if we do have cameras, who's monitoring them? We don't have a guard in the lobby. Is it time to move?

It was just after eleven when I got back to my apartment. I called for Maddy but got no response. I went to the kitchen and found a note stuck to the fridge saying she was out buying groceries and would be back before eleven. I yanked the note from the fridge, sending the magnet that held it in place flying to the kitchen sink. I fell into the couch and saw my reflection in the television. Just below the television, the clock on the VCR flashed 11:13 in bright red LED. It was after eleven. Maddy had said she would be back before eleven. I rubbed my eyes, cupped my hands over my face, and took a deep breath. My hands smelled of old lady. I had helped her pack an overnight bag, then brought her downstairs and put her in a cab.

Was she safe? She had offered to tell me her name. I asked her not to tell me. It was safer. She had my home telephone number and would call me in four days. On the way home, all I could think about were things

Erin might do to her if she found out she had been seen running from the scene. Not once, but twice.

Again, my mind started to concoct various sinister scenarios of what had happened and why Maddy wasn't back yet. Did Erin know about Maddy? Now I was concerned for Maddy's safety. I wondered what could be happening to her if Erin had found out we knew. None of what I was thinking was rational; none of the situations made any more sense than what had happened at the apartment earlier that day, but that alone was beyond anything of which I ever could have dreamt.

As I sat on the couch, I found a pen in the end table, flipped Maddy's note over, and tried to remember the address I had overheard on the officer's portable radio. If I called dispatch, I would have to ask one of the dispatchers to break one of the cardinal rules of confidentiality to give me the address. Odds were I would remember if I put some thought into it. Pen and paper were placed on the table; I sat back, sunk into the couch, closed my eyes, and let myself slip back to the hallway from a few hours earlier.

In my mind's eye, I could see Galen and Erin arguing at the end of the hall.

Two uniformed officers standing guard at the door were now paying attention to the discussion. Noise behind me. Noise in front. Radios blaring. Voices from Galen. Voices over the radio. "EMS and Fire have been dispatched." Yeah, I got that. To where? Where were they dispatched? The street name. A colour. Red. Orange. No. That makes no sense. It wasn't a colour. Or was it? Close your mind, listen to the voices. Too many voices, Galen arguing, the radio. Tune out the argument, focus on the sound of the radio. Shadows, dancing on the wall as they move about. Light overhead. Damnit, listen to the radio. What did they say?

The door creaked open. My mind snapped back and I lost my concentration. Opening my eyes, I saw Maddy pushing the door open and carrying two large bags. I jumped up, grabbed the bags from her hands, and lay them on the floor. I pulled her to the couch and sat her on the coffee table.

"Well, hello to you too," she snickered.

"Sorry, I have to remember an address. Remember how to focus on something to help you recall things? Ever done that?" I asked excitedly.

She nodded.

I went on to tell her about what had happened at the apartment I had just left.

"You're sure it was the female cop?" she asked.

"As certain as the old lady was. I just know how that female cop was acting when I was there. She got in a snit pretty quick when I suggested the video of the person was actually a woman and not a guy."

Maddy moved from the coffee table to the couch next to me. "The little girl who was killed the other day. It was a copycat killing, wasn't it? I mean, it wasn't the person we suspect it was. Oh my God." Maddy had a startled look on her face.

"What?"

"Shit. Shit. Shit." Maddy jumped from the couch and started to pace around the living room. "Shit. Shit. Argh." She began stomping on the floor as she paced. "What was the name? Damnit. *Murder on a Train*. No. *Strangers on a Train*. Hitchcock. Alfred Hitchcock." She turned to face me. *"Strangers on a Train."* She snapped her fingers, then pointed at me. *"Strangers on a Train."*

"K?" I had no clue what she was talking about.

"It's an old Hitchcock movie, sometime in the fifties I think. Anyway, the premise of the movie is two guys each want to kill someone in their lives. The problem is they would be suspects if they each committed their own murder. So, they trade murders. One guy kills the other guy's wife and the other guy would kill his business partner or brother or something. Doesn't matter. This way they have an alibi for the murders." Maddy continued to pace the living room. "Holy fuck. Oops, sorry. I just figured out who's killing the little girls."

I stood up. "Who?"

Maddy covered her mouth, "Holy shit. I think Erin the cop is killing the little girls."

Stunned, I sat back down. Maddy paced around, then turned to face me, "It all makes sense. The same person who committed the other child murders didn't kill the little girl who was murdered the other day. We all agreed on that. Right?"

I waited for Maddy to continue, then I realized she was waiting for me to agree with her. "Right."

"The killing today was almost perfect, except that she was spotted not only by surveillance but by an old lady who happens to know women." Maddy's voice was intense.

"What are the odds that we would have two serial killers in the same city at the same time? It was scary enough that we could have one, let alone two serial killers who are working together." I asked.

Maddy picked a package of baby carrots from one of the shopping bags. She crunched into one and offered me the bag.

"Let's just call one of your supervisors and see if they can give us some info on the call location. How good are you at lying your sweet ass off?"

I shrugged. "Can't hurt."

As Maddy put the groceries away, I dialled the supervisor's extension and let the phone ring several times before someone picked up.

"Hello." I didn't recognize the female voice.

"Hey, it's Ethan. Listen, I have a favour to ask." Then I paused.

"Can you hurry? I'm really busy."

Perfect; impatient, probably wants to get rid of me without too much of a problem.

"I heard a call to down in the east end. They found another kid. My niece lives around there. What was the address? I'm freaking out. I just want to make sure it isn't her."

I heard a few taps of the keyboard and then she said, "Rose Street. Good?"

"All good," I answered. The line went dead.

"Got it. Rose Street. Ready for a drive?"

Maddy grabbed her keys. "I'm driving."

Maddy drove like a medic on an emergency call. She weaved through traffic, pushing her luck at traffic lights and forcing her way through a few amber lights that even had me gripping the door handle and bracing myself against the dash for safety.

Travelling north on King Edward Avenue, she cut the corner tight turning right onto Cathcart Street and came to a sudden stop where it bends right and becomes Rose Street. Police had sealed off access to the street with scene tape and several cruisers. The media vehicles were parked along the east side of Rose Street all the way down to Bruyere Street.

Maddy parked her car along the north side of Cathcart. We exited the vehicle and walked along the barrier tape, which prevented the onlookers from crossing into the park area. Maddy and I walked along the road to where a bike path follows the Rideau River, then turns to connect with the corners of Cathcart and Rose Streets. That area provided us with the best vantage point to see the entire crime scene. We scanned the area for Galen or Lieutenant Lezcars.

On the northeast corner of Bruyere and Rose Streets, there is a large treed green space that borders the Rideau River. The extensive open area is bordered by a tree line that prevents a clear view from the homes on the west side of Rose Street and the houses on the south side of Cathcart. There's a clearing at the river's edge where the tree line gives way to the shore.

A group of police officers were standing in a circle there around a yellow plastic sheet; the same type of plastic disposable sheets we use on the ambulance. My heart filled with dread as I surmised that the EMS crew had pronounced the victim and covered her before leaving. I scanned the area and couldn't see an ambulance anywhere. They must've come, pronounced the victim, and left her on scene to preserve the evidence. The injuries would have to be definitive for me not to transport a child.

From where I stood, about one hundred feet from where the body lay, it was difficult to single out Galen from the rest of the detectives. Just out of view of the yellow blanket, along the east side of the walking path, a woman sat on the ground, hands and tissue covering her mouth, crying. Several other women sat with her, one with her arm over the crying woman's shoulders. I guessed she was the mother. Most of the crowd had gathered along the curved section of the road. There weren't many vehicles parked along the street, so I assumed they were people who lived in the local homes.

We stood behind the barrier tape and I continue to look for my friend. I tried to recall what he had been wearing earlier in the day, but with the events of the past few weeks, my mind was like day-old oatmeal left on the stove: mushy and not good for anything.

As I continued to scan the officers on scene, one person caught my eye. Erin had her back to me, and she turned and pointed to some area beyond the scene. She either hadn't noticed me, or had chosen to ignore me.

I elbowed Maddy to get her attention.

"Her, the one in the beige pants and white shirt. See her? That's Erin." I didn't want to point her out in case she turned around again. Maddy acknowledged that she knew to whom I was referring.

As we stood there, a uniformed police officer walked past and I drew his attention. After some convincing, I asked if he knew Galen and, if so, if he could discreetly tell him where I was without alerting anyone else. Instead of finding Galen in the crowd, the officer keyed his mic and radioed the message to Galen.

The first person to face me was Erin. She turned and was about to walk towards me when Galen pulled himself from the crowd and started to make his way to where we stood. Erin stopped short and turned her back to us.

Galen walked over, his expression and body language displaying his displeasure. He stood on one side of the barrier tape, Maddy and I on the other.

"I thought I told you to go home."

"Erin. She's the one. She's the girl who was dressed up as a man in the apartment. She's the one who killed the kids," I whispered.

"Make up your fucking mind. Either she's one or the other. Now you're saying she killed the kids and then used the belts to kill as well."

"No, just the one," Maddy interrupted.

"So, she's a cop, kills kids, and what else now?" Galen was raising his voice. Several of the reporters turned their attention to us. Galen noticed and lowered his voice. "Enough," he whispered.

Maddy felt the tension between Galen and I and interrupted us.

"Galen, stop, will you. Listen to me."

Galen turned to face Maddy, and his expression changed. "What?" Speaking to Maddy, his voice was calm and his tone less aggressive.

"I think, we think," she waved her thumb between the two of us, "that somehow, someway, we don't know how, but those two met, you know, the belt guy and her. And now, they're trading off kills."

Galen gave Maddy a puzzled look.

"I'm not sure why," she continued. "I think it was to give each other an alibi."

"Really? The world thinks Carl Ryan is dead. Why would he need an alibi?"

Maddy looked at me, surprised. "I hadn't thought of that. Galen, trust me. She's the one. We're certain of that."

"Do you have any evidence?" Galen asked.

"We do," Maddy exclaimed.

"Well? Let's hear it."

Maddy looked at me, and I shook my head.

"We can't tell you. But we're certain."

"Oh, you're certain, or is he? Maddy, do you speak for Ethan now, too?"

"Where did that come from?" Maddy was puzzled by Galen's comment.

"Go home. Leave the investigation to the police." Galen turned and walked away without saying another word.

I watched as Galen walked back to join the group that had gathered on the patch of green lawn. A spot in the group opened up and swallowed Galen into it. The group continued to stand in a circle, heads turning to one another, and an occasional arm would point to somewhere in the green space. Notes were being taken, but at no point did Galen turn his attention towards Maddy and me. Beyond the group, just off shore, I noticed they already had a team of divers on a small boat searching the waters for clues.

I turned my sights to the yellow plastic blanket that covered the body of the little girl. A soft breeze blew across the field, flipping the edge of the blanket, and causing it to fold over onto itself and reveal a child's bare foot. It was an eerie sight, the bare foot of a dead child sticking out from underneath the sheet. No one noticed at first, but then Erin turned her attention from the group and saw the tiny pale foot against the green of the lawn. She was unable to tear her gaze away from the child, hypnotized by the sight of the dead child's foot.

I elbowed Maddy. Maddy cast me a puzzled looked, I simply pointed in Erin's direction.

"That is so creepy. She can't stop staring at the dead kid."

"She didn't do it, didn't get the chance to see her. She wants to look at the kid's face, I bet. It's really bothering her. Look." Maddy pointed.

Erin's attention was no longer with the other investigators. She turned and pulled herself away from the group, stepping closer to the body. Slowly, almost hypnotically, she took a few steps closer. Lieutenant Lezcars called out, breaking Erin's trance. She rejoined the other investigators and didn't look back at the young body.

"My God, she's like a kid in a candy store. She can't keep her eyes off that child. The more I see her, the more I believe that old lady you spoke to was right."

*****

Lieutenant Lezcars flipped open his notebook and read wordlessly while the others in the group provided him with the silence he needed. He turned pages, scanned them, and flipped again. His lips moved in silence, he made side bar notes, and then went back to previous pages. He sighed deeply, looked into the blue sky, cracked his back, and looked at Erin Rodda.

"Are we boring you, officer?" he barked. The group turned to look at Erin, whose attention was on the yellow blanket. She spun her head around and apologized.

"No, sir. I was just trying to imagine what was going through the person's mind as they did something like this. I can only imagine what they were thinking."

"They? What do you mean, 'they,' officer?"

Erin stumbled for a moment. "They, he, she, figure of speech. The thought of it all. I mean, what has to be going through the mind of the person as they do this."

"Don't over think things, officer. Whoever is doing this is one sick son-of-a-bitch that I personally feel redefines my opinion on the death penalty."

"But sir, consider what the reasons are, what they feel when they do these things."

Lieutenant Lezcars pocketed his notebook, placed his hands on his hips, and stared down officer Rodda.

"There is never a good reason to kill; never." He pointed his finger at her. "You got that? Especially an innocent child. This discussion is over. If you care to argue the point, consider yourself off the team. Are we clear on that?"

"Crystal." There was contempt in Erin's voice. She clenched her jaw and kept quiet.

Lieutenant Lezcars turned his attention back to the group. "All signs point to the vic being from the original, not a copycat like the one earlier." The group nodded.

Galen made a motion, then suddenly stopped. Lieutenant Lezcars noticed.

"Speak up, man, as long as you aren't siding with the unsub at this point." He looked quickly at Erin.

"Sir, it's just that Ethan made a comment at the apartment this morning. He said that the body showed signs that indicated it was committed by someone else. The more I think about it, the more I tend to agree with him."

Erin was about to speak when Lieutenant Lezcars held up his hand to silence everyone.

"Enough. The Chief called in some help. We've gotten nowhere fast so the feds will be showing up tomorrow to take over. It is unprecedented to have this many homicides at one time in the city's history. We not only have to worry about municipal and federal politicians each having their say in what's going on, but the media coverage we're also getting is making us look really bad. We have until tomorrow morning before my ass is handed to me on a platter. That means each one of you on this team will be viewed in the same light as me: inept.

"Let's do our jobs, see if we can get a handle on things, and help out the feds when they arrive tomorrow. Got it?"

Everyone remained silent as they nodded.

*****

Maddy and I stayed behind the barrier tape, watching the investigators continue to discuss the case as uniformed officers guarded the perimeter and crime scene technicians gathered evidence. Maddy noted that the mother who had been sitting on the rounded section of the curb where the two streets blend into one another was now standing, and was getting ready to walk away. A friend wrapped her arm around the mother's shoulder, helped her gain her composure, and attempted to guide her away from the scene and towards the street. The mother resisted and kept straining to look back at her daughter, unwilling and unable to leave her child behind.

If the little girl had lived in one of the homes directly across the street from where she was killed, it would be devastating for the parents to look out the window and see the spot where she died every day. I couldn't begin to imagine what was going through the mother's mind, let alone comprehend the fact that the person or one of the persons responsible was standing only a few feet from the body.

Maddy bolted from my side, made her way to the east side of Rose Street, and went to the aid of the mother. I watched as Maddy gently took hold of the mother, supporting her, and the three of them disappeared into one of the townhouses on the south side of Cathcart Street directly across from the park.

I turned my attention back to the scene. By now, the sun was high in the sky, and the shadows were non-existent. All of the colours in the park were more vibrant, the grass an amazing hue of emerald green, the leaves a darker shade of hunter green. Tiny specs of bright light bounced off the tips of the waves in the flowing water in the Rideau River. For all the beauty of the day, I couldn't divert my eyes from the banana-yellow sheet covering the body of the little girl. Pulling my attention from the victim and scanning the area, I could understand why someone would've attacked the girl here. The Rideau River bordered the entire area to the north, trees lined the shore and the east and west boundaries of the park, and the only houses with a sightline to the park were the ones on the south side of Cathcart.

I sat on the curb watching the crime scene technicians walk through the park, looking under trees and shrubs, and turning over the deep grass. One person scanned the area with a metal detector. Galen and the rest of the team continued their site conference as they stood in a group, doing whatever they do.

A minivan pulled up to the scene and parked not far from where I sat. The driver and passenger exited the vehicle, walked to the back of the van, and pulled a stretcher out; it looked similar to what we use on the ambulance but considerably older. In all the times I had seen these guys on different scenes, oddly, I had never really noticed their stretcher before. On the stretcher, they had a black bag or a cover; I wasn't sure what it was but I knew what it was going to be used for.

The back doors slammed with a metallic thud as the two workers prepared to mount the curb with the stretcher and cross the grass to where the little girl lay covered by the yellow blanket.

I was suddenly struck with an idea. "Hey!" I called out to the two men as they were about to cross the barrier tape. I motioned for one of them to come closer. As the younger of the two men approached, I patted myself down to find a piece of scrap paper. I found an old receipt crumpled up in my pocket and mixed in with my money.

"Yeah?" the man asked.

"Have you got a pen?"

He pulled a pen from his breast shirt pocket.

"Can you do me a favour and give this to the female cop standing there?" I pointed to Erin. He acknowledged. I started to write on the back of the receipt.

"Why?"

I didn't reply; instead, I handed him the old receipt with the note on the back, and the only two bills I had in my pocket, a ten and a twenty, underneath. He flipped the receipt over, read it, shrugged, pocketed the thirty dollars and his returned pen, and went back to help push the stretcher.

As soon as he left, I scrambled away from the scene and mixed in with the larger crowd. I placed myself at the back so I couldn't easily be seen.

When the men with the stretcher arrived at the spot where the body was, they stopped, unfolded the large black cover, draped it over the stretcher, and lowered it to ground level. It was very professional, very business-like. The crew didn't look under the yellow blanket; they simply scooped up the body and placed it on the stretcher.

They were about to place her inside the black cover when a breeze pulled the yellow blanket off the body, revealing her legs and the floral dress she was wearing. It was similar to all the other dresses I had seen in the file. I wondered, if I ever had a daughter, would I ever let her wear a floral dress after what I had seen?

I thought the man I had paid to deliver the message had forgotten to deliver it, or was simply going to pocket the money. The cover was secured, the seat belts were fastened, and they were pulling away when the younger man stopped, returned to the group of detectives, and tapped Erin on the shoulder. He simply handed her the note, and had turned to walk away when she called out to him. Erin broke from the group and met up with him, and the two had a few words. He pointed in the direction where I had been standing before I'd moved. Noticing I wasn't there anymore, he simply walked away. Erin looked at the note, and then scanned the crowds as they stood on the street.

I lowered myself to hide within the crowd as Erin continued her attempts to locate me. Lieutenant Lezcars called out to her, and Erin slipped the note into her pocket and rejoined the group. She continued to turn around sporadically to see if I had revealed myself.

When I was confident I wouldn't be seen, I made my way back to the house Maddy had entered. I hadn't thought about the police wanting to interview the mother, and Maddy was still with her.

Looking back at the group, I watched Erin as she continued to return her attention to the crowd every few moments in an attempt to locate the person who had passed the note meant for her. Instead of knocking, I opened the door to the mother's house and walked in. The hallway before me went directly past the stairs on the right, to the kitchen. The hall opened up to reveal several people on the sofa in the living room consoling the mother of the dead child. I stood silently, watching the mother holding a picture, I assumed of her child. Maddy noticed my presence and excused herself from the room.

Maddy walked past me and I followed her to the kitchen. There were other people already in the kitchen who nodded politely at Maddy and me as we found a corner for some privacy.

"So what happened?" I whispered.

Maddy looked past me to watch the others in the kitchen leave.

"She let her daughter, Tiffany, out to go play with her friends first thing in the morning. She didn't know what happened until she heard the sirens."

"What about the dress? You'd think the mother would've read the papers or watched the news about the kids who were murdered."

"Come with me." Maddy grabbed my hand, pulled me back down the hall to the stairs, and led me upstairs to the little girl's bedroom. She opened the door to reveal a typical child's room. The wallpaper on the accent wall above the bed was a collage of vines and flowers. The bedspread was white, with large, open long-stem red roses.

"Most of her wardrobe is flowers. Tiffany loved flowers and dressed herself every day. Mom really didn't think about it. You know, the whole 'it'll never happen to me' thing. Tiffany went outside most days, met her friends, and played outside. Mom didn't worry about her whereabouts because this day wasn't unlike most days."

"Except it wasn't like most days," I countered. "K. We hafta get outta here."

Maddy looked at me oddly. "I'll explain in the car," I said. We made our way to the top of the stairs and I spotted Erin, Galen, and a few other detectives making their way towards the victim's house. They were still on the opposite side of the street. I stopped short as I felt panic overtake me. My first thought was to jump out the back through a second story window.

Instead, I held Maddy's hand, raced down the stairs, turned, and dashed down the hall past the living room to the kitchen. I pushed the kitchen door open into the backyard and froze. We were walled in by a six-foot-high wooden fence without a gate. I looked around the yard for something I could use to scale the fence, but it was free of any children's toys, tools, or garbage cans.

I went to the back wall, turned, ran towards the house, jumped, planted my foot on the brick exterior, braced my hands on the top of the fence, and pushed myself over. Stopping mid-way over, I rested my stomach across either side of the fence, motioned for Maddy, and pulled her up and over to the neighbour's yard before letting myself fall down.

Hearing a commotion from inside the victim's house, I peeked over the fence to see Galen and Erin through the door's window. I crouched down low at the base of the fence, and Maddy followed my lead. The door creaked open; one voice I recognized, the others I didn't.

"They went out this door?" Galen asked.

"They ran past and out the door. Yup," a strange female voice replied.

"There's no way out. You sure they went this way?" Galen questioned.

"Yes."

I strained to look through the tiny crack between the boards and could only make out partial forms of Galen and a few others. They all turned to walk back inside, leaving only one form standing on the back deck. Given the colour of the clothing, the slight form, it had to be Erin. Maddy placed her hand on my shoulder, trying to pull me away from the fence. I couldn't pull myself away; I had to know what she was doing.

The way Erin turned one way, then the next, I could imagine her looking around the yard to see how we had disappeared so quickly. Her body turned to face us then took a few steps forward when I heard her name being called from inside the house. She stood silently, unmoving, and then went back inside. I remained soundless for several minutes after the door closed, and then allowed myself to breath.

Inhaling deeply, I could feel myself relax. Maddy was already making her way to the back of the neighbour's yard. They had a swinging door to their fence that made our escape that much easier. Tucking low like we were making our way around a helicopter, we silently unlatched the lock, opened the door slowly, and disappeared behind the closing gate.

We walked down to the end of the row homes, peered around the corner, and noticed that neither Galen nor Erin were anywhere in sight. Casually making our way to the parked car, we kept an eye on the front door of the victim's house. I started the car and carefully drove away without attracting attention to our movements.

*****

Tom, Maddy, and I were sitting in a restaurant booth, three glasses of beer and an almost empty platter of nachos acting as a centrepiece. Tom refilled his glass with more draught from the pitcher and offered to do the same with our glasses. I placed a hand over my glass, while Maddy gladly accepted a refill.

"So, you're sure that female cop is the one who did it?" Tom asked as he scraped the platter for some of the hardened cheese.

"One hundred percent sure? No. But, there are just too many coincidences. It has to be her. If you had seen the way she was acting after I gave her that note. I mean, only a guilty person would do what she did."

"You're basing part of your conclusions on what she did after she read your note? That's pretty lame. What did the note say?"

"I only had a sec to think of something so I wrote, 'I know you did it.'"

"Well. That says it all. Why did you do it, anyway?"

I thought about what Tom had asked, and not having a good answer, I simply shrugged my shoulders.

Tom chuckled. "Does she know it was you?"

"Oh yeah. The way she confronted me in the hall. She's gotta know more than she's letting on. And I tell you, that old lady, she would've sworn on a stack of Bibles it was Erin who was dressed as the man."

Maddy finished her beer and placed the glass on the table. "Go on the offensive."

Her comment caught Tom and I off guard. "Go on the offensive? What the hell does that mean?" I asked.

"I have no fucking clue. But, do we really want to sit back and let her come to us? What's the saying, 'the best offensive is a good defensive,' or something like that? Let's go on the offensive."

Maddy's suggestion made perfect sense. I had no clue how to proceed, but I liked it.

"OK. How?" I asked.

Tom licked his fingers free of cheese. "I know. I know exactly how to do it."

Maddy and I looked at each other, then towards Tom. He scraped more cold, solid cheese from the platter, licked it off his finger, and looked up at us.

"What? Oh, you want to know now?"

"Now would be a good time."

"We have to create a diversion. We're gonna probably get into a lot of trouble, you know." He picked up a knife to scrape the platter.

Maddy slapped the knife free from his hand. "You gonna tell us or not?"

4:04 PM

Detective Nardone was cataloguing the files of evidence and placing them in banker's boxes, taking pictures of the white boards, and preparing for the transfer of ownership to the RCMP team when they would arrive the next morning. His jacket was unceremoniously tossed over a chair, and his tie had been slipped from around his neck and thrown on top of the jacket. It had slithered to the floor, but he'd left it there.

He had been in charge of the investigation, and now it was being taken away and handed over to another team. Detective Nardone hated losing; hated even more having to pass along his failures to someone else.

Detective Nardone picked up one of the boxes, walked to the corner, and placed it on the floor. He repeated this action with the second box, and as he was about to place it on top of the first, he paused, then flung the box to the far end of the room. The box smashed against the wall, the corner split, and the top went flying in the opposite direction as papers filled the room. He stood silently, watching the papers float to the floor. Picking up his jacket and tie, he was about to leave the room when the phone rang.

Detective Nardone briefly thought about letting it ring; instead, he sighed deeply, and picked up the phone.

"Detective Nardone."

"I have a message for Detective Rodda," the male caller said.

"Officer Rodda. I'm not sure if she's still here. Hang on, I'll put you on ignore." Detective Nardone pressed the "hold" button, hung up the handset, and peered down the hall. Not seeing anyone, he yelled out for Erin. No answer. He called again. He heard her voice coming faintly from the squad room.

"Pick up extension 108," he yelled.

Erin sat at her desk, picked up the handset, and punched in the extension.

"Hello."

"What did I write on the note?"

Erin's heart stopped; she suddenly felt cold and couldn't breathe.

"Tennant?"

"I know it was you. I'll prove it."

"Then why did you call?" Erin paused. "You want something, don't you? Otherwise, you'd have told Galen."

"I want to meet you."

"What do you want?" Erin's voice was getting agitated.

"Talk."

"Talk. That's all you want? Talk."

"For now. I want to know why."

"Where?"

"Someplace public. Lots of people."

"Where, then?" Erin was getting impatient.

"How about a coffee shop?" Tom, Maddy, and I had already decided where to meet, but I was acting as if this were a spur-of-the-moment decision. "Do you know the one on Alta Vista Drive, south of Industrial? The one by the strip plaza?"

"Time?" Again, she was showing her impatience.

"It's just after four now. Let's say five. Are you bringing Carl Ryan?"

The phone went dead.

"Well?" Tom asked.

"She's pissed, that's a given."

"She's gotta be guilty. Only a guilty person would agree to meet you," Maddy offered.

"Not really. She's a cop. She could be following a lead," Tom countered. "Do we tell Galen?"

I looked at Maddy and Tom. Their expressions offered no help.

"Either way, are we going to be ready? We have less than an hour, guys." I was worried that Tom's plan may be so wildly far-fetched that there was no way to pull it off.

Tom laughed. "Relax. I've got everything arranged. When the time comes, we'll be ready."

Maddy held up her hand. "We have to think of all the variables." She held up one finger. "She comes alone." Two fingers. "Carl comes along." Three fingers. "She comes with the police. Cause you know Carl won't come if the police are there." Four fingers. "She doesn't show up at all." Her thumb shot up. "She brings Galen." She paused. "Have I forgotten anything?"

Tom and I shook our heads from side to side.

Tom stood to leave. "K. I made all the calls. I'm heading out to get some of the stuff ready. Meet you there before five? I'll be parked out in the parking lot at the far end of the strip plaza."

153

4:59 PM

I walked into the coffee shop alone and took my place in line to order a drink. I scanned the room while I waited and saw Erin sitting alone in the corner behind me, her back to the wall, not far from the entrance. All the tables around Erin were free of other customers. Typical police behaviour. Back to the wall to prevent an unseen attack, watch everyone come and go, and the position provides a quick exit. Looking around the customer area, I determined that Carl Ryan wasn't in the room.

At the counter, I ordered a medium coffee, paid, and stepped to the side. My stomach was a mixture of butterflies fluttering in a sour soup. I felt nauseous and wanted to vomit. The server placed my take-out cup on the counter. I smiled at her, took my drink, and stood frozen for a moment, not sure I could do this. My whole body broke out in chills and started to shake.

Clenching my teeth, I gathered up my strength and walked towards Erin's table. One of the customers was walking past as they exited the shop and bumped into me. I apologized as I continued my way to the corner of the shop. When I arrived, she looked up at me, saying nothing. I sat down, placed my drink on the table, and crossed my hands on my lap. My legs shook under the table; I rung my hands together and felt them become clammy.

For several minutes, nothing was said. I stared straight ahead as Erin read her notebook. She finally flipped it closed, placed it in her purse, and looked at me. I could feel her eyes studying me. Finally, she spoke.

"You called me."

"I just have one question: why?" My voice cracked with nervousness.

"Are you wearing a wire?" she asked.

"No." Instinctively, I lifted my shirt to reveal that I had nothing to hide. "Satisfied?"

Erin's gaze didn't shift. She continued to stare not only at me but also through me, and was making me increasingly uncomfortable. I could feel myself beginning to lose control. If I had a panic button, I would've pressed it long ago as I fought the urge to run away.

"What do you want with me?"

To prepare me, Maddy and Tom had grilled me with questions Erin might ask. I felt like I was on trial, except the prosecutor had now asked a question for which I wasn't ready. Fight fire with fire.

"Why did you come if you aren't guilty?

"I'm a cop. I thought you had something to add to the case."

This was one of the comments we had rehearsed. Throw it back in her face.

"You were seen leaving the apartment where the girl was killed."

I was expecting more of a reaction from Erin; instead, her gaze remained fixed. She failed to react at all, except her left index finger began to tap the table, softly, with no noise, barely noticeable. The finger hardly moved; it was an instinctive stress reaction to being caught. Time for another blow.

"Why would you risk getting caught? I mean, no one suspected you. You teamed up with Carl Ryan, didn't you?"

The finger began to move more rapidly, still not making any noise. Her gaze remained focused on me. Erin didn't show any facial signs that she was stressed. I was feeling more comfortable now. Pulling the lid off my coffee cup, I placed it on the table, giving me a reason to look down. Her finger was moving so quickly now, even Erin must've known it was a tell.

I felt in control now, but had to hold back from feeling overly confident. Then it hit me.

"Carl sought you out, didn't he? He was the one who murdered that girl; the copycat killing. Being part of the investigative team, you knew if they ever started to suspect it was a woman, they would profile the person responsible. It could've led to you. You needed to deflect the suspicion. This was all your idea, wasn't it?"

Erin didn't flinch; she didn't show any signs of stress other than her finger twitch, and now her forehead started to glow. I had her. She knew it.

"Why?" I asked again.

"Have you ever felt an urge, an itch, that needed to be scratched, but you couldn't reach it, or no matter how hard you scratched, the itch never went away?" Erin paused. Her finger no longer fluttered on the tabletop.

I waited for her to say something more, admit to what she had done, but she just looked past me. Erin suddenly looked very sad, and oddly enough, I felt a wave of sympathy for her. There was a moment of silence that I didn't want to break in case she would suddenly blurt out a confession. I waited for a few more moments.

"You have an itch, that's why you—" I started to prompt before she cut me off.

"You have no evidence, nothing to add to the investigation; this is a fishing expedition. My being here is pointless." Erin took control of the conversation and deflected the topic away from herself.

The entrance door chimed as it opened and closed behind me. I turned to see several people walk out of the shop.

"Unless you have something more to add, I'm leaving, too." Erin stood, grabbed her purse, and then leaned in close and whispered in my ear, "That girlfriend of yours is very pretty. She reminds me of one of the girls."

I looked up at Erin to see her smiling back. Before I could respond, she was already at the main door. Several customers followed her out. I remained at the table as I watched her drive away. Minutes later, Tom walked in and took the seat vacated by Erin.

"Did it work?" I asked.

"We've got at least five tailing her right now." Tom stood and raised his voice. "Thanks, guys." Most of the customers in the shop responded with a raised coffee cup. He sat back down. "It's nice being part of a paramedic family, isn't it? If we had more time, I could've had half the platoon down here covering surveillance. The guys are in personal cars tailing her and will rotate coverage. Those of us with cellphones with keep in touch with each other now that we know her car and plate number. We've got the guys working in the rigs keeping an eye out for her car in case we lose her. If I were a betting man, I'd say she's going straight to Carl. And if we catch Erin with Carl, we have the proof we need, right? Not bad for a bunch of ambulance drivers, huh?"

"I wished I shared your positive attitude. Right now I'm worried about Maddy."

"She can handle herself," Tom reassured me.

5:30 PM

Two of the off-duty medics who had volunteered to help followed Erin as she pulled out of the coffee shop parking lot. Erin drove north on Alta Vista and made her way to the Queensway. The chase car maintained the same speed as Erin's car in order to avoid losing her at the lights. She turned west on Industrial, taking the far lane, then north on Riverside Drive. Erin accelerated quickly, with the chase car following closely behind. She took the westbound exit to the Queensway and merged with traffic. The chase care remained several cars behind and one lane to her right. As he kept an eye on her vehicle, the passenger's cellphone rang.

He tapped the little green button. "Yeah?"

"Where are you?"

"Coming up on Parkdale. We're a few cars behind. You going to take over and we can fall back?"

"You got it."

"We have to release the other teams that were heading east and south. I'll call them after you take lead on the tail." With that, he hung up.

The passenger dialled Tom's cellphone and gave him their location, then filled him in on who was taking over Erin's tail. He then called the other teams who had been placed in various locations and gave them a status update. They would redeploy south and north along the Queensway, west of Erin's location.

As the second team pulled onto the Queensway, they sped up, crossed several lanes of traffic, and then slowed down abruptly once they were a few cars behind. Erin noticed the car in her rear view mirror, and watched as they drove like rookie cops in training trying to follow someone. Again, the focus of the passenger in the pursuit car never left Erin, and the driver matched her speed in traffic. The first crew backed off as Erin thought they would, pulling back even farther.

Erin had spotted the car following her the moment she had left the parking lot. The car had stayed too close, and Erin had noticed that the driver never took his attention away from her car. Instead of taking the east exit as planned, she decided to head west, away from where she wanted to go. She drove as she normally would, allowing her tail to stay within view.

Erin knew that Ethan was behind this. She mentally gave him credit for concocting a plan so quickly. It's time, she thought.

Erin kept her eyes on the overhead traffic signs, and when the Parkdale Avenue exit approached she suddenly jerked her car right along four lanes of traffic, causing drivers to slam on their brakes to avoid a collision. She used her police training to skillfully guide her car across three lanes of traffic and down the exit from the Queensway.

Parkdale Avenue has a long exit that parallels the Queensway. Erin gunned the accelerator going down the off ramp. She looked in her rear view mirror and didn't see anyone following her. The light ahead was green as she maintained her speed and then made a hard turn right through the intersection. She headed north on Parkdale Avenue and disappeared.

"Fuck." The off-duty medic in the first car punched the dashboard as he blew past the Parkdale Avenue exit. "I'll get Tom on the phone."

5:45 PM

Maddy knocked at the front door repeatedly until Galen answered. The only thing separating them was the screen door. He didn't look pleased to see her. Only hours before, Maddy and Ethan had evaded them on Rose Street. Now, she was standing on his front porch.

Before he could say anything, Maddy took control of the conversation.

"Are you going to pout or listen to reason?"

"If you were Ethan, I'd kick your fucking ass. You have some nerve coming here. Now, if you don't mind, we're just about to sit down for dinner."

Maddy crossed her arms in defiance. "You going to invite me in or come outside? I don't want to talk to you through the screen door."

Galen pushed open the screen door, and Maddy stepped aside as he joined her on the porch. She walked over to the two white resin chairs, sat in the far one, and waited for Galen to join her. Against his better judgement, he sat down next to Maddy. She elbowed him in the right upper arm.

"You mad at me, copper?"

"No. I'm pissed at your boyfriend."

"Well, you aren't gonna like what we're doing now."

"Do I wanna know?"

"Nope."

"Then don't tell me."

"Yeah, but I gotta. Sorry, copper. If everything goes as planned, Ethan is having a little conversation with Erin right about now about our suspicions. If she leaves, we'll have a tail on her. We think she'll go straight to Ryan. If she stays, she may confess to Ethan. I'm sure there're things we haven't thought of, but we'll deal with it."

Maddy continued to tell Galen the plan that they had concocted.

"You know someone is gonna get killed." Galen stood and went inside the house. When he returned, he held a bottle of beer in each hand. Galen handed one to Maddy, took his seat, and tilted the bottle back.

"I should kick you in the ass, you know."

"I love you too, copper."

"Tell me again why you think Erin is involved." Galen stared straight ahead. "And why you feel Carl Ryan and Erin are in this together."

6:00 PM

The sun was still high in the sky over the west end of Ottawa as Erin pulled into the driveway where Carl Ryan had been staying. She slammed the driver's door and ran to the back of the house. She found Carl sitting in the same chair in which he had been when she had visited the night before. He didn't even bother to turn around or acknowledge her presence until she stood before him.

"We hafta get outta here. Now." Erin was panting even though it was only a short distance from the driveway to the back of the rental house.

"Why?" Carl's voice remained calm.

Erin went on to tell him what had happened throughout the day and what Ethan had tried to accomplish by setting up teams to follow her. Carl was still unaware that she was a police officer, so any reference to that was omitted from her story.

"I really hate to say 'I told you so' but you wanted to get this thing done and over with as fast as possible, which can only mean you thought the police were on to you. Grab a seat." Carl patted the spot next to him. "Let's chat and grab a bite to eat."

Erin kicked the cheap patio chair, sending it flying. Carl didn't react.

"We need to leave now," she insisted.

Carl raised his voice and pointed at Erin. "No. You need to get outta here. They have nothing on me. If you wanna play Bonnie and Clyde, that's fine by me, but don't make it sound like any of this is my fault. Got it?"

Erin stood silently before Carl. Since meeting him, Erin had assumed she was in charge, but she now realized that she feared him. Her handgun was in her purse but she had left it in the car. She took a few steps back in case Carl attempted to attack her. She calmed herself down, and in a slow, methodical voice, offered Carl an alternative to leaving. Erin held out her hands in front of her, palms facing Carl, in an attempt to show him she was calm.

"The only ones who suspect anything are the ones who set up that idiotic sting to try and follow me. I'm not sure exactly how many or who knows what. The only thing that I am one hundred percent sure of is that the police do not, and I repeat, do not, suspect me."

A coy smile came over Carl's face. He put his head down, and Erin was positive she heard him begin to laugh. As he stood, he was in a full laugh.

"Cop." He laughed again. "You're a fucking cop." He held his hand to his forehead. "I can't believe you're a cop."

Erin was stunned. Had she been so careless that she had let her only advantage slip?

"What? I'm not a…"

"Of course you are. It makes sense. When you mentioned you saw me in the crowd, I couldn't figure out why you were there. This is the only thing that makes sense. I have my own little cop in my pocket."

Erin tried to interject but Carl refused to let her speak.

"You're more valuable to me alive as a cop than dead or on the run." Carl was now in a very good mood. He stood, reached out, and hugged Erin. He wrapped his arms around her and squeezed tightly. "I've got a cop in my pocket." Carl used a child's voice.

Erin pried her arms up inside Carl's hug and pushed away from him. "Let's get one thing straight: I'm not your cop, and I'm definitely not in your pocket." She pointed her finger at him, wishing it were her handgun. "Don't you ever forget that."

"Calm down. Well, now that I know you're a cop, I need you around." Carl sat back down in the chair. "So you say that the cops don't suspect you but these idiots do. If they do suspect you, we need to stop them before they say anything. Who are they?"

"One of the other officers' friend, Ethan something."

"Can you find out who he is and how many might know?"

"How about a reverse sting?" Erin went and picked up the plastic chair, planted it facing Carl, and sat down. "I think I know how to get in contact with him."

Erin had a million scenarios playing in her mind, and she wanted all of them to end with Carl's death.

6:25 PM

Galen drove as Maddy used his cellphone to call Tom. He gave Maddy the details of how what they believed was a well-thought-out plan had gone horribly awry. They planned to meet at Ethan's apartment to regroup and formulate another plan of attack. Maddy disconnected and tossed the cellphone onto the car seat.

"Your phone?" Maddy asked.

"On what a cop makes? I don't know how anyone can afford these things. Fucking expensive. I got it as part of the investigative team. All they kept on telling us was to watch the minutes, whatever the fuck that means. Of course that all goes to hell in a hand basket tomorrow."

"What happens tomorrow?"

"We aren't in charge anymore. I guess the feces hit the oscillating blades and they called people in who can do a better job. They sat us down and I was told I'd be in uniform for the rest of my career because, as the Chief put it, I 'couldn't track a menstruating elephant in a snow storm.'" Galen's knuckles turned white as he gripped the steering wheel. "I can't be a uni for the rest of my career."

Maddy gently put her hand on his shoulder and wanted to say something, anything, but somehow felt responsible for what may have happened to his career. She wondered if she and Ethan had caused any of this to happen.

"And don't go blaming yourself. If anyone is to blame, it's that skinny ambulance driver boyfriend of yours."

"Hey, hey, don't call him that. You know he hates being called skinny." Maddy laughed.

Galen usually called Ethan an ambulance driver because he knew it always got a rise out of him. Galen's sullen look gave way to reveal a soft smile. He truly liked Ethan's new girlfriend.

A soft buzz broke the moment as the cellphone rang from the seat. Maddy picked it up.

"Should I answer it?"

Galen shook his head from side to side and Maddy offered him the phone. His large thumb pressed several buttons at once but still managed to connect the line.

"Hello."

"It's Erin. Sorry I freaked on you today."

Galen silently mouthed "Erin" to Maddy and tilted the phone so she could hear the conversation.

"It's OK. Don't worry about it. Sorry for the noise. I'm driving right now. The wife made me go out and get a pie to have after the barbeque." Galen made a guilty face to Maddy.

There was a slight pause before Erin spoke again. "It's actually a good connection. Listen, when you see your friend, can you tell him I'm sorry for yelling at him this morning. I was a little on edge. Bad night. You know how that is."

"I know. Don't worry about it. If I know Ethan, he's already forgotten all about you and moved on to bitch about something else."

"Great. It means a lot to me if you can do that. When will you be seeing him?"

"No clue. Probably the weekend. We usually get together at least once when we both have the same weekend off."

"K. Well, thanks again. Guess I'll see you tomorrow when we get our asses handed to us on a platter."

"Seven a.m. Sharp."

The line went dead.

Galen dropped the phone on the car seat. "What do you figure that was about?"

Maddy shrugged her shoulders, not sure what to make of the phone call.

Erin watched from a few car-lengths behind as Galen and Maddy turned to one another when their phone conversation ended. Erin blindly fumbled to place the phone back in her purse. Carl looked across to Erin.

"So what now?" he asked.

"We know Galen is involved somehow. At least we know he'll probably lead us to Ethan. I'm pretty sure that's Ethan's girlfriend riding with him. She looks like the description I got from the little girl's mother today. She was in the house grilling the family about what happened before Ethan came in and we lost them out the back door.

"If you want to keep me on the job, we may have a lot of clean up to do."

Carl nodded in agreement. "Did anybody see me do anything at the park?"

"Nothing. No one saw you."

"Good." Carl reached into his pocket, pulled out a small swatch of material, and kept it hidden in his palm. "Open your hand," he instructed.

Erin released one hand from the steering wheel as Carl placed the folded cloth in it and folder her fingers over. Immediately, she knew what it was. She brought the material close to her face and inhaled deeply. She closed her eyes briefly as images and fragrances overwhelmed her senses and her mind filled with pictures of the incident.

"Thank you for this."

"Least I can do. Now, let's focus on what we have to do to clear up this mess."

Erin placed her new souvenir in her purse, reached across and gently touched Carl's hand, and then took hold of the steering wheel again.

"I have to clean up this fucking mess. It's all on me." There was a short pause before Erin yelled, "FUCK," and slapped the steering wheel.

Erin's face was a bright hue of red, and beads of sweat dripped from her brow. She was angry. Not at Ethan, Galen, or Carl, but at herself. She had always been impatient, impetuous; taking risks when she shouldn't. Luck had always been on her side, but now her reckless behaviour had gotten her in trouble. Erin noticed she had progressed dangerously close to Galen's car. She changed lanes and slowed to match speeds with him.

Carl glanced to his left and realized that this petite, strong willed woman was going to be more of a handful than she may be worth. He wondered himself if he was getting into something he should let her handle on her own. As Erin kept her distance between Galen and Maddy's vehicle, he ran through his options in his head. He wondered if they could ever get everyone, even if they were successful in eliminating Ethan and the group of people who knew what was truly happening. Erin had mentioned that she was being tailed. By whom, he thought. Cops, friends, someone else— there was no way to know how many.

The more he thought about it, the more he began to worry this was going to end badly. There wasn't one scenario that ended well for both of them.

6:49 PM

Galen pulled into the parking spot of Ethan's building, and they both exited the vehicle and locked it. Out of habit, he looked around to see if there was a car close by that also pulled into the lot at the same time. Nothing. Several people walked past on the sidewalk; the street was almost deserted.

They walked towards the apartment building; Galen was still cautious and kept turning around to scan the area. He saw nothing that raised any flags. Galen opened the front door, allowing Maddy to enter first. He followed and used his personal key to gain entry into the foyer. He closed the glass door tightly behind him and they made their way to the elevator. Out of habit, Galen pressed the "UP" button repeatedly until the lift arrived.

The elevator chimed, the doors opened, and they went to Ethan's floor.

Two people ran from the back service door of the apartment building to the front foyer as the doors closed. They watched the numbers climb on the display until the elevators stopped on the sixth and fourteenth floors. Erin was wearing shoes with heels that made her look a few inches taller. She had on loose-fitting pants and a baggy jacket, and a ball cap was pulled down low over dark sunglasses. Her purse hung across one shoulder and rested on the opposite hip. Carl was wearing dark pants and a mechanic's striped shirt with a nametag sewn over the left breast pocket that declared, "Rob." Carl recognized the building. He had been in it when he had attacked the girl, and knew exactly where they had to go. Before he could say anything, Erin turned towards the front doors.

"Hold the door open for me," Erin ordered. She ran to the front vestibule, her hard soles clicking on the marble surface, while Carl held the door open. She checked the names on the sixth and fourteenth floors until she found what she was looking for. "Let's go." Inside, Carl was laughing.

Carl and Erin rode the elevator to the fourteenth floor, the doors opened, and she checked the wall placard for the direction of Ethan's apartment.

"1413. This way."

Erin turned right and walked briskly down the hallway. She reached into her purse and handed one handgun to Carl; she gripped the other gun tightly but kept her hand in her purse.

Before stopping at apartment 1413, Erin looked both ways down the hall to make certain the area was clear and that there were no hidden cameras. She stood on one side of the door, Carl on the other. She listened for voices and heard two male tones in the apartment. Patiently, she waited, with her ear pressed against the door. The voices were muffled but distinguishable. Erin waited to confirm it was the right apartment, and when she heard someone call out Ethan's name, she knew she was at the right place.

Erin held her finger to her lips as she brought the pistol up close to her face with both hands. With her back against the wall, she reached down and grasped the doorknob. Slowly, carefully, she turned it, making sure the door wasn't locked and holding the knob in position for quick entry. Erin waited for the voices behind the door to enter a steady conversation so she would know that their attention was away from the door. When Erin felt the moment was right, she gave Carl the nod, then she pushed the door open and rushed into the apartment.

As soon as Erin was past the door, Carl turned and ran for the closest exit, pushed the door open, and took the steps two at a time.

Pumped up on adrenaline, Erin stepped into the living room, her gun drawn. The room was empty; the drapes fluttered in the breeze from the open patio door. The voices continued a casual conversation somewhere in the apartment. She ducked into the kitchen; seeing no one, she slowly stepped down the hall, to the bedroom from whence the voices were coming.

Erin had been so focused on finding Ethan and Galen that she still hadn't noticed that Carl wasn't in the apartment with her. Heel to toe, she stepped down the hall to the bedroom. Ahead of her, the bathroom door was open, whereas the bedroom door on the left side of the hall was closed. The closer she got, the clearer she heard the voices emanating from the bedroom. She pressed her ear against the door and heard Ethan and another male speaking with each other. She reached across, turned the handle slowly, and burst into the bedroom to find it empty. Her head swivelled from side to side until she saw the stereo cassette tape recorder spinning and the small green lights blinking in unison with the voices.

"Fuck," she screamed.

"It's a bitch when things don't go as planned." Galen's voice was directly behind her. Erin froze.

Galen saw Erin's hand that held her handgun fidget.

"Yeah, I wouldn't do that. My gun is pointing at the back of your head and I'm betting I can squeeze the trigger faster than you can turn and raise your gun at me. Besides, sweetie, there's more than just me out in the living room."

Erin's hand relaxed. Galen reached down and took the gun from her. Erin turned around slowly to see Galen and Detective Joe Nardone standing at the bedroom door. Galen holstered his gun and leaned in close until they were nose to nose.

"Out of professional courtesy, I'm not going to cuff you. K? But don't try anything stupid because believe you me, nothing would make me feel better than to empty my cartridge into that pretty little head of yours."

Detective Nardone reached around Galen, grabbed Erin by the arm, and pushed her into the bedroom wall. She turned her face just as it slammed against it. Nardone jammed his leg between Erin's and spread them wide as he pulled her arms behind her back. With his glove-free hand, he patted her down, searched her purse, and found no other weapons. He did find a torn swatch of material that he recognized and handed to Galen.

Erin turned around to face Galen as he murmured, "Well, well. This looks awful familiar. I wonder where you got it from." Galen glared into Erin's eyes. There was pure hatred emanating from the way he looked at her. Galen turned and walked into the living room as Detective Nardone pushed Erin to follow.

7:30 PM

Erin expected to see Carl in custody; instead, she was stunned not to see him in the group gathered in the living room. At the front, Ethan and Maddy stood shoulder to shoulder with Tom and several uniformed officers. Detective Nardone shoved Erin back, forcing her to sit on the couch.

"Hey," she yelled as she fell.

Galen bagged the swatch of material as he chatted with the other officers in hushed voices. Ethan, Tom, and Maddy broke off and sat at the dinning room table. The three of them stared at the disgraced police officer sitting on the couch.

Erin nodded at Ethan. "You wanna tell me what happened?"

Ethan stood, walked over to the couch, and sat on the corner of the coffee table.

"What do you want to know?"

"How?" Erin, a broken woman, looked up at Ethan.

"I knew it was you. You were spotted at the scene running away by a witness who was one hundred percent positive it was you."

"How did you do this?" Erin looked around the apartment.

"Oh, you mean how did we stage this?" Ethan laughed. "It was actually Tom's idea—well, Tom thought about following you. Maddy and I came up with the idea to run the reserve sting."

Ethan went on to explain that the coffee shop had been filled with off-duty paramedics. They had planted crews of more off-duty medics in their cars on all major streets leaving the coffee shop so they had it covered wherever Erin went. They also knew that the medics would foul up the tail, not being properly trained and a little too excited. That was the only variable. Would Erin actually spot the tail? Maddy was confident she would. Someone who lived their life looking over their shoulders would spot a poorly executed tail.

Ethan knew that Erin didn't know where he lived, so it was only logical to assume that she would go to Galen's house and follow him to Ethan's place. In order to get Galen involved, Maddy had to convince Galen to be part of the act. While Maddy was with Galen, Tom and Ethan were recording a fake conversation on the cassette tape and moving his stereo system from the living room to the bedroom.

On the way from Galen's house to Ethan's apartment, Galen had called Detective Nardone and explained what they were doing. Nardone and a few uniformed officers had managed to take cover in two of the neighbouring apartments across the hall from Ethan's.

The only thing Maddy, Tom, and Ethan hadn't factored in was Carl losing his nerve and running away before they could trap the two of them in Ethan's apartment.

"The son-of-a-bitch bailed on me. I wondered where that low-life scum-sucking prick went to," Erin said through clenched teeth. "Did you catch him?"

Ethan look embarrassed. "He got away."

"Wanna know where he lives?"

Tom and Maddy were now standing behind Ethan. He looked up at them, then back at Erin.

"Of course."

Erin provided Ethan with the address of Carl Ryan. He stood, walked over to Galen, and whispered in his ear. Galen thanked his friend and went to Detective Nardone. He repeated to the detective what Ethan had done, whispering Carl's location into his ear. Detective Nardone looked past Galen toward Erin. She turned away, unable to face her commanding officer. Nardone went back to speaking with Galen.

Tom, Maddy, and Ethan returned to the dinning room table and each took a seat, leaving Erin alone on the couch. The three turned their attention away from Erin and on to Carl Ryan.

Erin sat, alone, dejected, embarrassed. She rung her hands, wiped the sweat from her brow, and looked extremely uncomfortable. Erin tilted her head to the right. The drapes continued to flow inward from the evening breeze. The longer she watched the slower the drapes seemed to move. The fabric drifted in the air, floated, then settled back down against the glass, until the next breeze. Beyond the balcony, the sun was beginning to dip in the west. Ethan's balcony faced east; outside his patio, the sky was a blend of orange, red, and black. She looked beyond the glass patio doors to the evening sky. Erin turned on the couch and faced the balcony, fixating on the way the drapes moved and then on the sky beyond.

7:45 PM

I was holding Maddy's hand as we walked towards the elevators. Tom pressed the "DOWN" button, stepped back, and hopped between feet as we waited.

"We gotta get downstairs fast. Should we take the stairs?" Maddy suggested.

"Are you kidding?" I laughed. "I'm not taking the stairs. I'll have a coronary or puke. Or both."

"How sweet. Such a lovely thought coming from my boyfriend." She gave my hand a gentle squeeze.

"Come on. Come on." Tom was still hopping from one foot to the other. The chime indicated the arrival of the elevator. The doors opened and we piled in, Tom pressed the "Lobby" button, and then stood back and repeatedly pressed the button to close the doors.

I had never seen Tom so anxious before; his gaze never left the LED floor display. Maddy snuggled in close to me in the corner of the lift as we watched Tom in amusement. The display counted down to "1," and Tom moved to the front of the box. When the doors opened, he dashed out, pushing open the security door and running through the vestibule into the parking lot.

By the time we made it to the outside of the building, we heard Tom's car rev as he made his way around the corner of the parking lot.

Maddy sat in the passenger seat, and I forced myself into the tiny back seat. Tom floored the accelerator and cranked the steering wheel hard to the left. The tires squealed as they caught the asphalt and then finally gained traction.

"How much time do we have?" Tom asked.

"Galen told his boss the address. My guess is a few black and whites will beat us there. Erin drove and still had the car keys in her purse. If, and that's a big 'if,' Carl went back to the house he rented, he'd have to get a cab, bus, run, walk, or steal a bike or a car. We may catch him before he gets back to the house. If you were Carl, would you risk going back to the house?"

Maddy thought about it. "He may be thinking that Erin would've been killed, or if captured, she wouldn't talk. And if he does go back to his house, it has to be for something important."

"The slimy bastard bailed on her. Did you really expect him to stick around? If he has something at the house, we may be able to catch him there," I said from the back seat.

Tom was driving his car as if it were an ambulance. I doubted he ever touched the brake. The car weaved between other vehicles; he drove into the oncoming traffic and swerved back into our lane. I never felt uncomfortable. Maddy, on the other hand, braced herself against the dash and pulled the seatbelt tight. Before shifting gears, Tom would rev the engine to the red line before shifting up.

"Crazy idea, guys." Tom paused. "Just saying, what if this was planned and she gave us the wrong address on purpose?"

Maddy turned in her seat to face Tom. "You mean she was one step ahead of us the whole time?"

The idea of what Tom and Maddy were contemplating was making my head spin. I attempted to play the scenario out in my mind and couldn't even begin to imagine the variables.

"If this was planned out, she's a genius. And if she did plan this, she's alone in my apartment with Galen and his boss."

The uniformed officers had been relieved when they'd dispatched the cars to Carl's address.

8:00 PM

Tom slammed on the brakes and the clutch, sending me crashing into the back of Maddy's seat. Behind us, I heard tires squealing and car horns blaring at us. One driver passed us on the right and gave Tom the finger. Tom threw the car into reverse, looked over his shoulder, and gunned the accelerator. The engine whined as the speed increased, and when Tom felt it was safe—or maybe safety wasn't even factored in—he stepped hard on the brake and simultaneously cranked the steering wheel to the left. The car started to spin; halfway through, he stepped on the clutch, pulled the stick from reverse to first, released the clutch, and gave it gas. The engine revved high, and Tom went from first to second and quickly into third.

Tom ordered Maddy to call Galen's cell.

"I don't know his number," she told him. She looked at me. "What's his number?"

"I don't have a clue."

*****

Detective Nardone and Galen were alone in Ethan's apartment guarding Erin Rodda. The two men sat at the dining room table as she continued to watch the curtain flutter like a flag in the breeze. The other uniformed officers had been dispatched to Carl Ryan's house or on other calls.

Erin sat on the couch, her head back and resting on a pillow, still watching the breeze as it pushed the curtain in and then let it relax before deciding to give it another good shove. She looked beyond the patio doors to the sky as it gave way to the dusk of the evening, unsure of which colour it had decided upon to dress itself before going with traditional black.

The screen door began to move open slowly; nauseatingly slowly. There wasn't any noise—no metal on metal grinding, no squeaky wheel bearings that needed to be oiled—it simply began to open.

Erin merely closed her eyes, not giving Galen or Detective Nardone a clue as to what was about to happen.

*****

Tom had one hand on the horn, while the other held firmly on to the steering wheel. We were whizzing past cars like fence posts. I looked at the speedometer. I couldn't see the speed but the needle was tilted past the centre point toward the right.

Tom didn't slow down when he turned into my apartment complex. The car hit the entrance curb, grounding out the undercarriage, sending sparks flying, and making a horrible metallic sound.

Tom slammed on the brakes at the entrance, leaving a long trail of burned rubber on the driveway. Maddy jumped out with me in pursuit. Inside the vestibule, I fumbled with my keys to get past the security door. I found the key and dropped the entire ring.

Maddy reached over me and ran her palm down every button on the call panel. Almost immediately, the door buzzer started to sound to grant us access. She pushed the door open and Tom and I ran into the lobby.

We stopped at the two elevator doors: three of us, two elevators, and two sets of stairs.

"I'll take the stairs to the right, Tom, you go left, Maddy," I turned and faced her, grabbing her by the shoulders, "you stay here, stand at the back of the lobby by the door. If they come out, run."

Tom handed her his cellphone. "If you see them, call Ethan's apartment. Keep calling until someone answers." Tom looked at me. "I'll wait for you at the top. Try not to puke, buddy." We both bolted for the stairs at the north and south ends of the building.

I stopped halfway down the hall and pointed at Maddy. "Call 911. Tell them…" I was lost.

"I got it. Go," she commanded.

I pushed the fire door open and took the stairs two at a time. Grabbing the metal railings on either side, I pulled myself forward as I climbed the steps. My pace was steady for the first few floors, but then my lungs started to burn and I felt myself getting winded.

Over the sound of my footfalls, I heard voices above me. I stopped and leaned over the centre rails to peer upwards. Two voices: one male, one female. I waited, and the voices stopped. *Calculated guess.*

"Erin," I screamed as loudly as I could. A head popped over the railing. Erin Rodda was looking down at me from a few floors above. Her hand came over the railing and a shot rang out. I jumped back as the bullet struck the concrete of the main level several floors down. The sound echoed in the stairwell.

"The door," I heard Carl yell out.

I broke into an all-out run up the stairs. They were going to enter one of the floors and try to take the other stairwell or the elevator down. I heard the heavy sound of the door closing. I stopped. My heart was pounding in my chest and I felt as if I really were going to throw up. What floor did they escape to? Should I continue up or go back down to the lobby?

Then I realized I had heard another sound when she had shot at me. Up, I screamed at myself.

With renewed strength, I climbed the stairs faster than when I had first started. Several floors up, I found what had caused the second sound I had heard echoing in the stairwell.

A shell casing lay on the landing of the twelfth floor. This was where they had gone into the building. Without thinking, I pushed the fire door open. Before I made it through, I saw Erin and Carl standing at the elevator, waiting for the lift to arrive.

Erin turned, broke into a full run towards me, raised her gun, and fired. I slammed the metal door shut and hid behind the concrete wall. I was breathing heavily as the bullets repeatedly hit the fire door. From the other side, the noise of gunshots ceased, to be replaced by the sound of the trigger being pulled and the clicking of the hammer not striking a fresh bullet. She was either out of bullets or would be replacing the magazine, if she had another.

I waited for a few moments and heard Carl say something before the fire door opened and closed at the far end of the hall. My door was opened just enough for me to peek through. The hallway was empty. I gathered my strength, took a deep breath, pushed open the door, and ran down to the opposite end of the hall. As I passed the elevator, it chimed and the silver doors opened.

Pausing at the opposite fire door, I pressed my ear against it and heard footsteps echoing in the stairwell. *One set, two, three?* Pushing the panic bar, I entered the stairwell, and looked below and then above. A lone figure was coming up the stairs. *Tom?* Above me, two sets of feet were running up the stairs. I decided to give chase.

When I arrived on the landing of the fourteenth floor, I thought for a moment about checking on Galen in my apartment, but instead stopped and kept myself pressed against the outer section of the stairwell.

"Tom." My voice echoed.

"Yeah."

"Check on Galen."

No response. I turned and started to make my way up the stairs. Finally, Tom answered.

"K."

I grabbed the railing and pulled myself up the steps. My leg muscles began to tighten and my lungs burnt with every breath. My mouth was wide open, trying to take in as much oxygen as possible.

As I hit the landing to the sixteenth floor, the fire door opened and was pushed hard to the outer railing. The door hit my left hip, sending sharp pain down my leg. My right leg buckled due to a kick placed behind my knee. I fell hard to the concrete landing and felt a punch to my right cheek. My eyes were closed in pain as what little air my lungs were able to hold was suddenly expelled by another kick to my right ribs. I coughed, spit blood, rolled onto my back, and opened my eyes to see Erin standing over me with her foot ready to come down hard on my face. Quickly, I rolled to my left. Her foot found the concrete landing.

Making a fist, I instinctively punched upwards to where a man would take a debilitating hit. My fist landed with enough force to cause anyone pain. Erin let out a whimper; I hit her again in the same spot. She buckled and fell on top of me. Placing my arms under her, I pushed her off, sending her into the concrete wall. The impact forced the air from her lungs; she opened her mouth, but air couldn't escape or enter until the forces in her chest equalized.

I got to my feet, my right knee sending lightning bolts of pain to my brain. As I was moving to turn her over onto her stomach, her right hand shot up and landed on the side of my left calf. I screamed in agony as she twisted and dug something into my leg. I fell backward against the far wall. Looking down, I glimpsed a knife protruding from my pant leg, and hot blood quickly flooded my shoe.

Impulsively, I reached down and pulled the knife from my calf. The pain doubled. Erin got on all fours and punched me in the open wound. I didn't scream this time. Tears welled up inside me as the pain became unbearable. I wanted to run away—crawl into a corner and cry. She punched my calf again. This time, I didn't feel anything. I had exhausted all the pain my body could tolerate. Instead, as she was still on her hands and knees, I grabbed her hair with both hands, lifted her up, and slammed her face down hard against the concrete floor. A sickening thud echoed in the stairwell.

I fell backward with my back to the railing. Erin was looking at me, her eyes open in a blank stare. A pool of blood formed around her head and flowed towards where I sat.

I couldn't look at her. With my right foot, I pushed her face away from me.

My left calf was burning. I had to see the damage she'd caused. I pulled up my pant leg and saw a large puncture wound to my calf. The knife had cut through my pants and deep into the muscle. I inserted my index and middles fingers of both hands into the hole and pulled in opposite directions. The material gave way around my lower leg exposing my leg from the knee down. I pulled the lower part of my pant leg over my shoe. Blood continued to ooze from the wound sending a steady stream from the wound to my shoe. Tearing the material into a strip, I dressed the wound and tied it snuggly enough to hold pressure but not so tight as to restrict blood flow.

Once my wound was dressed, I crawled to Erin and checked for a carotid pulse. Nothing. Her blood pressure was either so low that I wasn't able to palpate a pulse or she was dead. I hoped for the latter.

I stood and put weight on my leg. The pain was tolerable but constant. Looking up, I knew Carl only had a few floors to go before he was on the roof.

8:35 PM

I caught my breath, held on to the railing, and took a step. Pain. *What I wouldn't give for a shot of morphine right now.* Right or wrong, I reasoned that moving fast would cause less pain.

I paused, then sprinted up the steps. At each landing, I cautiously opened the fire door and looked down the hall. When I finally reached the last door, I stopped and froze. If Carl had managed to elude me by cutting across one of the floors to the other stairwell, he should've been in the lobby by now. And, if Maddy had called 911, the place should be crawling with cops by now. *So why risk it?* I wondered. *Why go onto the roof?*

I pushed the panic bar and the door creaked open. I stepped onto the gravel roof and held the door open with one hand while looking for something with which to prop the door. It was almost dark, and difficult to find anything on the roof. Instead of wasting time, I pulled a credit card from my wallet and fit it between the latch bolt and the frame. The door closed slowly but didn't lock.

Looking around, I knew that if Carl was up here, he would have the advantage. He would have arrived first; he may have been hiding, ready to strike, and would have had a chance to view the terrain before I had. Every part of me wanted to crawl back inside the hall and see if all my friends were all right.

The gravel crunched underfoot. I knew my wound hadn't stopped bleeding; blood continued to fill my shoe. Looking from side to side, then behind me, I was in full panic mode. Staring down at the gravel roof, it was impossible to tell if anyone had just walked there. There wasn't an impression, a sound—anything to indicate if Carl had made it to the roof. I wouldn't have risked coming up here, if I had been him. Unless he thought he could jump across to the next building. *Sure. If you're Superman.*

I decided that after one quick tour around the roof I would be done. *Let the guys with the bullet-resistant vests and radios and shit take the risk.*

I rationalized that my fear was due to blood loss. *Yeah. Right,* I told myself. If there was a scale for fear, I was past the "scared shitless" level. I was well beyond that. I don't think they had invented a level yet that described how I felt.

I made my way close to the edge, or to where I thought was close enough to the edge without having to add my fear of heights into the mix. As I turned right, the gravel continued to give away my path and location if someone was indeed up here. I kept a slow and steady pace. Suddenly, I thought I heard gravel crunching between my steps. My pace continued for several more seconds, and then I stopped.

I had heard it. I knew there wasn't an echo up there. There had been one more step after I had stopped. Directly ahead of me was a large, metal—something. To my right, a large air conditioning unit produced a low constant hum. To my left, twenty feet or so away, lay the building's edge. The step had come from behind. Those were my choices. I decided to...

Something smooth wrapped around my neck and pulled me back. I wanted to cough, breath, something; but I couldn't. My fingers reached up to feel leather. I had a leather belt wrapped around my neck that was being pulled tight. The pressure inside my head was impossible to bear. My eyes hurt and felt as though they were going to explode. I had never felt pain this intense come on so quickly. As the pain continued to increase, I was pulled back and dragged on the gravel. If I couldn't brace myself to fight back, I was dead. Carl knew that. He had the advantage.

I reached down and started to punch his legs. *Useless.* Out of desperation, as Carl was dragging me backwards, I let myself fall to the rooftop. I caught Carl off guard. The belt slipped away from around my neck as I hit the loose gravel. Instead of just lying there, I started to roll away. I tucked my arm in close and rolled several times to achieve distance from Carl, then hopped to my feet, only to see him rushing at me. *The best defence is good offense*, I remembered. I ducked low and ran at Carl, hitting him in the stomach with my shoulder.

I felt my shoulder plunge deep into his stomach and knock him flat on his back. Standing over him, my first instinct was to straddle him and punch him. In my weakened state, however, I was no match for him. Instead, I did what any coward would do: I started kicking him. As hard as I could. Anywhere I could. It didn't take long before I landed several good blows. Carl curled up in the fetal position as I continued kicking him. Non-stop, dirty, street-fighting kicks. I knew I had landed a few kicks to the head because I thought I had broken a toe, but I kept the assault going.

I continued the barrage of kicks as the pain from the knife wound increased. The blood soaked, make-shift dressing had slipped down and was hanging loosely around my ankle now. There was nothing left inside me but I kept going. I stopped only when I was completely spent.

"Please." There was a child's voice asking me to stop.

"What? Please? How many times did your victims want you to stop? How many times did you show them mercy?" I summoned every last bit of strength and kicked him one more time, then fell down. I couldn't stand anymore.

In the darkness, I could only imagine what Carl looked like: bloodied, swollen, broken. I wanted to sleep; instead I stood and hobbled my way to the door.

I made my way to the roof door and as I was about to grab the door handle, I heard gravel crunching, and turned to see Carl running at me. There was strength left in my body as I broke right and sent whatever reserves I had to my legs. The moonless sky offered nothing; it was now impossible to tell where the building ended and night began.

I felt like a rabbit darting left and right to avoid being caught by the fox or falling into the abyss.

As I broke left, the traffic offered me something I hadn't seen before. The headlights of the vehicles ended where the roof began, so I knew where the roofline was. I ran as fast as I could straight for the edge without looking back. Only feet before the building ended, I cut right and fell to the gravel roof, covering my head. I heard the crush of gravel under running feet behind me, then nothing.

For a moment I lay there expecting Carl to do to me what I had done to him, but there was nothing except the sound of the city in the distance. I crawled to the edge of the building and looked down. I thought I would see something, but I couldn't. The lights around the base of the building didn't reveal what I thought I would see. Just as well, I thought. I'd seen enough for one night.

I rolled over onto my back, wanting to get up, move, get away from this place, but my leg hurt, my face hurt, my toe hurt. I tried to speak but the only noise that came forth was a raspy bark. I closed my eyes, the sound of the city becoming more prominent as I drifted off.

The Next Morning

Ethan had been sleeping for over twelve hours, an IV of normal saline running. The right side of his face was swollen, and the bruising around his eye was still dark before it started to turn that wonderful shade of green and yellow. Maddy and Tom had taken up permanent residency in the two chairs in his room. Maddy was sleeping—she had been up all night—while Tom read.

Earlier, Maddy had spoken to the nurses and they had let her read his chart: fractured right zygomatic process (broken cheekbone), fractured first metatarsal (big toe), eleven sutures in left calf, contused larynx, multiple contusions (bruises) over his body.

Galen was outside the room with Detective Nardone. Galen watched as the hospital staff walked past, unaware of the events that had transpired, what brought these two police officers to their halls. Nor did they care. The bed would be filled with one patient or another. The events that brought them here mattered little to the hospital, they still had to care for the patient behind that door regardless of who he or she was.

It was almost another four hours before Ethan work up, his face still painful from where Erin had punched him. Medication had quelled the pain in his leg and cheek, but he was still exhausted. His room was empty. He was hungry and he really had to pee.

Good, he thought. *They didn't put a urinary catheter in. Thank God. And I'm really hungry. Can't be all bad if I'm craving a Lick's burger.*

He laughed at himself as he swung his legs off the side of the bed. The sharp pain reminded him of where his sutures were. He reached down and felt the pointy ends of the nylon sutures.

The IV was still running. He reached up, discontinued the flow, and removed the catheter from his right antecubital. Slight pressure was applied with his thumb in case he bled a few drops. He slid off the bed and put a little weight on his left leg. It was tight, but he reasoned he was still in better shape than the person who had given him this gift that would leave a nasty scar.

Ethan hobbled to the washroom, hiked up his hospital gown, sat down, and emptied his bladder. He closed his eyes and realized that he could probably sleep for another few hours. Ethan couldn't remember the last time he had been this exhausted. Even after he finished, he sat for a few moments longer with his eyes closed. Maybe the thought of leaving was not a great idea. A few more hours of sleep might be just what the doctor ordered.

The door to his room opened and he heard Maddy call out to him.

"In here."

Maddy walked in to see Ethan sitting on the toilet with his hospital gown covering his knees.

"You look like shit," she said with a smile.

"I'm sure I feel a lot worse than I look."

"Why are you up? You should be in bed getting rest." Maddy walked to his side and tried to lift Ethan up and escort him back to bed.

Ethan laughed. "I'm fine. Really. Leg is a little sore. Face feels like Tom backed the ambulance up over my head. But other than that, I'm fine." Ethan stood and wobbled, and Maddy righted him. "A little tired but I'm fine."

Maddy didn't put up an argument; she simply walked him back to bed and covered him with the white cotton sheet.

"Feel like seeing Galen?"

"Yeah, that'll be great." He would've preferred a little more sleep but Ethan felt he owed his friend that much.

Maddy opened the door, stuck her head out, and invited Galen and Detective Nardone to join her. Galen walked in as if he was entering a party—loud, Diet Coke in hand—while Nardone remained silent and took a seat.

"Hey, bud. Docs say you'll be fine. How're you feeling? You look good. Maddy says you'll be off work for a week or so until that shiner goes down." Galen always talked too much when he was nervous.

"I'm fine. Feel fine. Haven't thought about work yet." Ethan was already tired.

"You up to hear what we got so far?"

Ethan sat up in bed and propped up a couple of pillows to support his back. Maddy stood beside him and held his hand. As Galen prepared to speak, Detective Nardone took over.

"Anyway, the address Erin gave us was bull. The people who live there knew nothing about Carl Ryan. I imagine we'll probably never know where he lived."

"Did you find him? I mean, I couldn't see from the rooftop."

Nardone looked at Galen. Galen nodded.

Detective Nardone spoke for the two of them, "He ended up in the back seat of a Nissan. We'll be running DNA and other tests just to make certain it is Carl Ryan."

"And Erin?"

"Where you left her."

Ethan was stunned. He knew he had taken two lives in a matter of minutes, but to have it confirmed sunk it deep.

"You OK, bud?" Galen was truly concerned for his friend.

"Yeah. Fine." He wasn't. "What else did you find?"

"We have more evidence to show that she was involved in at least one more of the child slayings. She had another swatch of material from another case. That's all we had. Maddy and Tom brought us up to speed on the rest of what you knew while you were out."

"Any chance I'm gonna be in trouble for what happened?" Ethan's voice was subdued.

"None whatsoever," Nardone said.

"Can we keep my involvement quiet? Even omit me from the notes. I really don't want to be mentioned."

Nardone chuckled. "Kind of impossible, but we will downplay your involvement." He looked at Maddy. "Yours too."

"Listen guys. I'm really tired. Is there any way we can continue this another day?"

Not another word was said. Nardone left the room, and Galen came to Ethan's bedside and kissed him on the cheek. Maddy snickered. She kissed him on the lips. And then he was alone.

*****

I watched the door close as Maddy walked out. My eyes were heavy—well, eye; my right eye was already closed. The energy it had taken to get to the bathroom and back was all I had in me. I still wanted that Lick's burger.

Sleeping on my back was never my favourite position. I wanted to roll onto my right side but my face hurt when I rested it in the pillow. I reached down and scratched all around the sutures, and I swear I could feel the muscle damage Erin had caused when she'd dug that knife into my calf.

My mind began to drift off, thoughts became cloudy, a blur then "Thud." I knew that sound. It echoed in my mind. That sickening sound that had reverberated in the stairwell when I had smashed Erin's face to the concrete floor. Without thought of the consequences, I had used every ounce of strength I could muster. It wasn't intentional; it was adrenaline. I could still hear it.

I closed my eyes, and all I saw was Erin's face staring back at me as she lay on the floor, the pool of red beginning to form beneath her head.

Rolling onto my left side, I pulled the sheet up tightly around my neck, trying to shut out the sound of her head hitting the concrete and the look she had given me as she'd died.

I pulled the sheet up higher and started to cry.

About The Author

After graduating as a paramedic in 1983 from Fanshawe College in London, Ontario, Perry Prete moved to Windsor, Ontario, and then Brockville, Ontario, where he now continues to work full-time as a paramedic for the county.

He continues to write and operate a pre-hospital medical supply company.

With over thirty years of experience as a field paramedic, he draws on his career to bring realism to the calls depicted in his writing.